THE DIAMOND STUD
GA HAUSER

The Diamond Stud

THE DIAMOND STUD

Copyright © G.A. Hauser, 2011

Cover art by Alexander Richfield

Edited by Stacey Rhodes

ISBN Trade paperback: 978-1456-3531-8-6

The G.A. Hauser Collection LLC

This is a work of fiction and any resemblance to persons, living or dead, or business establishments, events or locales is coincidental.

All Rights Are Reserved. No part of this may be used or reproduced in any manner whatsoever without written permission, except in the case of brief quotations embodied in critical articles and reviews.

WARNING
This book contains material that maybe offensive to some: graphic language, homosexual relations, adult situations. Please store your books carefully where they cannot be accessed by underage readers.

First The G.A. Hauser Collection LLC publication: January 2011

Chapter 1

Chad DeSoto didn't answer the ringing phone.

On his knees in his bedroom in Dayton, Ohio, at six in the morning, Chad jammed a suitcase with his clothing, sweat dripping down his temple. It didn't matter it was mid-October. He was boiling hot.

Before his answering machine picked up, Chad stretched to his nightstand, tugged the plastic cordless phone off the top, and yanked the plug from the wall.

The phone clattered to the hardwood floor and the piece holding the battery in went skidding under the bed frame. He swore and resumed packing, feeling as though a ticking time bomb was under his ass.

A half hour later, wearing sunglasses, a ball cap, and leather jacket, a single diamond earring in his right earlobe, Chad jogged to his black Pathfinder and threw the overstuffed suitcase into the back. He glanced around the apartment complex in paranoia, touching the concealed revolver he had tucked into his inside jacket pocket.

The Diamond Stud

Wasting no time, he started the car engine, pulling out of the lot to hit Interstate 75. He didn't have a destination, but he knew it had to be far away.

Giving a quick glance at his gas gauge, Chad figured he had enough to get him beyond the state border. Once he hit Indiana he'd stop. Not until then.

It was before dusk, and felt like night. Chad was mixed with emotions; anger being the most vivid.

He left it all behind now. All of it. There was no place to go but up.

~

Ten hours later, Chad had made it to Iowa. His back ached, he was starving, and he needed to lay horizontal.

He turned off Interstate 80 at an exit just east of Des Moines. Needing a rest after the marathon in the driver's seat, he pulled into the lot of a Motel 6.

Even though he knew he had not been followed, he remained paranoid. Another concern he had was that his Ohio concealed weapons permit didn't cover every state. But he'd be damned if he was going to be without protection until he had put at least two thousand miles between him and Ohio.

When he stood next to his truck, his legs ached. He waited until he was sturdier on his feet, holding the fender. He had stopped twice in ten hours; two gas stations to fill up, and relieve himself. He hadn't eaten in twenty-four hours.

He had no one to blame for his dizziness but himself. He could have located food anywhere. He just wasn't sure he wanted to waste the time it took to eat it.

He staggered like a drunkard into the motel reception lobby. A table with coffee urns was set up against one wall and looked inviting. He'd avoided coffee during the trip to limit his stops.

The woman behind the desk glanced up from writing. She was plump and couldn't be more than twenty years old.

"I need a room for the night." Chad removed his wallet from his back pocket.

"Just you?" She handed him a form and a pen.

"Just me."

"While you fill that out, I need your ID and a credit card."

At having to show his name, Chad cringed, but what were the odds anyone would suspect he had left Ohio already. No one would find out unless they broke into his apartment and noticed the suitcase gone and the disarray of a hurried exit.

He handed the girl the two cards, filling out the form with as little information as possible. She typed onto a computer keyboard as he wrote. He handed her the form and pen, needing food and a bed desperately.

"Here you go." She gave him back his ID and credit card, and then wrote the number of his room on a cardboard slip, inserting two card keys into it. "Number two-ten." She pointed behind her. "If you go behind this building and turn left it's on the second floor, near the end."

"Thanks." He tucked his items back into his wallet. "Anything decent to eat around here?"

"There's fast food chains all along this road." She waved to the front of the hotel. "And a truck-stop diner in that direction."

"Okay. Thanks." He hated driving another few miles, but had to get something in him. He groaned in agony as he sat behind the wheel again, turned on the ignition and pulled out of the lot. A drive-thru burger chain restaurant was close by. He stopped at the menu and tried to focus.

"Can I help you?" a voice came from the speaker on the board.

"Yes, I'd like a cheeseburger, fries, and a chocolate milkshake, please."

"Anything else?"

"That's it."

The Diamond Stud

"Seven dollars and twenty-eight cents, please. Pull up to the next window."

Chad wanted to be in bed, not still in his car ordering crappy food. He parked at the next window and handed the young woman a ten. She gave him change and a bag.

"Thank you," she said, smiling.

"You're welcome." Chad set the aromatic white bag on the floor of the passenger's seat and drove back to the hotel.

He followed the directions he had been given to find his room and spotted the numbers on the doors. It was nearing six and the daylight was waning. Chad parked under the balcony where his room was located. He grabbed dinner and his suitcase and locked his car. Wandering along the side of the motel, he noticed a set of stairs near a vending machine and an ice maker. He climbed the cement steps, dragging in exhaustion.

Placing his suitcase down, he used the cardkey and opened the door. Instantly the scent of old cigarettes and dust hit him. He glanced back at the door itself and noticed a 'no smoking' symbol. Obviously someone had failed to comply with the notice.

He put his case down and closed the door. Without taking off his coat, he sat on the foot of the bed and peeled the paper back from the burger, taking a big bite. As he chewed he looked the room over.

It contained two double beds, a desk, a dresser, a television, and a sink outside the bathroom. A clothing rod with a suitcase stand was beside the sink.

He dug into the bag and stuffed a few fries into his mouth. As he ate, he knew he'd suffer for the food quality and the speed he was consuming it. He didn't care. He was famished.

Once he was down to the shake, and struggling to sip it through the straw, Chad slowed down and shook off his jacket. He felt the presence of the handgun in a small leather holster, weighing it down. Removing it, he placed it by his bedside and threw out the bag of trash in a waste can under the sink.

He stood in front of the mirror and inspected his reflection. His blue eyes were red from exhaustion and the blond highlights in his hair needed a touch up, not to mention he had hat head, from wearing a ball cap most of the trip. With his thumb and index finger he checked the back of his stud earring, making sure it was secure.

He opened a small bar of hotel soap and scrubbed his face, feeling filthy from the traveling. Before he stripped for the shower he made sure the deadbolt was locked on the door and even put a chair in front of it. He glanced down at his car from the window, moving the thick plastic lined curtain. The motel was filling up. Pickup trucks with boat trailers attached to them were backing in, lined up in a row beside his Pathfinder. *Good ole' boys out for a fishin' weekend.*

Hadn't he left that behind? Not yet. No. He'd have to drive a lot further west to be rid of that kind of man.

Sighing loudly, Chad removed his black muscle t-shirt, tossing it on the bed. When he patted his pants pockets to empty their contents, he looked at his mobile phone. He turned it on to see what calls or text messages he had missed, though dread nearly made him toss it on the bed and never turn it on again.

Two he deleted before he heard the voicemails the individuals had left. One text he read.

'Where r u?'

It was from his good friend Jett Warren. He felt badly. He didn't tell Jett he'd left the state. Chad took a deep breath and dialed his mobile phone number.

"Hey, girl!"

"Hi, Jett." Chad caught sight of his naked, shaved torso in the mirror's reflection.

"I was worried about you when you didn't answer your home phone or cell phone."

"I left Ohio."

"No! You shitting me?"

"No, I'm not shitting you. I'm in Iowa at a motel."

"No. Come on, Chad. Sweetie, you didn't have to leave. You could have gotten help. Please come back."

"No way."

"Where the hell are you going to go?"

"I'm not stopping until I hit the Pacific Ocean."

"Girl? Are you serious?"

"Yes." Chad ran his hand through his hair. He was so tired he dropped to the bed and lay flat, staring at the ceiling.

"I will miss you so much."

"I'm sorry, Jett...I had to. I couldn't deal with it anymore. I was getting myself sick with worry."

"But to just up and leave? Did you have time to pack all your belongings?"

"I have all I need."

"Baby..."

Chad knew Jett would be upset. "Look, I'm completely wiped. I was about to step into the shower and then rest."

"You call me every day and check in. You hear me?"

"Yes, Mother."

"You' damn right! Someone's got to look out for you. Sweetie, I'm heartbroken. Who am I going to whine to? Whose shoulder can I cry on when Mr. Right breaks my heart?"

"I'm a phone call away. And you can visit...when..."

"When? When you what? You don't even know where you're going. Chad DeSoto, you are one crazy muthafucka."

"Am I?" Chad was not smiling. "Or was I about to be executed. You don't know what was really going on, Jett."

The silence on the other end of the line felt thick to Chad. Finally Jett said, "You never told me it was getting worse."

"I didn't want you involved or to get hurt like I was back in May. You think I was going to chance someone waiting for you with a baseball bat? No way."

"I'm sick about it."

"Yeah, well, life sucks then you die." Chad rubbed his face. "Let me go. I'll either email you or text you when I get tired of driving and stop for the night. I don't keep the phone on while I drive."

"You be careful. I love you."

"You too. I'll keep you updated."

"You better. I'm going to go cry now. My best friend left me."

"Please don't make this any harder for me than it is." Chad felt miserable.

"I'm sorry, Chad. I must be on my period. I'm fine."

Chad shook his head. "Yeah, I'm bloated and depressed as well, girl, but that's life. Bye, my chocolate drop."

"Bye. Kiss, kiss."

Chad shut off the phone and placed it near his gun. He finished stripping off his clothing and stood in the tub under the hot water. A tiny bottle of hotel shampoo in his hand, Chad washed up, much better with food in his belly and without the endless highway in front of him.

Chapter 2

Chad had fallen asleep in front of the television. A noise of voices right outside his door woke him. He checked the clock—it wasn't even nine p.m. yet. He rubbed his face and stood, looking out of the window.

A man was loitering on a grassy strip behind the motel, Interstate 80 as his backdrop. With a beer in one hand, he was directing a truck with a boat trailer with the other.

Chad noticed four powerboats lined up in the parking lot next to his SUV. The beer looked refreshing. He checked the time again. He couldn't believe he had slept over an hour. "Fuck it."

Shutting off the TV, Chad dressed and put the holstered handgun back into his inner lining jacket pocket. He counted the cash in his wallet and made sure he had the hotel room key.

The minute he left the room, he could see a group of men together, drinking beer, as the final space in the lot was taken by the boat trailer. Chad leaned on the rail to admire the expensive selection of pleasure crafts. Fishing poles rested on the plastic covers as the men laughed and spoke to each other.

A teenager was throwing rocks into the brush between the interstate and the parking lot. Chad leaned down to see what he was up to. A pair of skunks were snuffling around the underbrush. Chad couldn't help but think the boy was an idiot. Hitting a skunk with a rock was not only cruel, it would stink up the whole area. *The rednecks followed me here. Just my fucking luck.*

Chad inadvertently caught one man's eye. The man smiled in a gesture of greeting. Chad gave him a fake one back. He headed to the cement stairs. His intention was to walk around the busy street in front of the hotel, looking for a gas station with a grocery shop to purchase beer.

A group of men, mostly middle-aged wearing flannel and ball caps, were standing near the bottom of the stairs, beer bottles to their lips, or laughing at a joke.

"Sorry." Chad couldn't get by without disturbing them.

They shut up and stepped back, staring at him. The gazes felt hostile. To test the waters, Chad asked, "You guys wouldn't know a close place that sells beer, would you?"

An older looking man said, "Have one of ours."

"No. It's not why I was asking." Chad began moving away. "Thanks anyway."

Another man said, "There's a place right across the main road."

"Cool. Thanks." Chad stuffed his hands into his pockets and heard them talking behind him as he walked off. He wondered if his frosted hair and diamond earring had tipped their gay-dar. It usually did.

The air was cool and felt damp. Chad noticed a heavy volume of traffic on the main street in front of the motel. The area was a Mecca for travelers in search of cheap motel rates and fast food.

He was mid-block, so he waited for the signal at the end of the street to change before he jogged across four lanes to the mini-mart store.

Even with a concealed gun he felt vulnerable, like he was a walking target. He was six-two, and had frosted blond hair, wore a tight muscle tee and skin tight jeans. It was who he was. He couldn't help it. He didn't do too much camp or obvious hand

The Diamond Stud

gestures to reveal his sexual preference unless he wanted to. It didn't matter. He heard it constantly. "Aren't all pretty boys gay?"

He didn't know if thirty-eight qualified as a 'boy' but his age didn't stop the accusations.

Avoiding eye-contact with exhausted travelers, Chad walked to the beer section and tried not to be picky. He grabbed a six-pack created by a smaller brewing company and brought it up to the cashier. He stood behind a tiny Asian man buying cigarettes and gas.

When the little man was finished with his transaction, he spun around, nearly bumping Chad. He excused himself and then gave Chad's crotch a closer inspection.

Chad looked down to see if his fly was open. It wasn't. With his eyes he followed the little man's exit. The man looked back at him several times, making Chad nervous.

"Can I help you?"

Chad broke his gaze on the man and placed the beer on the counter. He took a twenty out of his wallet and waited.

"Anything else?"

"No. Thank you." Chad peered behind him. There was a line of people. He cleared his throat and took the change and his receipt.

Standing just outside the door, he stuffed his money into his pants pocket and tucked the beer under his arm. Once again he stood at the busy street, waiting for a chance to jog across to the motel.

A light drizzle fell but he barely noticed it.

On his way back to his room, Chad again ran into the group of fishermen.

"Got your beer?" the older one asked, smiling.

"Yes. Thanks."

"Don't rush off. You can join us." Another one raised his bottle invitingly.

Drinking alone in my room or making small talk with a bunch of butch outdoorsmen? Butch men. Chad took one bottle out of the cardboard pack and held up the rest. "Anyone?"

A younger man with a Cincinnati Reds ball cap on said, "Fancy beer."

"Fancy?" Chad read the label. "You're kidding, right?"

Since he got no takers on his 'fancy' beer, Chad set the rest of the pack at his feet. He couldn't twist off the cap, since 'fancy' beer needed a bottle opener.

"See what happens when you have gourmet taste?" One of the men laughed, handing him a pocketknife with the bottle opener extended.

"Thanks." Chad popped off the top and returned the pocketknife. He dropped the cap into the six-pack holder and took a deep swallow of the cold beer.

"Where're you from?"

Chad didn't answer, still pressing the neck of the bottle to his mouth.

"Is that your rig? The one with the Ohio plates?"

Caught by his need for human contact, Chad made his own trap. Trust was no longer an issue. He trusted no one.

He deliberately didn't answer, changing the topic. "You guys going fishing locally? Or headed out of state?"

"We're headed up the Des Moines river."

Chad glanced at the license plate on one of the boat trailers. They were from Kentucky. He should have known by the accent.

Time to go.

He picked up the rest of his beer and said, "Been a long day, gentlemen."

A murmur of them saying goodnight followed. Chad didn't look back. He climbed the cement stairs to his room. When he

The Diamond Stud

reached the balcony a younger man was leaning on the rail, directly over where he and the others had been standing. He recognized him as the man he had spotted before he went for the beer. He'd been the one that smiled, directing the trailer.

Chad caught a strange look in his eye and kept moving.

The man said, "You going to drink all those yourself?"

He stopped and gave the man a closer inspection. His senses didn't pick up anything unusual so Chad held out the six-pack. "Help yourself."

The young man took one bottle out and nearly cut his palm trying to twist the cap. He hissed and shook out his arm in pain.

"Hang on. You need a bottle opener." Chad placed the cardboard carrier in front of his door and used his key to gain access. He picked up the beer and entered the room. The man was inside with him before he could invite him in, or not.

Chad spun around, watching the young man suspiciously.

"There's an opener attached to the bathroom sink." The young man pointed to it. "I know because my room is the same." He walked across the carpet and used the opener, tossing the cap in the plastic trash can.

Chad set the four beers on the counter by the television and stared at the man.

"You're gay, right?"

Chad's heart quickened. He knew he had a gun in his jacket pocket, so he tried to stay calm. "What gives you that idea?"

The man smiled and touched the tip of his nose in a cliché gesture.

"Anything else?" Chad tried not to be terrified. With a motel loaded with Midwestern sportsmen, he knew he'd lose in a war. "If you don't mind, I just want to unwind in front of the TV.

"Yeah. Me too." The young man touched his fly in what could have been interpreted as a proposition.

Chad took nothing for granted, especially a stranger's homophobia.

"I'm Bill."

Do I use my real name? No. "I'm Joe."

"Joe." Bill extended his hand. "Nice to meet you."

Chad shook it quickly.

"You should put those beers into the fridge. Keep them cold." Bill knelt in front of a mini refrigerator and turned it on. Chad could hear it hum. Bill loaded the remaining beer bottles into it and stood, flattening the cardboard they came in.

"I assume you're with the group going fishing." Chad finished the beer he was drinking and put the empty on the nightstand.

"Yup."

He felt the hair rise on the nape of his neck in suspicion.

Bill drank his beer, placed his bottle down near the TV and crossed the room towards Chad.

Instinctively Chad patted the spot in his jacket where his handgun was hidden. To his astonishment, Bill knelt down in front of him and touched his zipper flap, peering up as if asking permission.

"Holy fuck." Chad wondered if it was a trap. Make a play for the gay boy, then tell your buddies about it and beat him to a pulp. *Been there, done that, laid up in the hospital for weeks because of that.* Well, he hadn't been propositioned, just beaten unconscious with a baseball bat.

"I always liked the name Joe." Bill used more pressure against Chad's zipper.

Chad had to make a decision. *Now.* Take chance on a hot blowjob, or fight the mob later when Bill spilled the beans.

Naughty him. He wanted the blowjob. Particularly because Bill seemed so straight. So- good-ole-boy-ish. Every gay man's secret fantasy, seducing a straight man.

The Diamond Stud

Bill wasn't ugly or pretty. He was just a man. Nothing stood out on his features. He appeared clean cut and definitely ten years his junior.

Chad held his breath from nerves as his belt was unbuckled. "Are you gay?"

"No. Are you?" Bill smirked, popping open the button of Chad's jeans and tugging down the zipper pull.

Stop asking me that! "Uh. No." Chad figured he'd play the stupid game. He was armed. He could defend himself. It was obvious Bill didn't have a weapon. He was only wearing a flannel shirt and blue jeans. Nothing was concealed. Because his anxiety over a brutal beating was overshadowing his mood, Chad was soft.

Bill didn't appear to be a novice as he hunted him down in his briefs.

"I need to lie down. Sorry." Chad inched closer to the bed.

"Go ahead. Take off your jacket." Bill sat on his heels and waited.

Chad touched the weapon through the leather. He reluctantly removed his jacket, simply because keeping it on would appear more suspicious than taking it off. He folded it on the bed beside him, the pocket lip showing in case he needed to grab his weapon.

Bill sat down next to him, smoothing his hand up Chad's thigh. "You're a very handsome guy."

"Thanks. You sure you're not gay?"

"Nope. Are you?"

Gawd! Is there an echo in here? "Nope." Chad didn't know if he could get it up. Yes, he'd had a plenty of hook-ups and one night stands, but this wasn't a man from a gay chat room or the gay bar he tended at. It was a possible set up for something nasty. And if it weren't for his craving for sex, Chad would have chased the man out the first moment he opened his beer.

He couldn't remember the last person he'd turned down who offered to suck his dick.

But those past offers weren't in a motel in Iowa with a crowd of fishermen in neighboring rooms.

Bill hooked his finger into a belt loop. "Are you going to take these off?"

No. Down, but I'll be damned if I'm going to strip and be vulnerable for you.

Chad wriggled the tight pants lower on his hips.

"Gay guys like to wear snug clothing." Bill reached for Chad's earlobe. "And earrings in their right ears."

"Do they?" Chad's breathing accelerated from his nerves. *I am so stupid! He's going to kill me.*

"...dye their hair frosty blond..." Bill ran his hand through Chad's hair at the same time he exposed Chad's cock from his briefs. Bill's focus turned to Chad's soft dick. He gave it a long glance, then opened his mouth and enveloped the entire length.

The heat and wetness of Bill's mouth was too delicious to fight. Battling his horrific fear, *Please don't kill me, please don't kill me,* Chad struggled to get erect.

Bill closed his eyes and drew hard suction, holding the base with two fingers.

Good God, Billy-boy. You've done this before!

Chad bit his lip on a loud groan. One hand rested on the bed beside him, the other on top of his jacket pocket over the gun, just in case.

Bill opened his eyes and pushed Chad's shirt up higher, until his nipples were showing. He pinched one and Chad's hips jerked up in reflex. He was growing harder by the minute. Suddenly he imagined he could come. Would 'straight' Bill swallow?

It was silent in the room except for Bill's slurps. Outside the rumbling male laughter and voices continued.

The Diamond Stud

Chad felt the first pulsating rush of a climax. Bill sucked faster, harder. His nipple was tweaked again. It didn't take much after that. "I'm coming."

Instead of disconnecting and moving away, Bill moaned and pressed his palm over Chad's pectoral muscle.

Knowing he'd given Bill warning, Chad let go, arching his back and shooting his load.

Bill kept sucking and fisting Chad's cock strongly as he lapped at the slit.

Chad opened his eyes and caught his breath. *Right. Now do you kill me?*

Bill used his sleeve to wipe his mouth. He stood beside the bed, opened his jeans, and revealed a stiff thick cock.

As he stared at it, Chad wondered what was expected of him. To his relief, Bill jerked off over him. Cream spattered his pubic hair and semi-erect cock. He glanced at Bill's face. He appeared satisfied.

"Bill?" A voice called from a distance but they both heard it. "Bill?"

Looking more terrified than Chad was a moment ago, Bill tucked in his cock and made for the door. "Bye."

Chad was left blinking in surprise. He hopped off the bed quickly, clutching his clothing, and looked out the window. He expected a gay-bashing posse of anglers at his door, torches ablaze.

He dead-bolted it, slid the chair in front of it, and walked to the sink to clean up. As he wiped the spent cum from his skin with a soapy washcloth, Chad shook his head at his reflection. Taking chances was not wise. It's what got him into trouble in the first place.

Chapter 3

Before daylight Chad packed, left the motel keys on the desk, and carried his suitcase to his SUV. All the pickup trucks and boat trailers were gone. "I guess the early bird gets the trout." Chad used his key fob to open the back of the Pathfinder, tossing his bag inside.

He sat behind the wheel and prepared himself for another nine to ten hours of driving. Even in October the interior of the truck grew hot from the cloudless sky and if he cracked a window, he couldn't hear his music. The fan was the only thing he used to cool down, reserving his fuel.

Leaving the Iowa smell of pig and cow shit behind, Chad hit Nebraska. The game of cat and mouse with the eighteen wheelers was wearing on him. They'd drive up his ass, pass him at a snail's pace and then cut in front of him to crawl, making him pass them again. It was an irritating game. He had two choices; go ninety miles an hour and risk a huge ticket or possibly a reckless driving charge, or go seventy-five and play the match of death like in the movie, *Duel*.

The gas gauge seemed to drop as he watched. Chad estimated he could go another hour before he had to refill, but his bladder was beginning to complain. Since he left the motel, he'd been on the road for four hours. A sign for a rest area in one mile convinced him to stop to stretch his aching legs and relieve himself.

The Diamond Stud

Slowing down, driving off the exit ramp, Chad hated stopping for many paranoid reasons. He pulled into a spot close to the restroom building and shut off the engine. Prior to getting out, he grabbed his leather jacket off the passenger's seat and put it on just outside the car door. The morning air was cool but not icy. He closed and locked the vehicle, making his way to the men's room, again, slightly wobbly from too much time behind the wheel.

Old women were walking little hairy dogs, men with gray beards and protruding beer bellies smoked cigarettes at the picnic tables, and a steady flow of tired drivers entered and exited the restroom building.

Chad stood at a urinal and glanced around the room quickly. One stall was occupied, another man washed his hands at the sink, and a third man stood at the blower drying his hands. The noise from the dryer echoed like a vacuum cleaner in the tiled room. Chad relieved himself, knowing it was going to be four or five more hours until he'd stop again. He finished, fastened his jeans and belt and flushed the urinal.

Three more men entered the room, all making for the stalls or urinals quickly. Chad minded his own business and took his turn at the blower.

He passed vending machines on his way out. He was craving water but assumed the more he drank the more times he'd have to stop. His stomach grumbled. "All right." He shook his head in annoyance as he answered it.

Taking change out of his pocket, Chad inspected the selection. Sugar or salt, take your pick.

Someone was behind him. Since Chad couldn't decide, he stepped back. "Go ahead."

"Too many choices?" The man smiled and stuck a dollar bill into the slot.

"Yeah." Chad watched the man. The man chose corn chips.
"That looks like the one."
"Love those things." He bent down and removed the bag from the machine.
Chad fed the slot coins and pushed the same letter and number combination for the snack. He opened the bag and ate a few at a time. The man stared at him.
"Good?"
Chad peered around first, then replied, "As usual."
"Where you headed?"
Was it idle chitchat or did people turn nosy all of a sudden? Chad assumed that's the question everyone asked while on the road.
Before Chad answered, the man asked, "Reno or San Francisco?"
"Why would I go to either of those places?" Chad ate more chips, licking the salt from his finger.
"You look like you could be a pop singer at the nightclubs…or…"
Chad didn't want to hear the second choice. Wasn't all of San Francisco gay?
"See ya." He spun on his boot heels and walked to his car. Suspicion kept him peeking back to see if he was followed.
He wasn't but the man stared at him. Chad dumped the crumbs from the small bag of chips into his mouth, threw the empty bag out and brushed his hands off on his jeans. "A Reno nightclub pop singer? Moron," he scoffed to himself. "More like a lip-sync drag show queen. Du-uh!"
He started the engine of his car and locked the doors while he checked his mobile phone. Jett had texted him—'*i miss u!* :-*'— and again there were voicemail messages. Seven. Chad figured the cat may be out of the bag that he left the apartment. He had no clue what was going on, but it was possible they figured out

The Diamond Stud

he had vanished. He could picture his front door being kicked in and his apartment being searched. Or maybe the fact that his Pathfinder hadn't been in the apartment's assigned space for twenty-four hours was the key clue in his disappearing act.

He didn't listen to the messages. They would just upset him. The minute he could, he'd change his number. He shut the phone and made his way back onto Interstate 80 and the risky passing games with the truckers.

~

If Chad thought Nebraska was a big state, he dreaded Wyoming and Nevada. He couldn't drive another minute. Nine more hours behind him, once again hungry and achy, Chad pulled off the interstate just as he crossed the Wyoming border.

The chain fast-food eateries and low cost motels appeared before he hit Cheyenne. He rolled to a stop in front of a motel reception lobby and shut off the car. Waiting for a moment to collect his thoughts and open the car door, Chad noticed a sedan pull in beside him. He waited until the driver and passenger got out, entering the motel lobby first.

Chad exited his car and straightened his back with a groan. He opened the lobby door and stood back as the two men rented a room for the night.

One was clean-shaven, in his twenties, slightly overweight, but still attractive, wearing a dark blue water-proof jacket and baggy blue jeans. The other was forty-ish, tall and slender with a receding hairline, a mostly gray ponytail, and a beard. Chad thought he looked like Tommy Chong.

Since the check-in area was small, Chad couldn't help but overhear everything that was said. The younger man was allowing the older one to make the reservations. Instantly Chad imagined them as lovers, but that was because he imagined every male couple was. It was more fun that way.

"...one night," the older man said, glancing back and catching Chad's eye before he brought his attention back to the clerk.

"One king or two doubles?"

The men exchanged glances before the older one said, "The king will be fine."

Chad smiled to himself. How bold of you guys. *Overtly sharing one bed in Cheyenne, Wyoming? I'd have asked for two doubles and avoided any threat. But that's me.*

Trying to appear nonchalant, Chad pretended he was not eavesdropping. He walked near the glass door and inspected their car. *California license plates. Hmm. The plot thickens.*

Just as Chad spun around, the younger of the two men made eye contact and appeared to be deciding on whether to smile.

Chad did. *What the hell.*

The young man asked him, "Do you know a good place to find a decent meal and a beer?"

Shaking his head, Chad pointed to the clerk. "No clue. We'll have to ask him."

The Tommy Chong look-alike put his wallet back in his pocket and gave Chad a distrustful look; more the kind of gaze Chad was used to. The older man asked the clerk the same question.

Since Chad liked the idea of a beer and a good meal, he listened in to the clerk's answer.

"There's a place just down the main road..."

"Thanks," the older man said, gesturing to his friend to leave with him.

The younger man gave Chad a friendly wave. "Have a good night."

"You too." Chad waited for them to exit the lobby and approached the desk, giving the clerk his ID and credit card. "Just one night, please."

The Diamond Stud

The man typed his information into the keyboard of a computer and slid the credit card through a machine.

"Do you want a room near your friends?"

"Hmm?" Chad woke up from his tired stupor. "Want what?"

"Sorry. I thought you all knew each other."

"No. But I don't care where you put me." Chad leaned over the counter on his elbows, propping himself up.

He was handed a credit card slip and a plastic card-key. While he signed, the clerk said, "Room one-oh-five." He pointed to the right. "The room is in the building on this side of the lobby. First floor. There's an icemaker by the stairs to the second level if you need it."

"Great. Thanks. Uh, where was that restaurant you told those guys about?" Chad didn't want fast food again. He waited for the directions and nodded. After he climbed back into his SUV he stuffed the receipt into his glove compartment and backed out of the space to head to his room.

The car with the California plates was right next to where he parked. Chad figured he'd freshen up before he hit the eatery.

Since it was the same motel chain, the décor was identical to the last room, but this one didn't stink of stale cigarettes. The farther he drove from Ohio, the more Chad let his guard down. It just wasn't feasible for someone to track him. It would take the FBI with access to bank records and cell phones to know where he was. Chad had told no one. Not even Jett knew exactly where he was.

Voices from the next room came through the thin wall. Chad figured it was the men he'd met in the lobby. Although he wasn't comfortable around strangers at the moment, he wished he knew they were definitely gay. It would be a comfort just having a gay couple within shouting distance if trouble found him.

Chad placed his suitcase on the stand and took off his jacket so he could wash his face and hands. The reflection in the mirror showed him he was losing weight. One meal a day was not sitting well with his high metabolism.

He considered a shower, but his empty stomach took president. Standing tall, fluffing up his frosty blond locks, Chad picked up his jacket, deciding whether to leave the gun in the room. Wyoming was a reciprocal state when it came to having an Ohio permit, so he kept it on him.

After patting his pocket for the room key, Chad left, making sure the door had closed and locked behind him. Though he was exhausted, he forced himself to get back into the car once more and drive.

Five minutes down the road, where the clerk had said it would be, was another chain restaurant, but this one was an improvement on the drive-thru he had suffered the last evening. And the remaining beers in the truck were warm at the moment.

He parked and walked to the front of the restaurant. Inside it was noisy with bad acoustics, but Chad was used to loud bars and clubs from working as a bartender for over a decade. The one he had worked at in Dayton didn't come alive until midnight. The one gay bar in the entire area. Another mistake he had made—becoming a bartender there. His schedule had become so predictable, anyone could stalk him. Never again.

The hostess perked up and smiled. "Table for one?"

Chad glanced around teasingly. "Unless you've arranged a blind date."

She blushed and didn't return a comment on the joke. "This way."

In a small place in Chad's mind, he envisioned ordering take-out and sitting and eating it in the room so he could strip off his clothing and relax. But he figured he could spend one night eating at a table and not on the foot of a bed.

The hostess handed him a menu. He thanked her.

"Your server will be right with you."

The Diamond Stud

Chad thanked her again. He shook off his jacket and left it where it was tucked behind his back. Just as he opened the menu, Chad noticed the Tommy Chong look-alike and his younger friend being shown a table.

The younger man spotted Chad immediately and his eyebrows went upwards in an expression of surprise. Chad nodded politely to him. *You have to be a gay couple. Something tells me you are. But my, oh my...look at the age difference in you two. Tsch, tsch.*

The younger man nudged the older one, tilting his head in Chad's direction. The older man didn't look pleased.

Competition? Why the long face?

To the disappointment of the older man, the younger man raised his finger in a sign of 'one minute' and walked closer to Chad.

"I'm sorry if I'm bothering you."

"No bother," Chad said.

"If you don't want to dine alone, you're welcome to join us," he lisped. A campy gesture followed.

"Thank you. Why don't you guys just come sit here?"

"Pookie likes a booth." The man rolled his eyes sarcastically.

Pookie? Yup. Gay. Chad took his jacket with him as he stood. "Sure. Thanks."

"I'm Tim." Tim reached out for a handshake.

"I'm Joe." Chad shook his hand.

"Joe. I like that name." Tim grinned and led Chad to the waiting hostess and his partner.

The hostess said, "Looks like you found your blind date."

"Looks like it." Chad smiled and caught Tim's curious gaze.

"Introduce yourself." Tim gave his partner a playful slap on the arm as they took their seats in a booth, the two men opposite Chad. The hostess left them with menus.

"I'm Sal." The older man reached out politely.

Chad shook his hand. "I'm Joe."

"Nice to meet you, Joe."

Judging by Sal's expression of annoyance, Chad didn't think Sal thought it was nice at all.

"You sure I'm not intruding?" Chad didn't want to cause any discomfort to Sal. He knew how the man felt. When you're a gay couple, asking an unknown man to join your table was a gamble. No one knew that risk better than Chad.

"Sit!" Tim flipped his wrist, gesturing for Chad to stay where he was.

Chad stuffed his jacket between himself and the wall of the booth. A waitress appeared with a tray, putting three glasses of water on the table. "Can I get you anything to drink?"

The two men searched around the stack of menus for a beer and wine list. They shared the one menu as Chad waited his turn.

Tim and Sal ordered the same amber ale. Chad did as well. He figured it might offer Sal common ground and make him less anxious.

"Be right back." The waitress walked off.

While Sal inspected the menu, Chad caught Tim's dreamy stare. He picked up his own menu and investigated the salads.

"Love your hair."

"Thanks." Chad had a feeling Tim was fishing around for the answer to his gay-dar senses.

"Is that a half carat diamond in your ear?"

Sal looked slightly pinched. Was his partner flirting?

"No. Slightly under."

"Right ear?" Tim giggled. "You do know that's the sign for a gay man, right? Or did you not know."

"I know." Chad assumed Sal could take a deep breath in relief.

The Diamond Stud

"Honey!" Tim waved his hand. "I told you, Pookie. I told you he was gay." Tim said aside to Chad, "He never trusts my woman's intuition."

"I understand. It's a scary world out there." Chad sipped his water.

"Worse than usual," Sal said, his frown deepening the creases around his mouth.

"I can't agree more." Chad decided on a meal.

The waitress returned with their beers. "Do you need more time?"

"Joe?" Tim asked.

"I got it. You guys ready?"

"Yes." Sal said, "Cheeseburger and fries."

"I'll have the same. Swiss cheese, please." Tim piled the menus.

"I'll have the grilled chicken salad with fat-free ranch on the side." Chad handed her the menu stack. "Separate checks, please."

"Got it." The waitress left.

Chad raised his beer in a toast. "To being queer in a strange land."

Tim tapped his glass and said, "A-men, sistah!"

Sal touched his glass to the other two and said to Tim, "Tone it down. I don't need the disgusted sneers during dinner."

Tim appeared insulted but stayed quiet.

Chad drank his beer, dying of thirst. "Have you guys been getting hassles?"

"Not too badly. Just that Tim here," Sal thumbed towards his partner, "is too showy for both our goods."

"Don't start on me. You always put me down in front of other people." Tim glared at Sal.

"How long have you two been together?"

"Six months." Sal guzzled his beer as quickly as Chad was. "This is our first vacation together."

"We went to Fire Island!" Tim wriggled in the booth excitedly.

"You drove to Florida?" Chad cringed.

"Yeah. Never again." Sal shook his head.

"Jesus." Chad shivered, feeling every weary muscle in his body.

"Where're you headed, Joe?" Tim's leg made contact with Chad's under the table.

Chad had no idea if it was deliberate, and figured it wasn't. He moved his knee away. "I suppose California."

"You suppose?" Tim connected to Chad's leg again.

No mistake that time. Six months and a vacation later, these two look like they're on the verge of splitting up. A kept boy-older man relationship rarely stood the test of time. Chad had no doubt twenty years separated them.

"I'm still figuring things out." Chad and Sal both finished their beers. Tim sipped his.

"I noticed you have Ohio license plates." Sal wiped his lips.

Chad cringed, even knowing his sense of terror at what he had left behind had to be unfounded this far from home.

Tim seemed to notice Chad's discomfort. "You okay, Joe?" He touched Chad's hand.

Chad checked Sal's reaction to the contact. Sal had no idea Tim was playing footsie with him right under his nose. "I'd like another beer, then I'll be okay." Chad glanced around for the waitress.

"Got that right." Sal moved his empty glass to the edge of the table. "I'm sick of driving and we have a ways to go."

"We do." Chad raised his glass to the waitress, and mouthed, 'Two more?' She nodded.

"We live in Richmond Beach. Where are you headed?" Tim asked, his leg beginning to rub against Chad's.

"Not sure." Chad sat back as the waitress brought two fresh beers and took the empty ones.

"I'll check on your order," she said.

"Thanks." Chad raised the glass to his lips.

"Do you wax your eyebrows?" Tim rested his chin in his palm, staring at Chad.

"Yes." *I must be comfortable with these two. I'm letting my guard down.*

"Should I have mine done?" Tim fluttered his eyelashes at Chad, leaning over the table.

"Why don't you ask what Sal thinks?"

"He says he likes me just as I am." Tim puffed out his cheeks as if that were a bad thing to say.

Sal continued to look worn and pinched. He didn't react to the comment.

The waitress approached with two plates of food. A second server had the third. Once they were placed before the men, the waitress asked, "Is there anything else I can get you?"

Chad glanced at the other two. They were already stuffing food into their mouths, shaking their heads no.

She walked off.

With a mouthful of food, Tim said, "I really love your diamond stud."

Chad asked, "Are you trying to make your man jealous?" He stuck his fork into the romaine lettuce on his plate.

Sal bristled. "He does constantly."

"I do not. Nothing wrong with being nice." Tim shifted in the bench seat. "I'm just being nice."

"I know this may be inappropriate, but I have to ask." Chad wiped his lips with his napkin. "What's the age gap between you two?"

Sal winced and Tim said proudly, "Twenty-four years. He's forty-five and I'm twenty-one."

Chad didn't think Tim looked twenty-one. More like twenty-five or six, but he wasn't going to argue.

"He's my sugar-daddy."

Chad gave Sal his sympathy. Sal appeared as if he understood Chad's tacit communication.

"How old are you, Joe?" Tim gobbled his burger with robust energy.

"Thirty-eight."

"No!" Tim's eyes widened. "I wouldn't have said a day older than twenty-nine. No. Do you do anything?" Tim lowered his voice to a hissing whisper, "Botox or something?"

Chad laughed, continuing to eat.

"He's thirty-eight!" Tim dropped his jaw in an exaggeration of surprise. "Sal, do you believe him?"

Before Sal answered, the waitress appeared. "You guys doing okay?"

"Yup," Chad said.

She refilled their water glasses and left.

"Do you have a boyfriend?" Tim's eyes narrowed as if the question had an ulterior motive.

"No." Chad finished his second beer and devoured his salad he was so hungry.

"What do you do for a living?"

"Is this an interrogation?" Chad tried to sound humorous.

"Let the man eat in peace, Timothy. He's just been on the road like we have, for-fucking-ever."

"He calls me 'Timothy' when he's angry at me. Just like my father." Tim frowned dramatically. "I hate it."

When the last bite of salad was gone and the plate wiped clean with a roll, Chad felt the beer working through him. He

The Diamond Stud

waited until the waitress was in view and asked her for the checks.

"Are you headed back to the motel?" Tim asked.

"Yes. I'm exhausted." Chad rubbed his rough jaw and yawned.

"Here you go. I hope you have a nice night." The waitress gave them two folders with separate bills in them.

Chad used cash and tucked it into the black folder. "Thanks for asking me to join you. It was better than eating alone."

"No problem." Sal tucked his credit card into the black folder.

"Excuse me, gentlemen." Chad slid out of the bench, putting on his leather jacket. "I have to hit the little boy's room before I go."

Tim stared at him with large brown eyes, not saying anything.

Chad entered the men's room and headed to the urinal, adjusting his jacket, feeling the heavy weight of his handgun.

He relieved himself and looked forward to a shower and a night's rest.

"Joe."

Chad heard the whisper but didn't acknowledge it.

"Joe!"

He spun around and spotted Tim near him. Chad tried to finish what he was doing and not be distracted. Tim stood at the urinal beside him, opening his pants.

Chad glanced behind them. At the moment the bathroom was empty. He finished what he was doing, fastened his jeans, and flushed the urinal. He caught Tim checking him out.

When he stood at the sink to wash his hands, Chad noticed Tim trying to be quick to catch up to him. Once Tim was at his side by the next sink, Chad said, "Don't make your boyfriend jealous."

"I'm breaking up with him anyway."

"Does he know that?" Chad tugged paper towels out of the dispenser.

"He will. He's too old."

"That's harsh." Chad tossed out the paper towels.

"Hey, he got his money's worth."

"Right. On that note." Chad dug for his car keys as he left. It was pitch dark outside and cooling off quickly in the mid-October breeze. The sight of his Pathfinder and its driver's seat brought an instant ache to his legs and back. He dreaded the next two days, but that's how long it was going to take him to make it to the coast.

He dropped heavily into the seat and drove back to the motel. Once again the parking lot was nearly full with travelers making their way across the I-80 corridor.

Chad could imagine in the heat of summer how many people would be loitering outdoors. He was glad the weather had turned cold. The last thing he needed was noise of a tailgate party outside his room.

He slid his key into the slot and finally felt the road weariness consume him. After bolting the door, Chad stripped on his way to the bathroom, looking forward to a shower and relaxing in bed.

Standing naked outside the tub, he held his hand under the spray until it warmed up. He unwrapped the little bar of soap and stood under the water, moaning at the sensation of cleaning off the dust of the highway from his skin. He shampooed his hair, squeezing out the contents of a miniature plastic bottle and closed his eyes as he massaged his scalp. Using the rest of the shampoo, Chad shaved his jaw, chest, pits, legs and pubic area, where he sported a tiny tattoo of a warrior symbol.

He thought something loud banged outside the bathroom. Chad paused to listen. Unable to hear it clearly, Chad rinsed off and shut the water. Another loud pounding rattled his room. His adrenalin dumped in fear.

How could they find him? No way!

He grabbed a towel and raced out of the bathroom, wrapping it around his hips as his wet hair dripped down his shoulders. The knocking got louder and quicker in cadence.

Once his gun was in his hand, Chad walked slowly to the window and moved back the heavy curtain just enough to see out. Tim was there, shifting his weight anxiously, continuing to knock.

Chad blew out a breath in relief and tucked his gun back into his jacket. He opened the door a crack. "What?"

"He's a horrible bitch!"

"Did you break up with him now?" Chad held the towel at his hip.

"No. He just screams at me like I'm an idiot. Can I come in? I need a shoulder."

"Um." Chad glanced down at his naked chest.

Tim pushed against the door. "Please, Joe? Just for a minute?" He poked his head in. "Oh! Wow!"

The force behind the door increased until Tim wedged his body inside Chad's room. Chad closed it in a hurry and searched around for his jeans. "I wish you'd given *me* a minute."

Tim rushed him, stopping Chad from picking up the pair of pants that he had tossed over his suitcase. "Let me be your bottom-boy."

"Isn't Sal in the next room?"

"Yeah. I told him not to take a Viagra. I'm in no mood. I think I'm on my period…for him." Tim unlaced his shoes.

Chad stared at the wall which separated the two rooms. "I don't want to get involved in a lover's spat."

"Don't worry, honey. He just thinks I'm here to whine." Tim stripped his clothing off, leaving it in a pile on the floor. Chad could see numerous tattoos on Tim; one swirl design on the back of his neck, colorful floral patterns on each forearm, and a whooping crane adorning one calf. Tim turned down the bed and knelt on the sheets, his bottom high in the air and the pillow under his head. "You do have rubbers, right?"

Chad gave his luggage a quick glance. He did.

"Bet you're hung like a horse. Let's see it, you diamond stud, you."

"You have any idea how much trouble this could cause me?" Chad had enough to deal with.

As if he didn't care, Tim wasted no time scrambling off the bed and to his knees. He jerked the towel down with a sharp tug. Chad reached for the dresser for balance.

"Knew it." Tim lunged for Chad's cock and took all of it into his mouth. "Love shaved men and that tattoo on your pelvis is to die for!"

Bracing himself on a wall, Chad went awash with chills. "I feel like Warren Beatty in *Shampoo*."

"Hmm?"

"Nothing." Chad certainly didn't predict blowjobs at every port. Though he had a lot of success attracting men, Chad had learned to be leery of seducing the wrong ones.

Tim grabbed Chad's ass cheeks and drew hard suction. Chad orally fucking him, his cock stiff as a rod.

Tim leaned back, jerking his own cock. "Where's the goddamn rubbers?"

"No loud moaning. Ya got that?" Chad opened the zipper part of his suitcase. "I don't need Sal in here picking a fight or flattening my tires."

"He's probably already snoring. He's a grandpa." Tim returned to his previous position on the bed. "The guy's asleep by nine."

The Diamond Stud

Chad placed a tube of lubrication on the bed, kneeling behind Tim and tearing open a rubber with his teeth. "You're the one cheating, not me. Just don't get me involved in this. We fuck and you go. Understand?"

"Mmm!" Tim wriggled his behind. "Yes, sir."

Chad inspected the puckered pink hole in front of him. The scent of the same motel soap waft in the air. It was evident Tim had cleaned up after being on the road. He pinched a blob of gel onto his fingers and massaged Tim with it.

"Oh, honey!"

"Hush. The walls are too thin for that shit. My luck, Sal has a glass to the other side."

"I'm telling you he's snoring. I can hear him. Listen."

Chad stopped moving. A rumbling noise came from the next room. He laughed softly. "Still. Don't wake the guy up."

"Forget him. Screw me, diamond stud." Tim aimed his own dick backwards, winking at Chad with it.

"How did you know that was my nickname?"

"Like, as if! So obvious."

Chad fisted his cock a little to get it harder before pushing it against Tim's rim. Tim rocked back, allowing deep penetration. "I'm the eternal bottom to Sal's top. Go ahead, honey. I'm fine."

As chills rushed up Chad's spine, he held Tim's hips and kept pushing until his balls brushed Tim's ass. "You all right?" A flash of climactic sensation made Chad boiling hot.

"Hump away," Tim sang musically.

Chad stared at his sheathed cock thrusting into Tim's body. He loved to fuck, top or bottom. He just had to block the fact that this man had a partner in the next room out of his head. By early morning, when he was on the road, their spat wouldn't be his problem.

"My God, that feels amazing, Joe." Tim's moans were muffled by the pillow.

Chad felt his dick pulsate and quickened his pace. Exhaustion was trying to steal his orgasm away so he went for it. He assumed if Tim didn't like it, he'd say so. Going into overdrive, Chad piston-fucked Tim with the intention of coming and not edging the climax. He leaned over Tim and reached for his dick. Tim hissed air in a breath and arched his back.

Chad jacked him off just as fiercely as he fucked him. A deep grunt from Tim and hot spunk coating his fingers gave Chad the last push he needed.

He jammed his hips tightly into Tim's bottom and came, releasing Tim's cock to focus on his own pleasure.

Once the throbbing subsided, Chad pulled out, stumbling off the mattress, holding the condom at the base.

Tim rolled to his side and moaned. "I love you."

"Good. Get dressed and go back to your room." Chad worked the rubber off and washed up at the sink.

Tim stood beside him, rinsing a washcloth under the running water. "You interested in a toy boy?"

"No. Keep Sal happy and don't cheat on him again. He's a decent guy and there aren't many out there."

"Now you sound like my shrink." Tim dressed, looking as tired as Chad felt.

"Does Sal pay for that too?"

"Yes. Don't turn into a bitch on me." Tim sat on the bed to put his shoes on. "Kiss goodnight?"

"Nope."

Tim glanced at the stained sheet. "Well, at least I left you something to remember me by. Ciao."

Chad bolted the door behind him and listened as Tim opened the next room and settled in. There was no shouting, no noise. Chad exhaled in relief and used the wet washcloth to wipe the sheet as well as he could. He dropped down on the dry side of the bed, shut off the light on the nightstand and fell asleep.

Chapter 4

By six the next morning, Chad was on Interstate 80 once more, with a full tank and the destination of Salt Lake City in mind.

As he drove farther west the rest stops and highway exits grew sparse. There was no denying how enormous America was, miles of uninhabited acres, cattle grazing, and a skyline that went on forever. The truckers were once again his buddies and his beasts, as most were considerate in their actions, while a few terrorized motorists.

Orange highway construction cones loomed every few hundred miles. Even with early morning, non-commuting traffic, the quick pace of seventy to eighty miles per hour halted to forty-five constantly.

It amazed Chad that though lanes were blocked off from exit to exit, no one could be seen doing any work. Occasionally one pick-up truck in fifteen miles would be in the work zone. He would spot two men in hard hats smoking cigarettes as they leaned against the fender. Two men smoking cigarettes creating a single line of traffic that congested even the most deserted area.

He could only shake his head in wonder.

As the cones waned and the 'end of construction area' sign appeared, the cars would begin their free-for-all to pass the slower moving eighteen wheelers.

There was no doubt the vehicles with California license plates were the quickest to resume their ninety mile an hour pace.

Chad changed music CDs, running out of fresh tunes and wishing he could wear his iPod headphones. He was road weary more and more each day. He hadn't thought driving from Cheyenne to Salt Lake City would be that far. He was wrong. It was over four hundred miles and with the construction zones, that was going to be a long haul.

The pressure to his back and legs, not to mention his bladder, grew too much. Chad pulled off the road at the first sign of a gas station. The last thing he wanted to do was risk running on empty in an area that lacked a routine patrol of state cops or a service center within walking distance.

He drove to a gas pump and shut the engine. His body still vibrated with the sensation of moving. With his index finger he popped open the gas cap and tried to ease out of the car without appearing to be a hundred year old man. Once he was standing, he stretched out his back and checked gas prices. As he continued his journey west, the price per gallon had soared. Chad rubbed his face wearily and slid his credit card into the slot to pay.

The computer screen asked for his zip code. Chad hesitated, glancing around behind him. Under his breath he muttered, "Even in Utah I'm paranoid." He pushed his postal code into the machine and opened the plastic cap. Once the nozzle was humming with its toxic elixir into his tank, Chad leaned against his car and tried to feel well. In reality, he was dehydrated and hungry, which made him shaky.

After filling the tank and trying not to look at the cost, Chad took the receipt and decided to check out the selection of snacks in the mini-mart. He power-locked the SUV and walked to the glass doors, forcing his aching legs to obey him. The woman clerk glanced at him quickly. Chad thought he should be the one paranoid, but the quick-stop-type gas stations had 'stop and rob' written all over them.

The Diamond Stud

He spotted the video camera and tried to avoid it, walking to the cooler for a bottle of water. On his way to the cashier, he picked up a bag of cheese crackers from the shelf and waited his turn.

Standing, swaying, with a five dollar bill in his hand, Chad noticed a gray van in the lot and felt his blood go cold. He rushed to get a closer look, spotted a Utah license plate and sighed with relief. As he walked back to his spot in line, the clerk appeared wary.

Chad didn't respond to the odd look and paid for his items. He returned to his SUV, seeing a couple with two kids and a dog in the van. Letting out an exhale to release his stress, Chad stuck the water bottle into the cup holder, and opened the bag of crackers to munch as he drove.

He merged back onto the interstate, trying to sate his hunger and thirst and not have to stop again until the tank was on empty. Running away from trouble was exhausting. And his departure was only the beginning. He didn't know how he was going to find work, a home, or a safe haven once he arrived in California.

~

After driving for six hours, Chad felt wiped out. He hoped to do nine or ten, but his body was suffering the effects of one meal a day and too much worry.

Utah was like a lunar landscape; white barren planes with bizarre patterns of rocks, as if people had made designs and left no trace. The exits and rest areas vanished, and even in mid-October, it was boiling hot. He blew the fan again to save gas. When he opened a window, the noise of the passing wind was overwhelming, so he kept the windows shut and withstood the discomfort of the warmth.

Abandoned vehicles were more common in this salty wasteland. Not a sign could be seen of highway patrol.

The big rigs were using the left lane ahead. Chad spotted the reason, a broken down pickup truck was on the right shoulder. As he approached, signaling to move away from it as well, he saw a man in a cowboy hat, lying on the ground, searching under the bed of the truck, and an obvious flat tire.

"Yee ha!" Chad laughed. Coming closer, he actually met the man's eyes as he passed. "Holy crap!" Chad immediately pulled onto the right shoulder and hit the brakes to stop. He turned around, backing through his dust cloud until he was in front of the disabled truck.

Waiting for a safe space in the traffic which was flying by like a jet runway, Chad put the car in park and shut off the engine.

He walked over to a young man who was slapping the dust off his hands. A real cowboy. Chad had never seen one of those in person. Brilliant blue eyes, dark sideburns, tight faded jeans and a worn out denim shirt with the sleeves rolled up and unbuttoned low on his neck. Snakeskin boots topped off the incredible get-up. Chad made a note to dress that way for Halloween, if he eventually found a party.

"You need help?" Chad stood face to face with the man. They were the same height.

"Watch yerself." The cowboy grabbed Chad's arm and drew him a safer distance from the passing motorists.

The touch sent Chad into heat, which made his cheeks blush. It was already boiling hot on this tarmac and white landscape.

"Thanks." Chad extended his hand in greeting. "I'm Joe."

"Joe. I'm Charlie. Thanks for stopping."

"I'd want someone to stop for me if I was stuck in this hellhole."

When Charlie smiled, two dimples appeared. Chad needed to control himself. One of his favorite fantasies was being ridden like a rodeo bull by a feller in pointy boots and a ten gallon hat.

The Diamond Stud

"I located the spare." Charlie wiped his damp brow under his hat. "Now I gotta git it."

A loud tractor-trailer rode by. "Seriously, not a good spot to break down." Chad knelt and had a look under the truck bed. "Yup. There she is." He laid on his back and slid under. "Go ahead and lower it."

From where he was, Chad had a view of Charlie's body from the waist down. Perfect. Charlie began cranking the handle to release the cable. Chad moved over as dirt began to rain down from the undercarriage.

"You all right?" Charlie peered under the bumper at him.

"Yeah. She's coming loose." Chad shook the tire and it disengaged from the latch and cable. When it did, the tire came down on top of him. "Shit!"

Charlie crawled under the truck quickly. "Son-ova-bitch, Joe! You tryin' ta break a rib?" He dragged the tire off Chad's body.

Chad rubbed his chest. "I didn't expect that."

"I should've." Charlie inched back out from under the truck, sliding the tire with him.

Chad stood and brushed himself off. He hoisted up his shirt to see the result.

"You got yerself." Charlie leaned down to inspect the damage, tossing his hat into the bed of the truck.

"That's gonna bruise." Chad shook his head and rubbed the red skin.

"Yup." Charlie glanced up. His lips were inches from Chad's.

Chad's cock thickened and his exposed nipple went hard.

A speeding sports car beeping its horn brought Charlie out of whatever daydream he was in. Chad didn't have to wonder about his own. He wanted Charlie to lick his tit.

"Right. Let me get the jack over here."

Chad dropped his shirt over his chest again, waiting for Charlie as dust and dirt spun in the wake of the flying cars behind them. Charlie returned with the jack and tire iron, and knelt beside the flat tire. As he cranked, he began dripping in sweat, wiping his eyes. Chad rolled the spare closer, leaning it against the bumper.

"Want me to take over?" Chad asked.

"Yeah. Alright." Charlie stood, shaking out his arms from the strain.

Chad began cranking the lever until the tire was barely touching the road. He glanced up and watched Charlie remove his shirt, using it to wipe his face. It was instant meltdown for Chad. Charlie was lean and mean, like he worked as a farm hand or tamed wild stallions. "Motherfucker." Chad licked his dry salty lips.

"You got 'er. Let's get them lug nuts off." Charlie knelt beside Chad, straining to loosen the bolts.

"Those are some tight nuts," Chad said, tongue in cheek.

Charlie laughed but kept working until all five bolts were loose enough to take off by hand.

Chad inhaled the scent of cowboy sweat, his briefs damp from his excitement and warmth. He removed the nuts and made sure they stayed put.

"Crank 'er up." Charlie stood, hand on hip.

Chad continued working the jack, bringing the flat tire off the ground the rest of the way. Charlie hauled it off the axel and rolled it behind the truck bed.

Staring while Charlie moved, Chad drooled over every sinewy fiber showing from under Charlie's tanned skin. He used the jack to raise the truck up another inch for the spare, which was full sized and not a rubber donut.

Charlie brought it over after waiting for another gap in the traffic. "It's friggin' hot for October." He used his shoulder to wipe at the running sweat on his temple.

The Diamond Stud

"Ya got that right." Chad helped him aim the spare onto the protruding bolts. When it was lined up, they both pushed it on.

"Okay. Lower her down a bit." Charlie stood.

Chad released the lever and cranked the jack lower.

"That's good." He knelt down and began spinning the bolts on again. Chad helped until all five were connected. He sat down on his rump as Charlie tightened them, staring at the man's biceps and back, about to come in his pants.

Charlie made sure the lug nuts were snug, then began lowering the truck down and removing the jack from under it. "What a goddamn ordeal." Charlie tossed the jack and tire iron into the bed of the truck.

Chad picked up the spare. "Where you want this?"

"Just stick it in the bed." Charlie helped him toss the flat tire in the truck. When they were finished, wiping their hands on their jeans, Chad said, "I have water in the car." He walked to the Pathfinder and grabbed the bottle, returning to find Charlie sitting on the open tailgate, still brushing off his hands.

Chad joined him, giving him the water. When Charlie showed no hesitation in drinking from it, Chad's desire for him heightened. Charlie handed him back the bottle. Chad finished what was left.

"I can't thank ya enough." Charlie glanced at him. "Not too many stop nowadays."

"Like I said, I would like the help if I were stuck."

"Where're you from? I can't see yer plate from back here."

"Ohio. Don't hold that against me." Chad crushed the plastic bottle but he couldn't hear it crackle over the noise of freeway traffic.

"Why would I hold that against ya?" Charlie laughed.

"Never mind." He stared into Charlie's sky blue eyes. "So? Are you a real cowboy?"

"Yup."

"Yum." Chad corrected his faux pas. "Uh, I mean, really?"
"I heard ya the first time." Charlie laughed.
"Sorry. Now that I let my preference slip, you want to kill me? Kick some fairy ass?"
"No." Charlie smiled, shaking his head. "I still appreciate the help."
"I should let you get back to your rodeo, or rustling, or whatever it is you cowboys do." Chad hopped off.
"I don't know how to thank you." Charlie slammed the tailgate shut.
"I do." Chad glanced at the moving traffic.
"And what would that be?" Charlie gave Chad a wry smile and reached for his hat, popping it back on his head.
"Oh..." Chad shifted his weight and pushed on his stiff cock. "You don't want to know."
Charlie gazed out at the bizarre lunar landscape and the long stretch of straight highway first before he said, "Tell me."
"Can I suck your dick?" Chad winced, waiting for a punch in the jaw.
"Get in the truck." Charlie grinned.
"Yes! Yes!" Chad sprinted to the passenger's side. He opened the truck door, tossed the plastic water bottle inside, and grinned at the horse bridle and other riding tack on the floor. Before he got in he said, "This isn't a trick right? You don't pull out your six guns and shoot the queer, right?"
"Here's my six-gun." Charlie opened his jeans.
At the sight of his erect dick, Chad leapt into the truck face first, his feet sticking out of the passenger's side. He grabbed the base of Charlie's cock and sank it into his mouth. The scent of man-sweat made Chad swoon. He writhed on the seat, rubbing his dick into the leather under him, sucking like he meant it. After all, sooner or later, someone may call the highway patrol. He'd already lost an hour of drive time, but what an hour it was!

The Diamond Stud

Cowboy cock!

Charlie moaned and his thighs tightened under Chad's weight. A spurt of pre-cum on his tongue sent Chad into orbit. He humped the truck and drew stronger suction on Charlie's fabulous cock. Wishing he could touch him naked, Chad gripped Charlie's balls through his jeans. Charlie grunted and his hand finally made contact with Chad, digging into his hair as if asking him to suck deeper.

The second Chad pushed his finger against the root of Charlie's cock, Charlie came. Chad whimpered and swallowed down a delicious load of cowpoke spunk.

He didn't want to stop. He milked that one-eyed-trouser-snake until nothing more came out. When he was done, he slid back to his feet on the dry dirt outside the truck and wiped his mouth.

Charlie was gaping at him in awe.

"Good?" Chad laughed at his expression.

"Never had a man do it before."

"Yes!" Chad did a happy dance, punching the air.

Charlie pushed his soft cock back into his pants and fastened his jeans.

"But you will now?" Chad grinned mischievously.

"No. I don't know." Charlie smiled shyly.

"Thanks, babe. Now we're even." Chad backed up so he could shut the truck door.

"You're one funny guy." Charlie shook his head.

"You be careful riding the range, Chuck." Chad winked.

"And you be careful riding them gay-boys."

"Deal." Chad shut the truck door and was grinning ear to ear as he walked back to his SUV. He waved as Charlie waited for him to pull out first.

Chad looked at his grime-covered hands in glee, knowing where they'd been. He started his car, merged back onto the freeway, and gave a last wave as Charlie left the interstate at the next exit.

He was going to have some great cowboy fantasies to jerk off to tonight.

~

Slightly energized from servicing a cowboy, Chad kept driving until he hit Elko, Nevada.

With Utah, Wyoming, Nebraska, Iowa, Illinois, and Indiana behind him, Chad imagined a drive from Florida being unbearable. He wondered if Tim and Sal were bickering non-stop or had made peace.

Dusk was overlaying along the horizon. Pink, lavender, and light blue cirrus clouds feathered the deepening violet. In Chad's opinion, there wasn't anything more American than a panoramic view of two diesel locomotive engines pulling a line of one hundred freight cars in front of a backdrop of cattle grazing.

The vast wasteland of Utah and Nevada was peppered with tiny oases of civilization. An exit with the same motel and fast food selection appeared. Though the states kept changing, the name brands stayed the same.

Chad parked and took a minute to check his phone. He cringed at the numbers connected to the voicemail messages, and deleted them without listening to them. Would they never leave him alone? Chad was beginning to believe he would have to fake his death to be free.

Jett had left several text messages. Judging by the anxious tone of them, Chad called to reassure him he was okay.

"Baby!" Jett said when he answered. "I'm worried sick! What you doin' to your mama?"

"You should be less worried about me now that I'm nearly two thousand miles away from there."

"Where in the name of Princess Di are you?"

"Elko."

The Diamond Stud

"Elk-ho?"

Chad laughed. "Yeah. That'll work."

"Then go get yourself a nice young gigolo and enjoy."

"Sucked a cowboy's cock." Chad grinned, checking out the lodgers entering and exiting the motel reception area.

"No! A real cowboy?"

"A *real* cowboy."

"I want the details."

"Believe me, if I wasn't so tired, I'd give you a blow by delicious blow description." Chad glanced at his jacket which was on the passenger's seat. He was deciding whether to take it with him while he checked in, since it had a gun inside it, or leave it.

"Where did you meet a cowboy?"

"He had a flat tire in some no man's land area of Utah. I swear, Jett, it's like being stuck on Uranus."

"Ooh! Love when you talk dirty."

"I know you do, my chocolate honey-butt. Okay let me get a room and wash up and eat. I'm wiped out."

"Do you even know where you're going to live?"

"No."

"I'm worried sick! Mama is worried sick."

"Girl! You know what I left behind. Be happy for me."

"Aww, I am, precious. I am."

"Love ya."

"You too."

Chad disconnected the call and took his jacket with him. The evening brought much cooler temperatures with it so he put it on, touching the heavy gun through the leather.

Once he had checked in, he brought his suitcase to the room and put the warm beer into a bucket of ice. Standing at the sink, Chad washed his hands and face before he left the motel and hunted for his dinner.

Without a friendly gay couple to eat with, Chad purchased a meal at a fast-food drive-thru. He resisted the burger and fries duo and bought a salad and baked potato instead then headed back to the motel.

Very glad he was done driving for the night, Chad tossed his car keys and the room key on the dresser, shook off his jacket, and sat on the foot of the bed.

He pointed the television remote at the set with the aromatic bag of food on his lap. There wasn't a large selection of channels so he stopped at one broadcasting local news and removed the salad to eat first.

Chad craved a shower and to shed his filthy attire. He was running out of clean clothing and couldn't remember whether the motel offered a washer and dryer on the premises.

According to the television anchorman, not much was happening in Elko, but Las Vegas and Reno seemed to be newsworthy. Chad devoured the salad quickly and moved on to the baked potato. In between bites, he drank from a bottle of water.

Voices and footfalls sounded right outside his door. Chad stopped eating and put the volume on mute. He waited for them to pass. They didn't.

Someone knocked.

"Shit!" Chad put the food on the dresser and trembled as he reached inside the pocket of his leather jacket for his gun, removing it from the holster.

The knock grew louder.

Chad stood, gun pointing down beside him, and looked out of the peephole. A couple he did not know was outside his room.

"Who is it?"

"Peter?"

"No. Wrong room."

"Sorry, man."

The Diamond Stud

Chad moved the heavy curtain on the window so he could see outside. His heart was pounding and his breath puffed against the glass. He couldn't see them, but heard their voices receding.

Chad pushed the latch aside and cracked open the door, looking out. The couple was at the next room, being allowed in. He shut and bolted the door, leaning his head against it and closing his eyes to recuperate. How long could he live like this? Was he driving himself crazy or was he going to be found eventually?

"I'm overreacting. There is no way anyone can trace me. No way." Chad put the gun back into the holster and placed it on the nightstand. He used a chair to brace the door and felt queasy. After the scare the food looked unappetizing to him. He tossed the rest of it out and waited until he felt safe before he took off his clothing to shower.

Whatever sensual heat that lingered from his fun with the cowboy dissipated into fear. Seventy-two hours of traveling without proper food and water took its toll. And that didn't include the anxiety over the future. Chad hoped what he'd left behind, stayed behind. He was fooling himself if he thought uprooting his life wasn't screwing with him mentally.

In need of a shower, Chad tugged off his belt. His clothing had loosened slightly. He was a big man. One meal a day wasn't providing the calories he needed.

Once his nerves settled, Chad finished the bottle of water and remembered the beer he had left in the ice bucket. He took a dripping bottle out and touched the glass. It would take a couple of hours to chill it properly. This room did not have a refrigerator.

Chad sank the two bottles into the ice until they were nearly submerged. He glanced at the barricaded door and began stripping off his clothing. "No. No way anyone can find me." He shook his head and took a shower.

Chapter 5

All night Chad tossed and turned. The beer did nothing to help him rest. He needed tequila to knock him out. Though he had fallen asleep in front of the television, he didn't stay asleep through the night.

There was no laundry service at the motel. Chad put on the cleanest jeans he had and left the room before dawn.

In agony, he sat behind the wheel again, the rest of Nevada and the width of California still in front of him. What would he do once he hit San Francisco? He had to work. His savings weren't going to last.

Entering the interstate, getting back in line to play tag with the speeders and truckers, Chad knew he was running himself down recklessly. *I have no choice.* He smoothed his hand over his hair and down his lobe to his earring. He toyed with the diamond stud, spinning it gently. Day four. This time he wasn't going to stop until he ran into the Bay area fog.

Nevada's Great Basin met the foothills of the looming Sierra Nevada Mountains. Chad admired the picturesque view, but the grade of the roadway became a grind on the gas and brake pedals. A line of big rigs crept with an effort uphill in their own private lane, while they rode your bumper down the other side.

Though he had seen a sign for Reno pass by miles ago, Chad didn't know if he had crossed the state line into California. Suddenly, on a steep decline, highway state patrol cars swarmed

The Diamond Stud

like wasps. He struggled to keep within the legal limit and not wear his brake pads to metal.

Red and blue lights of a patrol car lit up directly behind him.

Chad glanced over at his jacket with the gun hidden inside it. He knew his license plate was tagged with the information that he had a permit to carry...in Ohio. California was not reciprocal.

"Fuck." Though he didn't know California law, he assumed carrying without a permit was punishable by death, or terminal incarceration, the guillotine, or something horrible.

Chad pulled over to the shoulder and figured he'd deal with the fallout. Just as he slowed to half his speed, the patrol car veered around him and attached itself to the pickup truck in front of him. Chad held his breath. Yes, the cop was stopping someone else. He blew out a loud exhale and resumed careening down the roller-coaster-like roadway, slightly dizzy from the stress.

Just as he recuperated from the image of a CHPs officer arresting him and carting him off to jail, a bizarre string of toll-booth-like barriers blocked the road. But this was no toll.

State insignias from the Department of Food and Agriculture, including warning signs, gave Chad a heart attack. Never in his life had he seen anything like it before on a national interstate highway.

Gulping down a dry throat, Chad stopped at the booth and barrier. A uniformed man approached his window. Chad quickly rolled it down.

"I see you're from Ohio."

"Yes." Boiling nervous heat instantly made Chad sweat.

"Do you have any plants or animals with you in the car?"

Was he hearing straight? Plants or animals? Chad shook his head. "No."

"Open the hatch for me."

Chad reached for the inside release. He popped it open, watching his rear view mirror. The only thing Chad had in the back of the Pathfinder was his one suitcase.

The SUV's hatch was closed and the man approached Chad again. A trickle of sweat ran down Chad's sternum. Was this the USA or Russia? Who allowed a state to act like a different country?

"Have a safe trip," the uniformed agent said.

Chad drove off. "What the fuck was that? You have to be kidding me." He had never heard of anything like it. Yes, in an airport, maybe border patrol, but never from state to state.

He stared into his side mirror. "Okay, take it easy. He's stopping everyone. Quit stressing." Chad used his shirt to wipe his moist face and kept on driving.

Signs for Sacramento appeared. Chad was tempted to stop. The journey from Elko was grueling and he was feeling like he should no longer be behind the wheel.

"How far could it be?" He rubbed his jaw stubble and calculated the miles. "No. Three hours to San Francisco? No. Oh, God, I can't do three more hours."

It appeared he was back in civilization. Every exit held a hotel, restaurant, shopping mall, and of course, fast food chains. The vast emptiness of Utah and Nevada gave way to urban life. He was relieved. At least if he broke down here, he'd survive and not keep his fingers crossed for a kind motorist.

Daylight waned, Chad stifled a yawn. "No. I can't do it." He left I-80 once more and cursed himself for not completing the journey. But where was he going to go in San Francisco? He didn't know a soul.

East of the city center of Sacramento, Chad located a plethora of hotels near an outlet shopping center. He parked by the entrance and treated himself to luxury after the cheap motels all week.

The Diamond Stud

The upscale hotel clerk behind the desk greeted him with a smile. "Hello, can I help you?"

"Hi. I need a room for one night." He removed his wallet and gave the man his ID and credit card.

"Two doubles or one king?" The man typed on the computer keyboard.

"King, please." Chad was handed a credit card slip and signed it. All along the walls were glass picture frames with a variety of air force shoulder patches in them.

The clerk assigned Chad a room and gave him his key. "We have a wine and appetizer social between six and seven-thirty and complementary breakfast between six and ten a.m."

"Great." Chad liked the idea of free booze and food.

"It's right down there in our lounge."

Chad looked towards a big screen television, tables and chairs, and a counter with the fixtures for a buffet, minus food. "Cool."

"Just let me know if you need anything."

"Do you guys have laundry service?"

"We have a coin operated washer-dryer by the elevator or you can give your items to room service and we'll have it for you in the morning."

"Okay." Chad handed him a five. "Can I get quarters?"

The man smiled and gave Chad the change. "Just a heads-up. There's a group of Air Force guys staying here. They tend to take over the place and the Wi-Fi service gets slow." He laughed. "But they're great guys."

Chad tried to fill his tight pocket with twenty quarters gracefully, avoiding dropping them all over the tile floor. "Air Force guys? Really?"

"Yeah. They come from all over to go to Travis."

"Travis? The band?"

"No. The Air Force base." The man glanced at the computer screen. "I see you're from Ohio. I guess you've never been to this area."

"Nope. But there's an air base in Dayton." Chad thought about a hotel filled with uniforms. It had possibilities. "Thanks." He left the building to get his suitcase, returning and heading to the elevator. He could see the coin-op laundry facility through a glass window in a door.

One more night on the road. After riding one floor up, Chad walked the long hallway, rolling his suitcase to nearly the end. He used his key and took a look inside. "Not bad." A small fridge, microwave, and sink, made for a petite kitchen area, a desk with internet wires and a lamp was positioned beside a large television, and the bathroom was spacious and sparkling clean.

He removed his gun, putting it inside the room safe. From now on he'd have to keep it unloaded, locked, and in the back of his SUV.

Have faith, Chad...they did not bother to look for you once they realized you'd abandoned ship. Please, God, please, tell me no one is searching for me.

It was after four and the little booze party wouldn't start for two hours. Chad dumped his suitcase on the bed and sorted the clothing. Everything needed washing, even the items he was wearing. Because of his hasty departure from Dayton, he didn't have time to box up every piece of clothing he owned. Did he have regrets? Maybe a little. But at least he had his life.

Chad stripped completely, putting on a pair of running shorts. He stuffed his entire wardrobe into a pillowcase and held a handful of coins and his hotel key. Walking barefoot down the carpeted corridor, Chad felt his nipples harden in the cool air conditioning. It may be October, but it was eighty degrees outside.

The Diamond Stud

It wasn't until he was standing in front of the laundry room door that he caught his first sight of camouflaged fatigues. A young man in a dark t-shirt and sweat pants was stuffing his uniform into one of the washers.

Chad had to use his room key to gain access. The minute he did, the young man spun to look.

"Hi." Chad smiled shyly.

"Hi." The man smiled back.

"Are you using both washers?"

"No. Be my guest." He stepped aside.

Chad crammed everything from the pillowcase into the washing machine. A vending machine offered a selection of laundry soap, fabric softener, and dryer sheets. Chad bought a small box of powdered soap.

He heard the young man feeding his washer with quarters.

"Are you stationed here?" Chad asked, dumping the detergent into the washing machine.

"No. I'm stationed at Fort Lewis."

"Fort Lewis...Fort Lewis..." Chad shut the washer door and read the panel to see how many quarters it was going to eat.

"Washington."

"D.C.?"

"No," he said, laughing, "Washington state."

"Duh...sorry. I'm clueless." Chad folded the pillow case. "Do you have any idea how long this thing takes?"

"It says here," he pointed to the printed writing on the front of the machine, "twenty minutes for the washer, thirty for the dryer."

"It must be nice to be feeling sharp. I feel brain dead." Chad noticed the young man glance at his naked chest quickly. He gave him a closer inspection, trying to detect any attraction. The washer began its cycle the minute Chad gave it enough money.

The young man didn't answer. A strained silence followed until the man said, "Well, nice meeting you." He opened the door to the laundry room.

"You too." Chad followed behind him.

Two men in uniform were laughing as they stood at the elevator. His young friend joined them, chatting comfortably. Chad kept quiet, standing behind the three, holding the pillowcase against his chest.

They entered the elevator. Chad pressed number two and asked, "Two or three?"

"Three," one man answered.

Chad depressed the button and the light came on. No one spoke while they rode up one floor, very slowly. The door opened and Chad left the other three behind. He glanced at them. They were all staring at him as the door slid closed.

Chills covered Chad's skin. He walked briskly to his room, hoping the wine social didn't turn into a beat up the gay-dude party. Back in his room, Chad tossed the pillowcase beside him on the bed and sat down to think. If he didn't get wine and food in the hotel lobby, he'd have to figure out what to eat and most likely drive there.

He moaned and flopped back on the bed.

~

Dozing in and out with the television on, Chad had showered, shaved, packed his clean clothing, and craved alcohol and food. He opened his eyes to see a commercial for the local political race being broadcast and shut off the set. He sat up and scrubbed at his eyes. It was after six. Time to brave the boys in beige.

Chad put his boots on and tucked in his shirt. He glanced at the mirror, combing his fingers through his hair and making sure he looked presentable. His wallet and car keys locked up with his gun, Chad slipped the room card key into his back jeans pocket and headed down to the main floor.

The Diamond Stud

The minute he exited the elevator he heard laughter and male voices. A few dozen men, some in uniform, but most not, were standing at the buffet, smoking cigarettes on the outdoor patio, or eating at the tiny tables for four.

Chad felt like the only outsider in a room full of military buddies. Being a gay man, it was either a dream come true or a prelude to his homophobic homicide. It was hard to be invisible. His frosted blond hair, six foot-two inch height, tight clothing, and not to mention the diamond earring in the *right* lobe, Chad may as well have been wearing a sign that read 'Queer here'. He avoided direct eye contact and figured he'd fill a glass with wine, a plate with food, and eat in his room.

Through the back patio doors, Chad could see a gas barbeque grill blowing out a cloud of smoke as hamburgers were being charred. A woman brought a fresh supply of buns and salad to the inside buffet table as the burgers were cooked.

While he waited his turn at the food, Chad inspected three bottles of wine; chardonnay, merlot, and a Riesling. He chose the merlot, filling a plastic cup to the rim. The line for food moved an inch. Chad chugged the contents of his glass, pouring another. The man behind him gave him a slight smile.

"Long day," Chad said.

"I hear ya."

Since the door had been opened to conversation, Chad asked, "Are you from Fort Lewis too?"

"Yes. We all are."

"Oh." Chad picked up a paper plate, put the full glass down for a moment, and scooped tossed salad on it. "Are you all being reassigned?"

"No. We're going on a tour at Travis Air Base."

"And the Air Force puts you all up in a Holiday Inn? How generous of them." Chad opened a bun and used tongs to put a cheeseburger on it.

"They get a group discount." The man laughed softly.

"I can imagine." Chad placed a plastic fork and knife on his plate, picked up his wine and looked around for an open seat.

Maybe the men were nice. Maybe he could eat here and get seconds without having to navigate the elevator and long corridor.

Since the man in line didn't pursue more conversation, Chad held his plate and cup and stood behind a vacant seat where two men were sitting at a table for four. "Is anyone sitting here?"

"No. Go ahead." The man in uniform gave Chad a once over before he continued to talk to his friend.

Chad felt as if he were intruding, but had committed himself. He took the chair, which faced the big screen television and patio, and gulped his second cup of wine.

The two men finished their food and stood, tossing out the garbage, leaving to light up and smoke outside. Chad was alone at a table for four. He felt like a freak but figured he'd finish his food and go. No harm done.

He noticed a man in uniform trying to find a place to sit. Chad tilted his head to him. "I don't bite. Honest."

The young man put his food down, sitting across from Chad. "Thanks."

"No. Thank you for serving." Chad wiped his fingers on a napkin and began eating the salad once his burger was demolished.

"What do you do?" the young man asked, taking a big bite of his food.

"I'm a traveling salesman." Chad was going to say he was running away to join the circus, but he didn't want to sound condescending. A traveling salesman seemed very benign. Exactly what Chad wanted.

"What do you sell?"

The Diamond Stud

"Office supplies." Chad had to think quickly. No controversy please. What was he going to say? Drag queen? Gay bartender?

The young man nodded, chewing his food.

"I need more wine. You want me to get you some?"

"I'm good."

Chad stood, dumping his empty plate into the trash and getting on line for another glass of merlot. He poured the remainder into his cup and an efficient staff member brought out a fresh bottle. Taking a sip, Chad noticed two other men had joined his dining companion. No way was he returning to that seat outnumbered three to one.

He gazed at the television which was broadcasting a twenty-four hour, right-wing news program. He turned his nose up in disgust and investigated the patio.

It was long and narrow, fenced in to block out the competition, which happened to be the motor lodge he had been using all across the country. White wrought iron tables with matching chairs, as well as potted plants invited him to stay outdoors. He sat by himself at a table, and sipped his wine.

There was a crowd of men by the barbeque grill and another group scattered near it, smoking while they ate. Like inside the hotel lounge, some men were in their uniform pants and beige t-shirts, others in running shorts and tennis shoes. Two women, both in complete military dress stood out. Chad thought they were very butch-looking. If not butch, certainly tough. Chad couldn't imagine battling either of them in a war.

The tiny cups of wine weren't doing their job. He wasn't even buzzed. An older man holding a plate of food in one hand and a low calorie bottle of beer in the other gave his table consideration. Chad didn't know whether to be cordial or not. Nothing seemed to make these men friendly.

Well, I'm not a bitch. Chad smiled. "You can join me."

"Thanks." The man relaxed behind his plate of food.

"I didn't even see the beer. Where was it?"

"On the opposite side of the wine. There's bottled beer and a keg."

"Sweet." Chad didn't like the big name-brand beers, so he figured he'd keep to his wine. "How long have you been in the military?"

"Since I was a cadet. So that makes it twenty years this November."

"Any plans to retire?"

"When I hit thirty years on duty." The man smiled.

"I'm Joe." Chad reached across the table.

"Dennis."

When Chad shook his hand, he checked the left one for a wedding band. No rings. Not married? Or married and not wearing a ring? *Gay...not gay? Homophobic...liberal? The nightmare continues. Whom do I trust?*

"It's nice that the hotel staff cooked food for us." Chad finished his third cup of wine, craving more.

"Yeah. This hotel always hosts the air force. They do a nice job."

"Are you from Fort Lewis too?"

"Yes."

"Is that were your family is?" Chad leaned on his elbows, trying to get a read on his man.

"Most of my family is back east. I'm on my own in Washington."

Not married. So far so good. "How long do you guys have to stay here?"

"Around three weeks." Dennis finished his burger, wiping his mouth on a napkin before putting it on the empty plate.

"Will you get sent to Afghanistan or Iraq?"

"Most likely Afghanistan. But not right away. My unit just got back."

The Diamond Stud

Chad cringed and expressed his sympathy. "I can't imagine."

"No. Most civilians can't." He smiled as he said it, but Chad knew Dennis had probably been through hell.

"Thank you for serving." Chad couldn't say it enough.

"You're welcome."

He wanted more wine, but had a nagging sense that if he went to get it, Dennis would either move on, or the table would fill with his buddies, like it did on his last conversation. There was something about Dennis' eyes he liked. No, Dennis wasn't young, or a pretty boy, but his was very attractive in a military, clean-cut, masculine kind of way.

Chad knew his craving for straight men usually got him into hot water. He couldn't help it. It was who he was. And after all, he got a straight cowboy and what he figured was a bi-curious fisherman. Two more notches to the bedpost. Could a military man be his third?

"It makes me want to enlist." Chad glanced behind Dennis to the rest of the men. No one was giving their conversation a second look. He was glad. Chad didn't need a whole troop of GI's to tear him apart.

"They won't take you."

"Too old?" Chad blinked.

"Don't ask, don't tell. Even with the repeal, it's not easy being a gay guy in the service."

He choked in surprised. "Should I run before you shoot me? Get a head start?"

"No." Dennis chuckled, shaking his head.

"What gave it away?"

"Where do I begin?"

"Never mind." Chad knew he had 'gay' written all over him. He tugged on his earring out of habit.

Dennis said, "Yes, that was one of the main clues. Right ear."

"I had no idea how widespread that knowledge was."

"Sweetie, you're on the west coast."

"Did you just call me 'sweetie'?" Chad's dick twitched.

Dennis appeared shy suddenly, eyes cast down.

Chad leaned closer to him, over the white iron table. "You have a girlfriend?"

"No."

"A boyfriend?"

After a soft laugh, Dennis said, "No."

"A jack-off buddy?"

"I haven't had sex in three years."

Chad sat upright in the seat and his jaw hung open. "Whaat?" He lowered his voice, "You have to be kidding me. Why the hell not? You're very attractive."

"Me?" Dennis pushed his fingers into his own chest. "Sure."

"I'd fuck ya. Or visa-versa."

The look on Dennis' face was tough for Chad to read until he said, "I can't even remember what it's like to kiss."

"Shut up. No way." Chad shifted on the chair. "Hey, come to my room. I'll fix you up."

"I'm tempted." Chad glanced over his shoulder at the crowd.

"Sneak there. I won't tell." Chad added, "I won't ask or tell. Dumb law. Good riddance to it."

Dennis rubbed his forehead as if he were dying to accept.

"Look, I'm in room number two-ten. I've got everything we need for a nice hot bout, so don't worry. It would be my privilege to service a serviceman. No one should go without it for that long."

Dennis still looked conflicted.

"Let me get you another beer." Chad slid out his chair.

"No. Uh. I'll get it." He rose up, picking up his empty plate.

"Right. Can't be seen talking too long with the queer?"

"Pretty much. If I do come to your room tonight, I have to be careful."

The Diamond Stud

"Two-ten." Chad felt sorry for him. "Don't forget."

Dennis nodded, dumped his trash in a garbage can near the doorway, and then entered the hotel.

Chad scanned around the patio. After a few suspicious glances from the group he was ignored. "Right. I'm done." He opened the glass door to the lounge, instantly hit with loud talking and laughing. One more stop at the wine table, and he carried his plastic cup to the elevator. When it opened, three more GI's stepped out. Chad entered the elevator, pushing number two and sighed. "That clerk was right. They're fucking everywhere."

His card key in one hand, the full cup in the other, Chad walked the long hallway, hearing muffled conversations through the walls as he went.

He closed the door behind him, set the glass down, and got himself comfortable. With four pillows propped against the headboard of the big king-sized bed, Chad channel surfed, sipping his wine.

~

Dead asleep and dreaming about lip-syncing Diana Ross' *You Can't Hurry Love* on a cable television contest, Chad woke with a start.

Someone was tapping at his hotel door. He glanced at the digital clock and turned on the light beside his bed. It was nearly two a.m.

In just his briefs, Chad scrambled out of the bed, his heart pounding behind his ribs. He looked out of the peephole. Dennis was there, checking up and down the hall, shifting his weight anxiously. Chad unlatched the security bolt and opened it. Wearing a t-shirt and shorts, Dennis rushed in, closing the door quickly. "My roommate is asleep."

"Roommate?"

"Straight, married staff sergeant. Not gay friendly."

"Right. Get the hell over here. We have no time to chat." Chad held his hand and led him to the bed.

"Christ, you've got an amazing body."

"You like?" Chad puffed up his chest.

"I like. But I'm so out of practice. I feel like a kid."

"Let me bring back your groove, military man." Chad licked his chin with the tip of his tongue as he ran his hand over Dennis' closely cropped hair.

Dennis immediately connected to Chad's mouth in a kiss.

There was no doubt Dennis had plenty of beers for courage. He could taste it. Chad wondered if he was tipsy. He didn't care.

He stepped back and helped Dennis remove his t-shirt and gym shorts. Dennis toed off his sneakers, holding Chad's arm for balance.

Chad gave him another lingering kiss and said, "Lay down." Dennis rested face up, watching Chad.

In anticipation of Dennis showing up, Chad had already placed the condoms and lubrication on the nightstand. He stripped off his briefs and played with himself to get Dennis excited.

Dennis dragged his khaki boxer briefs off and exposed a semi-erect dick. Chad crawled up from the foot of the bed, nuzzling in. He inhaled Dennis' scent, and liked it. Chad used his hands to part Dennis' legs. He needed to make him hard, so he held the base of his cock and sucked to his hand, toying with his balls and scrotum as he did. Dennis groaned and spread his legs wider. "I swear if you keep sucking, I'll come."

"You want to come in my mouth?"

Looking sheepish, Dennis shook his head.

"Okay, cookie. I get it." Chad smiled and worked Dennis' cock until he indicated he was edging his climax. "I'm close…"

The Diamond Stud

Chad reached for a rubber and put it on for him, coating it with gel. Once Dennis was prepared, Chad got to his hands and knees. "I'm all yours."

Seeming as nervous as a sixteen year old virgin, Dennis moved behind Chad, holding Chad's hips. "Tell me if you want me to stop." He put his cock against Chad's rim.

"Oh, hell no." Chad rested his cheek on the pillow. "Don't you dare stop until you're satisfied."

"I'm not going to take long." Dennis began a rhythm of sliding in and out.

"After three years? I'm surprised you didn't spontaneously combust the minute I got my mouth on you."

Dennis thrust deep and fast. "I'm coming. Sorry."

"Sorry?" Chad said, "You have nothing to apologize for."

A few more lingering thrusts and Dennis pulled out. "That was fantastic."

Chad sat up, helping him take off the rubber. "Oh, honey. I can't believe you waited three years."

"I had to. I'm risking my reputation right now."

Chad could see him shake. "Right. Give me that. Go clean up and get dressed." He took the used condom and nudged Dennis to stand.

Dennis entered the bathroom.

Once he had thrown out the trash, Chad shook his head sadly. Nothing in life was fair. Just as he thought he was in hell, he realized so was everyone else. He placed Dennis' clothing on the bed so he could dress easily.

He returned from the bathroom and began putting on his briefs, shorts and t-shirt. "Thank you so much, Joe."

"My pleasure. I'd say anytime, but I doubt I'll ever see you again."

"Where do you live?" Dennis slipped on his tennis shoes.

"I have no idea." Chad laughed but the feeling of being homeless made him frightened.

"I have to go."

"Please be careful." Chad touched his cheek.

Dennis pecked his lips and headed for the door. Before he vanished, he winked at Chad.

Chad heaved a big sigh and locked the door. He stood in the bathroom and stared at his reflection. The bruise from the tire that had fallen on his chest was still red. "What a long, strange trip it's been."

The Diamond Stud

Chapter 6

The same group of men from last night's wine social were having the free breakfast buffet the next morning. Chad thought he would be up early enough to miss them. He was wrong.

He poured a large cup of coffee for himself and placed it on one of the empty tables, going back for food. The selection was very good; hot scrambled eggs and sausage patties, whole wheat bread, and fresh yogurt and fruit.

Chad piled his plate high and sat behind his coffee, stuffing his face.

Dennis was in full uniform as well as the rest of his unit, obviously ready for their day at Travis.

"Why does it always rain on me?" Chad sung to himself, while Dennis didn't acknowledge he existed. *Yes, it would be suspicious if he said hi. Lord knows! Gays serving in the military? Gasp! Choke! No one will ever really get used to it.*

Chad camped it up in his head. It was safer there. He knew better than to lisp, wiggle as he walked, or make foppish hand gestures. *Maybe when I get to San Fran I can be my queen self. But not here.*

That lesson was learned when he was four, at kindergarten on a Dayton public school playground. He had been bullied, teased relentlessly, and beaten as a very young child for being 'different', and more recently nearly beaten into a coma. Not to mention a week ago, he dealt with threats of murder. That was enough for Chad to rein it in. He drew the line at wearing baggy unflattering clothing, keeping his hair brown, and *never*, would he take the earring out of his right ear. *I'm the 'Diamond Stud'! Fuck you if you can't deal with it.*

But his inner dialogue was all talk. He was terrified to be caught alone and in peril simply because of whom he chose to love. *Been there, done that. Hated being in the hospital with broken bones!*

His meal devoured, Chad sipped his coffee, thinking of going back to the buffet for seconds. A large group of GIs entered the lounge, clogging up the food line. Chad reconsidered a refill, sick of being the ignored civilian. He tossed out his paper plate and returned to the room to get his things. It was time to hit San Francisco. He had to live in a liberal environment and socialize around his own kind to survive.

Wheeling his small suitcase behind him, Chad stopped at the desk and handed the clerk his key. "Do you need me to sign anything?"

"Nope," the clerk said. "Let me print up your receipt."

Chad checked the cost, folded the paperwork and stuffed it into his jacket pocket. "See ya."

"Bye."

He stood behind his Pathfinder and used the remote to open the hatch and heaved his suitcase into it. With great reluctance, he unloaded his handgun, and placed a wire lock through the open barrel, disabling it. The bullets were separated from the revolver, and he was not happy about it. He hid it in the truck and closed the hatch.

"Right. Follow the Yellow Brick Road." Chad sat behind the wheel and had direct access to Interstate 80 West a block away from the hotel. Though the sight of that highway was as enticing as a rat with rabies, Chad knew the end was nigh. Three hours.

But where do I go from there?

The Diamond Stud

~

The gas gauge was beginning to warn him he was getting low on fuel. It maybe only three hundred miles, but it felt like the longest leg of his trip. The construction and traffic for this Friday morning commute made it more like an eternity. The merge ramps were short and loaded with cars so the highway came to a complete halt in places. Poor design and too many commuters equaled accidents.

The clear blue sky gave way to fog. Chad grew excited, knowing that meant the coast was near. He passed Berkeley and read signs for the Bay Bridge. "Six dollars?" Chad swore under his breath at the charge for a toll. "How come nobody warns you?" He shifted to get his wallet out of his jeans as he drove, trying to remember if he had cash left. The highway lanes spread out to the toll booths. Long lines gave Chad the time he needed to dig out a ten and make sure he was in a cash lane.

It didn't matter if it was a short journey, he was sick of being in his car. Rolling down the window, resting his head in his palm, Chad approached the booth, inch by inch.

He handed the man the ten and received his change. "Thanks."

"Have a nice day."

"You too." Chad faced a reverse effect on the other side. A multitude of lanes all cramming into four, one a restricted commuter lane. "Right. No more driving the interstate during rush hour. Lesson learned."

The end of I-80 appeared the minute he was on the west side of the bridge. There was no question Chad was glad to see the back of that eternal road. He left the madness of the highway and turned off to explore the local streets. The first service station he saw he stopped at. *Three-fifty a gallon? Oh, honey, you're not in Kansas anymore.* Chad pulled to a pump and shut off the car.

Once he filled the tank, he entered the mini-mart and searched for a city map and local newspaper.

With his purchases in his hand, Chad stood in line at the cashier and noticed the clerk wearing a rainbow wristband. The relief Chad felt at a sign of things to come was worth the trouble it took to get here.

"Hey." Chad smiled at the young man.

"Hey." The man smiled back, scanning the map and paper, taking the twenty dollar bill Chad handed him and giving him change.

"Do you know of any area of town where I can rent a room quickly?" Chad asked, putting the money into his wallet.

"Depends what kind of area you're looking for."

"The gay kind."

The man laughed. "Castro District."

"Of course."

"Good luck."

"Thank you." Chad took his map and newspaper, and left, sitting in the SUV to check out the area.

He realized he was already on Market Street so he began cruising it. Men were everywhere, some holding hands with other men. Small businesses sported posters of half naked males or erotic play toys in their window displays.

"Yes! Yes!" Chad needed to be on foot to get a closer look. He drove around looking for an open parking space and parallel parked in a tight gap. The second he had fed the meter, Chad danced around, spinning on his heels and waving his hands in the air. "I'm home! I'm home!"

"Welcome home, handsome." A man gave him a wicked smile as he walked past.

"Thank you, gorgeous." Chad waved at him. "Christ, I just want to fuck my way around the city. But…first things first." He felt like a child who has just been given his first two-wheel bike. Free to explore and spread his wings.

Each shop was better than the next. There were so many gay men to ogle, Chad kept being distracted from his task.

He approached a wooden fence that had been used to post advertisements and want ads. Chad inspected the plethora of flapping papers, feeling the cooler temperature now that he was between the Pacific and the bay. He zipped his leather jacket and raised the collar. One piece of printed paper caught his eye. 'Room for Rent'. Chad took out his mobile phone and tilted his head sideways as he read the phone number off one of the tabs on the bottom.

"Hello?" a man answered.

"Hey, I'm standing in front of a sign that says you have a room to rent. Is it still available?"

"Yes."

Chad read a few of the details. "So it's on eighteenth street and Market?"

"Right. Where are you coming from?"

"I think I'm only a few blocks away. Can I check it out?"

"Absolutely. Just ring the buzzer for the top flat."

"Cool. Be there as soon as I can walk to you."

"I'll be here."

Chad tore down the flier and looked for street numbers. He asked a passing couple, "Eighteenth is that way?"

"That way." They both pointed in the opposite direction.

"Good thing I asked." Chad imagined a sexy three-way with the two men and winked.

As the couple walked away Chad heard one man say, "Christ, he was hot!"

Twirling around light poles, Chad pretended he was Gene Kelly in *Singing in the Rain*, dancing and laughing as he made his way. No one threatened him. No one beat him up.

In fact, he was getting smiles and applause; some men hooked his arm and spun in a do-se-do.

Chad kept track of the house numbers and stopped short at the correct one. He had a look around the neighborhood. "Wow. This is right in the middle of everything. Location, location, lo-fucking-cation."

The flier in his hand, Chad read more of the description as he buzzed the doorbell. Behind the wooden door he heard the clomping of feet down stairs.

"Hi," the dark-haired heavyset man with a goatee said as he opened the door. "Come on in."

"What a place!" Chad followed the man up the stairs. "I know I'll love it."

"It's a bit pricy. But it's worth it." He gestured for Chad to enter the living room.

A fireplace was the first thing to catch Chad's eye. On an adjacent wall, bay windows faced the front of the building. It was furnished beautifully with a Victorian-esque gray velour lounge and a black leather saddle-back chair. It was entirely hardwood flooring and a Persian rug and black and glass coffee table accented the style.

"I love it." Chad touched the velvety couch and noticed a dining area attached to the living room containing a dark colored table and chair set. "Did you decorate it?"

"Yes. I'm glad you like it. Do you have furniture?"

"No. I have to buy some."

"Maybe not. This is the room I want to rent."

Chad was led to a small bedroom. A double bed with a cherry wood headboard was already inside it, with matching nightstand and dresser. "This comes with it?"

"It does if you need it."

"I need it!" Chad sat on the bed with a bounce. "Can I stay immediately?"

The Diamond Stud

"I usually like to check references and credit reports first." Chad took out his cell phone and dialed. "Jett?"

"Hello, sugar! Which state are you in now?"

"Heaven. Look, babe, I'm trying to rent a room and the man needs a reference. Tell him how amazing I am."

"You got it!"

Chad gave the man the phone. "Here you go."

"Who is it? Your employer?"

"No. My best friend."

"Hello?" the man said, turning to the hall.

Chad smiled and lay back on the bed, admiring the Victorian era crown molding and window dressing.

From this side of the conversation, it sounded as if Jett was raving about him. Chad smiled. Well, he was a decent guy.

"Right...okay. Thanks." The man handed Chad back his phone. "What's your name?" the man asked, as if testing him.

"Chad Desoto."

"Birthday?"

"Jett knows my birthday?" Chad put the phone to his ear. "You know my birthday?"

"Honey! I threw you a surprise party on your thirty-fifth. Don't insult me!"

"How drunk was I?" Chad removed his wallet and handed the man his Ohio driver's license.

"Okay, 'uncle'. I give up. So? You made it? You found a place to live?"

"I hope so. I don't want to spend another night in a hotel." Chad cupped the phone. "Okay?"

"Sure. Let me get the rental agreement." He left the room.

When he was alone, Chad sighed loudly. "Men hold hands on the street here, Jett. I can't believe it."

"That's San Fran for you. I am *so* jealous!"

"Come out. Fly here. Don't drive."

"I can't afford it. And I don't have any vacation time. You know how nasty the place I work for is." Jett paused. "I'll be fired if they see me on the phone."

Chad checked his watch. "Shit. Sorry. I'll let you go."

"Kisses!"

Chad made kissing noises and hung up. He hopped to his feet and found the man returning with a pen and paper. "I don't even know your name."

"Fernando Cruz. But everyone calls me 'Nan'."

"Are you gay?"

"Yes, but I have a boyfriend, sorry." Nan smiled.

"Don't be. It would be awkward if there were sexual tension between us." Chad brought the form and pen to the dining table and read it over. "Is this info confidential?"

"Yes. Absolutely." Nan gave Chad a magazine to write on so he didn't damage the wood top of the table.

Chad slipped it under his paperwork and began filling it out.

"Here's your ID."

"Thanks." Chad stuffed it in his wallet.

"I require a month and a half up front deposit."

"Okay." Chad tried to calculate the amount compared to what he had left in his savings account. He needed work. Now.

"So why did you leave Ohio?"

Chad stared into Nan's brown eyes. "Have you ever been to the Midwest?"

"No."

"Don't go. They think LGBT is a country music hit. And that 'corn-holing' is a game you play with beanbags."

Nan laughed, sitting with Chad at the table.

"My checkbook is in my car. Oh. Where do I park?"

"On the street. There's no garage or anything."

The Diamond Stud

He finished filling out the form, taking the ad from his pocket and rereading it. "I get my own bathroom? And there's a washer and dryer?"

"Yup. I'll show you."

Chad followed Nan to the hallway. A small bathroom with white fixtures, including a pedestal sink and shower stall, was all his.

"The washer and dryer is located off the kitchen."

A newly remodeled narrow galley kitchen with a window at the far end impressed Chad. "I can't believe how beautiful this place is."

"I'm glad you like it. I tried to keep the period look without changing too much of the details. And we're on a corner here, so there's no noise at all from neighbors."

"Why is it still available?" Chad looked out of the kitchen window at the street below. Same sex couples strolled leisurely.

"I just hung that flier this morning." Nan chuckled.

"Damn! Fate!"

"Do you have a job?"

"No. But by tonight I will."

"What do you do?"

"I'm a drag queen!" Chad threw up his hands dramatically. "And a bartender on the side."

"Love it." Nan shook his head. "Do you need a hand with your stuff?"

"I have one suitcase. So, no." Chad patted his pocket for his car keys. "Let me walk back to my car and get you that check."

"Hang on. Here's a key." Nan reached towards a set of small hooks from a key-rack and gave Chad one.

The ring was attached to a rainbow medallion. It made Chad's eyes tear up. He dabbed them quickly and reached out for an embrace. "Thank you for trusting me."

Nan hugged him, rubbing his back. "You feel wholesome. What can I say? And you also look like you've been through an ordeal."

Chad parted from the hug, wiping his eyes. "Mind reader or psychic?"

"I don't need to be either to see you need some TLC."

"Your boyfriend better appreciate you!" Chad wagged his finger.

"He does. So don't make him jealous."

"Never. Okay, sweetie, I'll see you in a few minutes."

"Don't worry about it. You have the key, take your time. Explore."

Chad cupped Nan's jaw and kissed him lightly on the lips. "You are wonderful."

"Oh! Don't do that. I can't think you're hot." Nan nudged him. "Go."

Laughing as he went, Chad descended the stairs to the street level, waving at Nan as he stood at the top landing, smiling at him.

~

Chad stopped in his tracks at the sight of a bar located on the corner of a busy intersection. He shielded his eyes and gazed into the glass window. It was closed because of the early hour, but there was a bear of a man inside, sitting at a table doing paperwork with a laptop computer in front of him.

He tapped the glass to get the man's attention.

"We're closed!" the man yelled through the glass door.

"You looking for a bartender-slash-entertainer?"

The man was about to shake his head no. Chad could feel it coming. He unzipped his jacket, hoisted his shirt up and used his index fingers to massage his nipples, grinning at the man.

"Very funny!' The man shook his head.

"Come on. At least talk to me."

The Diamond Stud

To his delight the man stood and unlocked the door. "Get your ass in here." He locked the door behind Chad.

"Chad DeSoto." Chad extended his hand.

"Wayne Newington." He clasped Chad's hand.

"Look, I have ten years of experience bartending, more than that lip-syncing in drag, and will work for peanuts."

"I don't have a full time position."

"Does that mean you have a part-time one?" Chad figured he'd get an income and worry about a second job tomorrow. As the man considered his offer, Chad said, "Just tips for the first month?"

"I can't let you do that. I have to at least pay you minimum wage."

"Deal." Chad snatched his hand before he could reconsider.

Wayne said with a smile, "I don't remember offering you the job."

"You did. You said you had to pay me minimum wage. Hang on, I'm wearing a wire, I'll play it back for you." Chad began to open his pants as a tease.

"You're quite the character." Wayne smiled.

"You have no idea. Your customers will love me. Literally." Chad tucked his shirt back in.

"Oh, boy..." Wayne rubbed his forehead. "Okay. Sit your tight butt down and let me give you your tax forms."

"I love it here. Everyone is so nice!" Chad sat at the table on the opposite side of the man's laptop. He sighed happily as he stared at the passing pedestrians.

"Where are you from?" Wayne placed a pen and paper in front of him and joined him.

"O-hell-o." Chad removed the 'room for rent' ad from his pocket to copy his address.

"I'm originally from Indiana."

Chad stared into his brown eyes. "Then we're kindreds."

"Pretty much." Wayne watched Chad write. "Tell me about your act."

"I get dolled up and sync anyone you want. Barbara, Liza, Aretha...you name it. Or I can just get naked and show off my big dick."

"Bet you look amazing in drag."

"I do." Chad sat up proudly. "That's why I left the bigot-bible-belt. B-B-B for short." Chad kept filling out the form. "Wow. What the hell is the tax going to be like? I had one form to fill out in O-hell-o."

"Sweetie, how long have you been in California?"

Chad checked his watch in a comic gesture. "Let me see. Twenty hours? Maybe less."

"Everything is more expensive here. And the state will take over your paycheck and life."

"Goody! A nanny-state. I'd take that any day to be free to put on my false tits and eyelashes."

"My customers are going to love you, Chad."

"Yup. They will. I aim to please." He slid the finished paperwork over.

"Bet you suck like a Hoover."

"Do I! Want some, boss?" Chad licked his lips.

"Yes, I do. But I better not. My husband will be pissed."

"Husband? Did they bring back gay marriage while I was stoned?"

"No. We got married before Prop Hate." He showed off his gold band.

"Anytime you want the cum sucked out of you, I'm here." Chad smiled. "Keep the boss sweet. He gives you more hours that way."

"I don't ask for sexual favors from my staff. But I know what you mean."

"When's my first shift? Please say tonight."

The Diamond Stud

"Yeah. I can tell you're either a glutton for punishment or desperately need money."

"Yes and yes."

"Ten 'til closing."

Chad reached over the table. "You got it, Mr. Newton."

"Newington."

"I knew that. But Wayne Newton just has a certain ring to it."

"Gee, that's the first time I've heard that joke."

"Told you I aim to please."

"Go. Get some rest and come back fresh."

Chad stood, slapped his own ass and hammed it up. "Fresh!"

"You're trouble!" Wayne wagged his finger.

"Can I bring a get-up? Hm? Do a quickie before closing time?"

"Sure. Why not?"

"Yes! Yes!" Chad danced around, throwing his fists into the air.

"You're easy to please."

"I am." Chad stood still and purposely made a silly expression. "That's very observant, Wayne. Not too many people know that about me."

"I bet there's a lot people don't know about you."

Chad's jovial mood dropped instantly.

"You okay?"

"Yeah. See ya ten to ten, boss."

"See ya, Chad."

Chad waited as Wayne let him out of the bar and relocked the door behind him. He stood for a moment, trying to think. *A bite of food, shopping for my outfit and wig, then back home for my beauty sleep.*

~

When Chad returned to his new abode, Nan wasn't there. He carried his purchases up the stairs and into his room, dumping them on the bed. Sitting down, he removed his boots and socks, trying his new pink high-heeled pumps on for size. He waltzed across the hardwood flooring, swaying his hips side to side. Next was the jet black wig with flowing long hair. He tilted his head and gave it a test run as well.

Hurrying to the hallway bathroom mirror, he fussed with it, making the long strands flow down his shoulders and back. "Hello, boys." He pursed his lips. In excitement, he raced back to his room, grabbed another bag of goodies and emptied the contents into the sink. He opened the lipstick and applied it, next, heavy black eyeliner.

As he struck a pose for himself, he heard, "Wow."

Chad glanced over his shoulder seductively at Nan. A young Asian man was standing beside him, staring. "Why hello, handsome."

"Chad, this is my boyfriend, Le Trung."

In his high heels Chad towered over the lithe young man. He held up his hand daintily to be kissed. "The pleasure is all mine."

Le awkwardly shook it instead of kissing the back of it, like Chad intended.

"You too big to be woman."

"I know. More of me to love." Chad put his hands on his hips.

"That's my line." Nan chuckled. "Is this just for fun?"

Chad took off the wig and shoes. "Yes and no. I got a job bartending at Twin Pecs bar."

"Already? That is so cool."

"Oh! My checkbook." Chad scrambled to his bedroom, threw the wig and shoes on the bed, and ferreted through his suitcase. The gun was still in its lock, unloaded but tucked into his clothing. He intended on putting it between the mattress and box spring, but got overly excited with his purchases.

He sat down on the bed to write it. "To Nan?"

The Diamond Stud

"Fernando Cruz."

"Right. Duh." Chad filled in the check. "Um, how much?" He cringed, knowing it would be high.

Nan glanced at Le. "Just give me a thousand."

"Yipes. What was I supposed to give you?" Chad hoped his tips were going to make up for this big spending spree.

"Twenty-five hundred."

"Gaaak!" Chad tore off the check and handed it to him.

"Will it bounce?" Nan read it.

"Not if you deposit it now. If you wait a week?" Chad shrugged, "No guarantee."

"Wipe off make-up. Let me see you without painted face." Le pointed to his own eyes.

"Where are you from, little boy?" Chad returned to the bathroom, opened a bag of cotton balls he had bought, as well as a bottle of baby oil to remove the make-up.

"Viet Nam."

"I see." Chad cleaned his face and washed it as well. He patted it dry and stood next to Le in the hall, saying, "Ta da!" reaching out his arms to the sides.

"You handsome man. No do paint no more."

"Come 'ere, you baby-doll." Chad picked Le up and swung him back and forth. "I could eat you up!" Chad ran kisses all along Le's neck until he was wriggling and laughing hysterically.

"Great," Nan said, "Now he'll be whining how much he wants you."

"Naw...he knows he's got a man." Chad set Le back on his feet and walked to his room. "Gotta get my power nap in, guys. Nighty-night." As he closed his door he heard Le say, "I want him."

Chad chuckled and piled his purchases onto the floor, crawling under the blankets and closing his eyes.

Chapter 7

Chad stood in the shower stall shaving everywhere but his head. Luckily he was fair, born a towhead blond, and didn't have a dark five o'clock shadow. He'd shaven his body so many times, he had a system; beginning with his jaw, moving on to his pits, his pubic hair and balls, finally his legs.

After he had finished, he stood dripping in the stall and felt excitement at starting a new job. A new life. As he dried off with a towel, something sinister was trying to edge out the fun. Fear.

The last time he had done a drag performance he'd nearly been killed. The beating was so severe he had stitches on his forehead, a split lip and broken ribs, and was unconscious until he woke up in the emergency room. He was laid up for weeks.

"Stop." He closed his eyes and inhaled. "Do not torture yourself. You are in San Francisco now." He stepped out of the shower stall and tossed the towel over the rack. To soothe the shaved skin, he used cocoa butter moisturizer. Chad covered his body in cream, massaging it everywhere, including his pubic area and balls. While his hands were slick he tugged on his cock a few times, wondering if he wanted to jerk off. Though it felt nice, he decided not to.

After wiping off the mirror, he put light mousse in his hair, running his fingertips through the frosty length and giving it that perfect disheveled look.

The Diamond Stud

With both hands he leaned on the sink and gazed into the steamy mirror. He stared at his eyes. Bright sky blue.

Out of nowhere, his mother's voice came to him. *I love you, I always will.*

At her memory Chad choked up. He missed her. She had been gone for four years and ever since she'd been taken away from him, things went horribly wrong. Her influence had been what kept him safe. It was a fact he didn't know until she died.

"Stop!" he screamed at his own recollections, echoing in the damp room.

"Chad?" Nan stood outside the door. "You okay?"

Chad swung open the door and embraced Nan, trying to contain his emotions.

"What happened?" Nan rubbed his back.

Battling the pain, Chad opened his eyes to see Le staring at him from behind Nan's back. "Hello, my Asian doll."

"Why you cry?"

Chad stood straight wiping his face. He had no modesty, nor any reservations about being naked in front of his roommate and his boyfriend. "Bad memories. I'm okay. But if I have red eyes and a puffy face, my makeup will look horrible tonight." Chad laughed but it wasn't a happy laugh.

"Anytime you need to talk, Chad." Nan frowned. "You know we're here."

"I know." Chad nodded. "Let me finish. I have to get going." Chad went down the hall to his room. He took a deep inhale to calm down, then dressed in a pair of skin tight white slacks, commando, and a dark blue, equally tight, muscle t-shirt. He hung a heavy, silver curb link chains around his neck and wrist, and checked the earring back of his stud, making sure it hadn't come loose. He placed his wallet, keys, and mobile phone into the inside pocket of his leather jacket and put it on. He glanced at the spot where he'd hidden the gun, then sat down to put his socks and black boots on. With the bag containing his drag gear slung over his shoulder, Chad threw a kiss at Nan and Le who were watching TV together in Nan's bedroom.

"Good luck!" Nan said.

"Thank you, sweetie. I'll try not to wake you up when I come home." Chad closed the door and trotted down the stairs.

The evening was cold and damp but it felt invigorating to him. He was within walking distance to the bar, so he picked up his pace and made sure he wasn't late.

~

Jeremy Houston sipped his apple-tini trying not to think about work. Accounting paid well, but with the end of the year looming, tax season was around the corner. The workload became manic until the last filing date, and even then, new customers popped in late constantly, begging for help with the IRS.

Twin Pecs had become his favorite Castro haunt. He considered himself a regular since he had stopped by every Friday and Saturday night for the past few months. Jeremy was shy and didn't have a large social network, or make friends easily, so he tended to sit by himself at the bar. This place was something special. He loved the ambiance of the older, more mature clientele. There was nothing he disliked more than college boys high on coke and ecstasy making morons of themselves on the dance floor.

The bar interior appeared to sparkle in the dark evenings. The selection of alcohol bottles glittered like the Manhattan skyline during Christmas. Polished brass and stained glass hanging lamps, plus the festive decorations for Halloween made this spot feel like paradise. The juke box wasn't overwhelming, so you could have a conversation without straining your vocal cords.

As he sipped his drink, Jeremy noticed the owner, a big bear of a guy named Wayne, with a strikingly handsome tall blond

The Diamond Stud

man. Wayne introduced this man to the regular bartender, Trent, and showed the blond into a back room.

Jeremy leaned over to catch the man's rear view in the clinging white slacks, which was just as attractive as his front.

Just as he tried to get Trent's attention, Jeremy noticed the handsome, frosty blond with the diamond stud in his ear appear behind the bar and begin shaking and creating the exotic mixed drinks. Before Jeremy asked for a refill, the stunning man snatched the empty glass from his fingers and said, "Let me guess." The man sniffed the remnants of booze. "Apple-tini."

"You're good!" Jeremy straightened his posture at this new addition to the staff.

"Coming right up."

He didn't know if it was the flattering light or his drought of having sex, but Jeremy was instantly smitten by this man's sensual appeal. A drink was placed before him. Jeremy caught hold of the man's arm and asked, "What's your name?"

"Is that so you can get your drinks faster, or...?" He batted his lashes flirtatiously.

"Or!"

"I'm Chad." Chad shook his hand.

"I'm Jeremy Houston and I'm in love!" Jeremy never acted like this, but there was something contagious about Chad's bubbly personality.

Chad reached for Jeremy's face across the bar, held it tight, and kissed him, sticking his tongue into his mouth. At the unexpected act, Jeremy nearly fell off the barstool in reaction.

Once he retreated from the kiss, Chad winked and moved on to fill more requests for drinks.

"Holy shit." Jeremy licked his lips for a trace of Chad's taste and assumed the competition for this super-hunk's attention would be fierce. He put a twenty dollar bill on the bar with the intention of giving it all to Chad.

Chad was in his element. A room full of mature gay men who seemed happy, gainfully employed with disposable income, and not a homophobic sneer was anywhere on the horizon.

Though he had dated and 'serviced' older men, he hated to admit, since he was in his late thirties, younger men were attracting his attention. Not twinks, but not middle-aged guys either. 'Tweenies'. Someone in their late twenties who wasn't too young or too old for him to have a relationship with. *A relationship*. Chad couldn't remember the last one of those. He and Jett gave it a shot for two weeks when they first met, but soon found they were better friends than lovers.

With a quick glance he checked on Jeremy's drink to see if he was ready for a refill. Chad thought Jeremy was adorable. He was jarred out of his daydream to see another man who needed his attention.

"Yes, my love?" Chad leaned across the bar towards the plump older man. "What can I get you? The sky's the limit."

"Don't flirt unless you mean it," the man said, smiling.

Chad acted insulted, putting his hands on his hips and thrusting out his crotch. "Oh, honey! Does this body look like it's mean?" He licked his finger and touched his bottom, hissing like steam.

Laughter surrounded him and the man said, "How about two beers. The lager on tap."

"I can do that." Chad winked and pumped the handle. His co-worker Trent brushed by him to get ingredients for his cocktail. Trent grabbed Chad's ass as he passed.

"Ooh! Naughty!" Chad made face at him and smiled. "Can you do it again?" He caught Jeremy smiling at his antics. Chad was glad. The man obviously had a sense of humor. "Your tini run dry, gorgeous?" He filled the pint glass and waited for the foam to subside.

The Diamond Stud

"Are you trying to get me drunk?" Jeremy asked.

"Mm. Are you easy when you're drunk?" Chad handed the man one glass of beer, working on the next.

Trent brushed behind him again. "You sexy fucker. I can't get enough of your ass in those pants. You'll turn this place on its head."

Chad met Trent's gaze. "Give me a kiss." He made kissing noises at him. "With tongue."

"I will!" Trent warned. "Don't tempt me."

The plump, bearded man took the one glass of beer and handed it to his friend. He waved a twenty at Chad. "Keep the change, blondie."

"You got it, big boy." Chad stuffed the bill down his shirt so it stuck out like he had cleavage. He gave the man his second beer and winked.

He rung up the tab and dropped the change into a glass for his tips. The bar was packed and Chad was in heaven. He spotted Jeremy staring again. Sauntering back, Chad leaned his elbows on the counter and propped up his head. "You like me, don't you?"

"Why shouldn't I like you?"

Chad could see his blush even in the dim light. "No. I mean *like*-like me."

"I barely know you."

"True." Chad stood straight and sighed loudly. "I'm a stranger in a strange land. Poor me."

"Really? Where you from?"

"I'll never tell. Shh. Top secret. I'm undercover with the FBI." Chad exaggerated a scan of the room. "Here's my gun." He gave his balls a good squeeze, trying to show off his package through his white pants.

"Geez. What a cock tease!"

"Never!" Chad rushed to get the next drink order, gazing back at Jeremy's smile.

Jeremy never stayed past midnight, but this new guy was too good to be true. It gave him the worst case of a school boy crush since sixth grade when he fell in love with Bon Jovi.

Wayne and Chad exchanged some nodding of the heads and gestures. Jeremy wondered if the owner was telling Chad his shift was through, since right after, Chad vanished into the back room.

Maybe it's just a break.

Jeremy nursed his drink. He didn't like getting drunk, but loved his mixed drinks. This time he did apple-tinis, tomorrow night he may switch to the chocolate-tini or a vodka Collins. It didn't matter what he ordered, the bartenders knew how to make them, and make them strong.

The crowd had not thinned, if anything it had filled up to maximum occupancy. Jeremy needed to use the restroom. He tapped the man next to him, the same man who had been beside him all night, and said, "Boy's room again. Will you watch the seat?"

"Sure."

"Thanks." Jeremy left to take care of business.

When he came back he noticed the juke box music was louder and the lights, dimmer. *Is this what happens here after I go home?*

All the men on the first floor were craning their necks towards the second floor. Jeremy wondered how hard it would be to get back to his seat. As he excused himself to try and find it again, he heard whistles and cheers.

He spun on his heels and tried to see what was causing the commotion. "Oh my-fucking-God!"

The Diamond Stud

Chad was dolled up in drag, lip-syncing into a phallic shaped microphone. He was wearing a skin tight black spandex micro-mini skirt and a pink v-neck sweater over false breasts. Long black hair shimmered down his shoulders and black fake eyelashes and heavy makeup nearly concealed his identity. His legs were covered in beige hose and his pink pumps made him appear like a giant.

Jeremy nearly fell over in surprise. Chad camped up the role to perfection. Gloria Gaynor's *I Will Survive* was blasting from the audio speakers.

Watching Chad descend a step, then stop to perform, gave Jeremy a nice view up his ridiculously small skirt. Though Chad may have tried to strap down his bulge, it was too big to tame. And from below Jeremy could easily see his high cut g-string or thong and a set of spectacular balls inside it.

He was glad he had emptied his bladder, because he was getting wood.

Chad spun around, wriggling his bottom, and the sight from underneath of two perfectly rounded bare cheeks had Jeremy in heat. The crowd erupted in cheers, whistles, and catcalls.

As he stared in awe, Jeremy could not get over Chad in drag. Though Chad was big and sexy, his features and fair coloring gave him the illusion of femininity. He was the consummate drag queen and had obviously spent a lot of time practicing. His lip-sync was flawless.

By the time the big finish came, Chad was standing on the first floor of the bar, the entire upper floor was crowding around to see him from above.

Chad threw back his head and opened his arms as the applause thundered around him.

Jeremy clapped like mad. Did this little local bar ever advertise that they had entertainment? Jeremy didn't think so. He wondered if Chad had convinced the owner to give his customers a special treat.

"Thank you," Chad said, smiling and nodding. "Thank all of you…you dirty, dirty old men!" Chad hammed up a shocked cliché gesture, opening his painted lips and touching his cheek.

Jeremy chuckled to himself as the crowd calmed down. He stared at Chad until he realized the man in high heels was making a beeline for him.

Jeremy's five foot nine inch height suddenly felt extremely tiny next to the tall man in three inch pumps.

"Hi."

"Hi." Jeremy gazed at the incredible skill Chad had used to apply his makeup.

"Come here often, sailor?" Chad tickled Jeremy's cheek. "I mean, cum. C-U-M."

Before Jeremy could think of a reply, someone goosed Chad, making him jump. He reacted playfully, yanking his mini up and exposing his fabulous ass. "Honey!" Chad said, "Don't touch it unless you use your tongue!"

Jeremy enjoyed the sight of Chad's thick cock and balls in the little thong pouch. Offers to lick Chad's rim abounded, but Jeremy could only see and hear one thing. Chad.

He lowered his skirt, brushing it into place as if he were a proper lady. "They're incorrigible." Chad made a face in disgust but he was obviously enjoying the attention. "Don't ya love it?"

"Hell yeah." Jeremy licked his lips.

Chad's electric blue eyes narrowed on him.

Jeremy got lost in the color.

A bell rang and Trent shouted, "Last call!"

"Let me help him out," Chad said. "Uh, you leaving?"

"You want me to stay?" Jeremy's pulse raced.

"Only if you want to." Chad shrugged.

"I'll wait for you."

The Diamond Stud

Taking a second to decide what to do next, Chad cupped Jeremy's cheek and kissed him again. This time it was slow and sensual. Jeremy nearly passed out.

By the time Jeremy reacted, reaching to touch him, Chad was walking behind the bar, serving the enthusiastic patrons.

Jeremy stood still in the midst of the mayhem, as twenty dollar bills were waved at Chad like he was a go-go boy in LA.

Chapter 8

Chad had no idea the reaction to his charm and his act would be so overwhelming. At the rate of the generous tipping, he didn't think he would need a second job right away. Cash was sticking out from between his fake boobs, and he was filling rounds of drinks so quickly that Wayne had to be pleased.

Seeing Jeremy standing in the background, his seat no longer available, Chad poured a cup of coffee for him, topped it with whiskey and waved him over. Jeremy hurried between patrons to take it. "On me." Chad pulled cash out of his bra and rang it up.

"Thanks." Jeremy took a sip and choked. "Is this coffee?"

"Irish coffee." Chad grinned wickedly.

"Wow."

Chad blew him a kiss. He didn't know why he picked Jeremy out from the crowd, but the feeling that Jeremy was nice, truly nice, drew Chad to him. Previously Chad enjoyed his playtime with sex hook-ups, yes, but he needed friends, close companions like Jett, to spend quality time with. Jeremy had an aura about him. Chad strongly suspected that Jeremy was a good, kind man.

After harrowing experiences, Chad learned if he didn't have allies, he had nothing.

Just past two a.m. Chad finished his first shift at his new job. He changed back into his white pants and muscle tee, scrubbed the makeup off his face, and hustled to help Trent, Wayne, and their glass washer, Juan, to clean up for the night. With the four

The Diamond Stud

of them loading the washer, and scrubbing the floors and tables, they managed to get done in an hour.

Though he should have been exhausted, Chad was elated. He had a large amount of money from his tips and checked with Wayne to see if he was happy with his work. "Well?"

"See you tomorrow night." Wayne grinned.

"You're the best!" Chad kissed Wayne's cheek and waved to the other men. He retrieved his drag gear and stood by as Wayne unlocked the door to let him out.

Jeremy was standing right outside the door in the cold.

"You could have waited inside," Chad said, staring at his sweet features.

"I didn't want to get in the way."

Since the bars were closing, a number of people were still lingering on the street, heading home or socializing.

"Do you want to come to my place?" Chad asked.

"Do you want me to?"

"What kind of question is that?" Chad smiled.

"Okay."

Chad gestured to the right direction and began walking with Jeremy.

"Where did you park?" Jeremy asked, his hands deep in his jacket pockets.

"I walked here. I live a few blocks away."

"Oh. Cool."

The silence felt awkward to Chad. Maybe this wasn't a good idea. They were both tired and obviously struggling to make conversation. Chad knew it would seem rude to send Jeremy away after inviting him.

He stood in front of the door to his flat and as he turned the key he said, "I have a roommate, so let's be quiet."

"'Kay."

Chad let them in and climbed two steps before he stopped. "You do want to come up, right?"

Jeremy echoed Chad's earlier line, "What kind of a question is that?" and chuckled.

"A dumb one." Chad continued walking up the staircase. The apartment was dark and silent. Putting his finger to his lips, Chad headed to his bedroom and hung his outfit on the door handle of the closet. He took off his jacket and boots staring at a nervous Jeremy. "You okay?"

"Uh, are we just going to have sex?"

Chad asked, "Isn't that the idea?"

"I thought maybe we could talk."

"Talk?"

"You know. Get to know each other a little first." Jeremy hadn't removed his coat.

"Get to know?" Chad dropped to sit on the bed. "You want to get to know each other at three a.m.?"

Jeremy lowered his eyes, staring at the floor or something lower than Chad's eyes.

Chad was deciding if he was too tired for this crap or if Jeremy was worth it. He gave Jeremy another inspection. "All right, honey. At least join me." He patted the bed.

Jeremy removed his jacket and shoes while Chad scooted to the far end, lying on his side, propping his head on the pillow. "You first."

The blush showing in his cheeks, Jeremy chuckled. "Okay. Are you from California?"

"Nope. Next."

"Have you ever been in a relationship?"

"Unless you count two weeks as a relationship, nope. Keep going."

The Diamond Stud

"This is your idea of a conversation? You have to be kidding, right?" Jeremy seemed to be keeping his sense of humor, which was a good thing according to Chad.

"Nope. Next?" Chad teased.

"Okay, I give up." Jeremy flopped to his back on the bed.

"Surrender, Dorothy!" Chad scooted closer, resting his hand on Jeremy's chest.

"I surrender. You negative?"

"Yup. You?"

"Yup."

Chad rested his knee cross Jeremy's thigh, caressing his chest. "How old are you?"

"Twenty-nine. You?"

"That number's unlisted." Chad had figured he had Jeremy by nearly ten years. He licked Jeremy's sideburn.

"So mysterious. Why?"

"Shh. I'm busy." Chad ran his fingers down Jeremy's body to his jeans. He felt Jeremy touching the diamond in his earlobe and smiled.

"Are you a stud?" Jeremy asked softly.

"A diamond stud."

"You fuck around a lot?"

"Maybe." Chad met Jeremy's dark eyes. "Should I stop what I'm doing?"

Jeremy blew out a loud exhale which sounded like frustration. "I don't want a onetime thing."

"I can make you come twice." Chad smiled.

"Seriously? I'm a hook-up? You courted me all night for a single fuck?"

Chad blinked and retracted his hand. "Uh. No?" Did he? No. He thought Jeremy would become a friend. Even better, a friend with benefits.

Jeremy sat up, giving Chad a look that was not impressed.

"What did I say? I'm not from here. I don't know the protocol for casual sex. Isn't this right?" Chad touched where he'd become erect in his slacks. It caught Jeremy's eye so Chad nudged his dick for him.

"I don't want casual sex." Jeremy went to get up.

Chad gripped him by his elbow. "Don't go."

"Look, we both want different things. What's the point?"

"What do you want?" Chad released his hold and waited to see if Jeremy would put his shoes and jacket on. He didn't.

Jeremy tucked his leg under him and faced Chad on the bed. "I want a boyfriend."

"Okay. So, you pick the biggest flirt in the bar?"

The blush was back to Jeremy's cheeks. "I'm stupid when it comes to relationships. I know. I always get hurt. I'm the nice guy everyone wants to be friends with."

"Excuse me?" Chad choked. "You're the hot fucker I want to have sex with."

"Once? A conquest and you're on to the next?"

"Well...I..."

Jeremy got off the bed and put on his jacket.

"Now you're going?"

"Yes."

"Come on, Jeremy. I didn't mean to make you upset. I've been through a lot. I have no idea what I'm doing, what I want, if I'm going to be killed tomorrow."

"What?" Jeremy stopped in his tracks. "What did you say?"

Chad swallowed the lump in his throat. "Don't leave."

"Who's going to kill you?"

"No one. I'm just kidding."

Jeremy sat on the bed again. "Chad, what the fuck?" He reached out for Chad's hand. "Chad?"

"All I wanted was hot sex. I don't want to talk." Chad punched the pillow angrily, curling into a ball.

The Diamond Stud

"What do you want me to do?"
"A bar full of men and I pick Mr. Let's-have-a-talk."
"Right." Jeremy stood, putting on his shoes.
"Do I repulse you?"
"What? No."
"Are you a virgin?"
"No!"
Chad took off his shirt. "Too old?"
"Are you kidding me? You're perfect."
"Perfect and unfuckable?"
"No. Very fuckable. Chad..." Jeremy shook his head in frustration. They met eyes.

Chad climbed off the bed and cupped the back of Jeremy's head, digging through his thick, short hair. It was as soft as rabbit's fur. Leaning down, Chad urged Jeremy towards him. Their lips met, brushing each other. Chad used the tip of his tongue to explore Jeremy's mouth. A whimper came from Jeremy and his hands were cool when they touched Chad's naked back. When Jeremy opened his mouth, Chad deepened the kiss. The grasp on his back tightened, sending a delicious rush to Chad's cock.

They twirled tongues, mashed lips and exchanged moans of approval. Keeping his mouth occupied, Chad nudged the jacket off Jeremy's shoulders, letting it drop. He opened the buttons of his cotton shirt, spreading it wide, cupping his hairless round pectoral muscles. Jeremy's kissing became more passionate and he slid his hands to Chad's ass, squeezing a cheek in each palm. Chad felt his cock throb in his pants. He nudged Jeremy's shirt down his arms, and that too fell to the floor.

Chad kissed his way to Jeremy's erect nipples, lapping at them with his whole tongue. When he found his way back to Jeremy's mouth, Jeremy ground their cocks together, working Chad's glute muscles like kneading dough in each hand.

Chad picked Jeremy up and spun around, laying him across the bed. He stood back to look at him, waiting to see if he would halt their progress. Jeremy didn't. His eyes wandered down Chad's body to his crotch.

He looked at himself. A stain of pre-cum dampened his white slacks and his cock was visible through the fabric where he had gotten hard.

Jeremy got to his knees on the bed, sucking at the tiny stain.

Chad closed his eyes, letting his head fall back, petting Jeremy's hair. Jeremy fondled Chad's cock excitedly, running up and down its length with his teeth and hands. His top button was opened roughly, then his zipper.

Opening his eyes, Chad watched as Jeremy peeled back the tight fabric, releasing his erection.

"Holy Christ." Jeremy wriggled in excitement, smoothing his fingers over the length.

"Do you want to fuck me, Jeremy?" Chad's cock tried to bob as it thickened, but Jeremy held it firm.

"Yes." Jeremy licked the tip of Chad's dick.

"You sure you don't want to talk?"

"Shut up," Jeremy laughed. "Get on the bed."

Chad laid on his back as Jeremy kept his grip on the base of his dick and stuck it into his mouth the minute Chad was horizontal.

"Play with my balls." Chad tried to remove his pants.

Jeremy sat up, tugging Chad's pants off. The minute Chad was naked, Jeremy spread his thighs and borrowed between them.

Chad hissed a breath through his teeth and bent his knees, touching Jeremy's shoulders and head affectionately. While Jeremy held his shaft upright in two fingers, he gave Chad a hell of a tongue bath. "Baby, baby..." Chad moaned.

The Diamond Stud

Jeremy stopped to catch his breath. He wiped his mouth with the back of his hand. "Do you have the lube handy?"

Chad stretched to the nightstand and tugged open the top drawer. "In there."

Jeremy climbed off the bed, and removed his jeans and briefs. When his cock flipped out of his clothing and pointed upwards, Chad said, "Nice dick."

"Thanks." Jeremy jerked it a couple of times. He removed a condom and a tube of lubrication, placing it next to Chad on the bed.

Chad put his hands behind his head to watch. Jeremy squeezed a drop of gel on his fingers and met Chad's gaze. They didn't exchange thoughts verbally, but Chad figured he could read Jeremy's. *No more conversation. Time for an orgasm.*

The touch of Jeremy's finger to his rim made Chad tense his muscles, but he soon went limp on the bed for him. Jeremy scooted low again, putting Chad's cock back into his mouth.

Chad stretched his arms to the sides of the bed and held on for dear life. Jeremy may not be interested in sex for sex's sake, but he certainly knew how to please a man.

While his cock sank into Jeremy's mouth, Jeremy slipped his fingers inside Chad's body. Chad moaned and felt goose bumps rise on his arms. Enjoying friction inside and out, Chad rocked with the rhythm, fucking Jeremy's mouth as his fingers fucked him. Pressure increased internally and the sensation of pleasure was intense. Though Chad tried to edge the climax, he was being sucked over the cliff. "I'm coming..."

Jeremy amped up the speed of both acts until Chad threw his head back into the pillows and arched his back. He choked on his grunt and came in Jeremy's mouth. Clenching his jaw on a howl that would wake Nan, Chad squeezed the bedding mercilessly as the orgasm was slow to subside. He forced his eyes open and found Jeremy sheathing his cock, going for his ass.

Chad scooted lower, holding his knees for Jeremy to get inside him more easily. Jeremy knelt between Chad's legs and pushed in, sliding deep into Chad's well lubed hole.

Jeremy's gaze lingered on Chad's cock as he hammered inside him. Chad touched himself for Jeremy's pleasure, raising his balls against his dick and stretching them out for him.

The veins in Jeremy's neck showed through his skin. Jeremy jammed his hips as close as he could get against Chad, and Chad felt his cock shiver deep inside him. "That's it," Chad said.

Grinding and pressing against Chad, Jeremy seemed to be enjoying the aftershocks as well as the initial climax. Chad smiled at his expression of lustful fulfillment.

Glistening with perspiration and catching his breath, Jeremy pulled out, holding the base of the spent rubber. He sat on his heels and used his arm to wipe the sweat from his forehead.

"The bathroom is in the hall."

"Okay." Jeremy climbed off the bed, holding his cock and the drooping, filled condom. He waited for Chad to show him the way.

They tiptoed to a doorway and Chad turned on the light as they stepped inside. He watched Jeremy remove the rubber and handed him a washcloth.

Neither spoke as they cleaned up. Chad checked his face in the mirror before they returned to the bedroom. He looked exhausted. The four day journey, late shift, and stress had taken their toll.

When they entered the bedroom, Jeremy began getting dressed.

"What are you doing?" Chad asked.

"Don't you want me to go home?"

"Walk to your car at four a.m.? No!" Chad peeled back the blankets. "Get in here."

"That's why? Because you don't want me to get mugged?"

The Diamond Stud

"Will you shut up and get over here?" Chad patted the spot beside him.

"Don't worry. I'll leave early in the morning." Jeremy seemed reluctant to join him.

"If I wasn't so tired, I'd have a snappy comeback to that." Chad shut off the lamp on the nightstand. He reached for Jeremy under the covers and dragged him close so he could spoon him. "Goodnight, Teddy bear."

"Goodnight, crazy man."

Chapter 9

Jeremy woke to find Chad still asleep beside him. He inspected the room more closely in the morning light. It was a pleasant space with high ceilings and simple furnishing. Jeremy imagined an apartment in this location would be very pricy. He remembered the roommate mentioned from last night, but had no idea who rented from whom.

He adjusted his position on the bed so he could stare at Chad while he slept. Chad's hair was dark ash blond at the roots and frosted to nearly pure yellow at the tips. His jaw stubble was barely noticeable but for the sun making it glitter. The diamond stud in his ear was impressive. Jeremy wondered if it was real.

Some of the previous night's conversation came back to him. Things that disturbed him.

I want a boyfriend.

Okay. So, you pick the biggest flirt in the bar?

That's exactly what he did. He fell for the most aloof guy in the bar. Did he chat with one of the older men beside him? One that sat next to him all night and even saved his seat when he took bathroom breaks? No. Did he make conversation with some of the less extravagant customers, with graying temples or inviting smiles? No.

Jeremy knew his choices sucked. He either became infatuated with the men his buddies dated, or ended up the 'friend' and shoulder to cry on. In the gym, at work, at the art museum and

The Diamond Stud

bookshops, he was 'that guy'. The invisible shadow you assumed would get the hint or be satisfied with a one night hook-up. Either that or he was the avid listener over a cup of coffee to someone mooning over someone else.

Great. Now I have to find a new bar to have a drink on Friday and Saturday night.

How embarrassing would it be to see Chad seducing a different man every weekend? *Horrible!*

He crept to the edge of the bed to get dressed and leave.

Chad's hand grabbing him startled him.

"Where do you think you're going?"

"I assumed you would kick me out the minute you woke up."

"You know what happens to people when they *ass-ssume?*"

Jeremy smiled. "Okay. Can I piss and brush my teeth?"

"Only if you come back."

"Promise."

"Pinky promise."

Chad raised his pinky and Jeremy hooked it and shook. "Help yourself to my toothbrush."

"Thanks."

"Better yet. I'll come with you." Chad emerged from the bed sporting imposing morning wood.

"Did you say you had a roommate?" Jeremy looked for his pants.

"Yup. Nan." He opened the door and strutted down the hall.

"Nan?" Jeremy hopped into the leg of his jeans as he followed. "Is that a man or a wo—" Jeremy stopped short at two people sipping coffee, staring at him from the dining room.

"Man." Chad said, smiling as he went into the bathroom.

"Hi." Jeremy waved shyly. "I'm Jeremy."

"Hi, Jeremy," the man with the goatee said.

"How ya doing?" Jeremy wondered how many men Chad had brought home for his flings. "I'm going to...um."

"Nice meeting you!" He grinned.

Jeremy slipped into the bathroom to see Chad leaning over the sink brushing his teeth. He closed the door. "You parade around nude in front of your roommate?"

"Should I be ashamed of my body?" Chad thrust his hips towards him, his big cock swinging as he did.

"No, but."

"No? Butt?" Chad spun around and stuck his bottom out.

"Nice butt?"

"How…how many guys have you brought home so far?"

"One." Chad handed him the toothbrush, loaded with paste, and stepped back from the sink to use the toilet.

"One? Who? Someone from the bar?"

"He was adorable. Brown hair, brown bedroom eyes. Sucked me like a Dyson."

"Oh. Great. Thanks a lot." Jeremy stuck the toothbrush in his mouth, frowning.

"It was you, ya dingdong!"

"Oh!" Jeremy spat out the toothpaste and rinsed his mouth. He watched Chad pee.

"Like golden showers?" Chad made a move to tinkle on him.

"No!" Jeremy jumped back.

"How about real showers?" He tilted his head at the shower stall as he gave himself a shake and flushed the toilet.

"Uh. Sure."

"Uh. Why do you sound so hesitant? Uh." Chad reached to turn on the water in the shower as Jeremy took his turn urinating.

"Because I keep waiting for the kiss off." Jeremy focused on his stream and jumped when Chad yanked down his pants from behind and planted a big kiss on his ass cheek.

"Consider yourself kissed off." Chad knelt behind him, gnawing on his bottom.

The Diamond Stud

"Can't a man piss in peace?" Jeremy struggled to keep his aim.

"Mm."

The chewing on his derriere became more sensual. Jeremy finished what he was doing and glanced back at Chad as he closed his eyes and enjoyed the foreplay. "You're wasting water."

"Killjoy." Chad slapped his ass with a loud crack and stepped into the shower. He poked his head out and asked, "What are you waiting for?"

"You want me in there?"

"Holy crap. Are you serious?"

Jeremy dropped his pants to the floor and stepped inside the small stall.

"Houston, we have a problem."

"You remember my last name?" Jeremy gaped at Chad.

"Yes. Do you remember mine?" Chad swapped places so Jeremy could wet down.

Thinking hard, Jeremy said, "You never told me."

"I didn't. Gold star for you." Chad licked his finger and pushed Jeremy's nipple like a button.

Jeremy washed his hair with the herbal scented shampoo. "Well? What is it? Or do you keep your secrets because you work for the FBI?"

"Diamond."

"Bullshit."

Chad played with Jeremy's genitals running hand over fist with his soapy fingers. "Jack of Diamonds."

"Jack of Shit." Jeremy braced himself on the wall as Chad worked him.

"Bond. Chad Bond."

"Shut up. Don't tell me. I don't care."

"DeSoto." Chad fisted Jeremy's dick briskly.

"Who?" Jeremy lost track of the conversation as the desire to come increased. He felt Chad closing in on him and opened his eyes.

Chad held both their cocks together and crushed them in his palms.

"Holy shit." Jeremy stared at the act and his breath caught in his throat. He'd never done this before. He tore his gaze from their winking slits and looked at Chad's chest. The man was a wall of sinewy muscle, big and strong. As he announced, "I'm coming," Jeremy choked on his words.

Chad increased his fisting and grunted as the cream of both their dicks flowed over his knuckles and dispersed quickly from the shower. "Got my morning climax. Now I need coffee." He rinsed off and rubbed his chest, as if feeling the stubble from where he'd shaved.

Jeremy leaned against the tiled wall to recover, wiping the water from his eyes. "Wow. That was intense."

Chad pressed his body against Jeremy and came within a breath of his lips. "You like me? I mean *like*-like me?"

Jeremy was head over heels, and terrified to admit it. "Of course I like you. Do you like me?"

"Do you want me to like you?" Chad licked Jeremy's neck.

"God yeah...uh, I mean. Sure. Why not?" Chills raced over Jeremy's spine as Chad lapped at his earlobe and jaw. "Do...do you like me?"

Chad made his way to Jeremy's mouth and kissed him. Jeremy's knees went weak. He prayed Chad did. This was dangerous territory, falling for a flirt. But the heart does what it does, in spite of the head's warning.

"Let's dress and get coffee." Chad shut off the water, pulled back the curtain and handed Jeremy a towel.

"At least you want to get dressed first."

Chad smiled at him wickedly and winked.

The Diamond Stud

After pouring Jeremy and himself a cup of coffee, Chad joined his roommate and Le at the dining room table. "Jeremy, this is the guy who was nice enough to let a maniac stay with him." Chad gestured to Nan. "Fernando Cruz, and his Vietnamese boy toy, Le Trung."

Nan said, "Are you insinuating I'm older than he is?"

"Yes." Chad laughed, the coffee cup to his lips.

"You older," Le said.

"Shh!" Nan waved at him to be quiet.

"I can't get Chad's age from him." Jeremy rested his elbows on the table. "He's being secretive."

"I know it. I got it from his driver's license." Nan smiled smugly.

"Uh uh..." Chad wagged his finger in warning.

"Come on," Jeremy said, laughing. "What are you? Thirty-one, two?"

"I'm impressed," Nan said.

"Did I guess right?" Jeremy asked.

"No, you—"

"Uh!" Chad poked Nan in the shoulder, then answered Jeremy with his tongue firmly planted in his cheek. "Yes. Right on the nose. Thirty-one." He slanted his eye at Nan to keep his mouth shut.

"Big deal. You're three years older than me." Jeremy shrugged.

"Changing the subject..." Chad set his mug on the table. "I need to buy food so I don't eat all of Nan's yummy munchies, get my hair done, and find a gym."

"There's a salon and a gym right here in the Castro." Nan pointed in a direction through the wall. "J-Reds for hair, and Gildie's Gym for your bod."

"Driving distance or walking?" Chad stood and brought his mug to the sink to rinse.

"Walk. I can show you where they are." Nan followed Chad into the kitchen. "And you're welcome to eat my food until you go shopping."

"I'll grab breakfast out this morning." Chad glanced back at the other two men in the dining room who were talking softly.

Nan smiled at Chad.

"What?" Chad wiped his hands on a dish towel.

"You two are a perfect match."

"Are we? Why?"

"Chad and Jeremy? Duh!"

"Is that supposed to ring a bell?"

"Okay, you're not that old, but my Uncle Levi had their LPs."

"You had an Uncle Levi?" Chad teased, "Oy!"

Nan whacked him playfully. "He was married to my mom's sister Conchita, so he's my uncle-in-law. Google 'Chad and Jeremy' if you don't believe me."

"LPs…like in music records?"

"Yes!" Nan took his mobile phone out of his pocket and scrolled through the applications. He typed in the singing duo, handing the phone to Chad.

Chad took the fancy iPhone and admired it. "I need one of these. I have a phone that only calls people. I'm such an old fucker."

"What? Thirty-one?" Nan pursed his lips.

Jeremy stood at the doorway with his empty mug. "Am I interrupting?"

"You ever hear of these guys?" Chad showed him the tiny screen.

Jeremy took it. "No."

"Uncle Levi has their LPs." Chad chuckled.

The Diamond Stud

"Who?" Jeremy gave Chad the phone, but Chad gestured to give it to Nan.

Le said, "Chad and Jeremy. I know they music."

The other three spun around to stare at him. Chad laughed. "Shut up. You do not."

"Do. Have *Before and After* on iPod."

"Now I've seen everything." Chad shook his head. "Okay. What's your plan, handsome?" Chad held the nape of Jeremy's neck, massaging it.

"You want me to make myself scarce?"

"Up to you. How much tedium can you stand? Me getting my head bleached and working out at a gym?"

"Got ya."

Chad needed to make sure Jeremy did not take the comment to mean he didn't want to spend time with him. "Excuse us, gentlemen." He physically spun Jeremy around and marched him back to the bedroom. "Sit."

"Yes, Master."

"Oh?" Chad got a charge of electricity from Jeremy's reply. "BDSM friendly?"

"You were saying?" Jeremy evaded a direct answer.

Chad jumped on him and pinned him to the bed. "And you call me a cock tease." He brushed his lips against Jeremy's.

"I'm getting mixed signals. First I got the hint that you wanted me to get lost, now..."

"Now..." Chad chewed on Jeremy's neck and jaw. "The famous dynamic-music duo will rock this room." Chad kissed his way down Jeremy's chest to his zipper flap. "Hard as a brick. Yum!" Chad ran his teeth along the length of Jeremy's cock through his denim. *That's why I love younger men.*

Jeremy let out a long, low, whimpering moan.

"May I suck you, kind sir?" Chad leaned on his elbows and rubbed hot friction on Jeremy's cock.

"Yes." Jeremy went to open his pants.

Chad slapped his hand playfully. "Master says, let me do it."

Jeremy laughed nervously. "I've never done S&M."

"Never too early to learn, oh-young-one." Chad tugged open Jeremy's pants, dragging his briefs down with them.

"Why do you act as if you're way older than me?"

"Uh!" Chad shook his head. "Don't blow the mood while I blow your trouser snake." He lowered Jeremy's pants to his ankles and relaxed beside him. Taking his cock into his palm, Chad nuzzled against it, kissing it from base to tip. Jeremy let out another sensual moan of longing. "For an average sized guy, you have one big dick." Chad licked under the head.

"It's not big. Yours is big."

"Is not. Yours is."

"Is too. Just suck."

"Okay." Chad enveloped as much as he could of Jeremy's cock into his mouth.

Jeremy gasped and thrust out his hips.

Chad stared at Jeremy's treasure trail which stopped short under his navel. The man didn't have one hair standing on his chest. Chad touched his sternum and didn't feel stubble. He was insanely jealous but knew as Jeremy aged he may grow more hair.

Jeremy held Chad's hand and brought it to his mouth. When he sucked on Chad's middle finger Chad became distracted from what he was doing. He stopped, opened his pants and took his erection out of his briefs. "I can take a hint too, you know." Chad straddled Jeremy's face. "There. Suck that instead."

Without hesitation Jeremy aimed Chad's cock at his mouth and drew deep suction.

Before he resumed his part of their sixty-nine session, Chad said softly, "I think I *like*-like you."

"Good," was replied with a full mouth.

The Diamond Stud

Chad orally fucked Jeremy while he enjoyed sucking him. In tandem they increased the intensity of the blowjobs, moaning harmoniously. "Mm!" Chad felt the urge to come and wanted Jeremy to know. He jerked his hips in a sign and loudly hummed, "*Mmm!*"

Jeremy got the message and accelerated his pace as well.

Chad came, his focus on his own climax, just as a load hit his tongue. He swallowed and milked Jeremy's cock while his own was tugged strongly.

They both released suction together, and Chad rolled to his back on the bed to recuperate. Jeremy crawled over his chest, cupping Chad's balls as they bulged out of his pants. "I *like*-like you a lot."

Chad choked up slightly with emotion. He grabbed Jeremy's jaw in both hands and kissed him, tasting his essence on Jeremy's tongue. They made out for ten minutes, just kissing, teasing tongues and pecking lips.

Jeremy leaned back and stared into Chad's eyes. "I know you have shit to do before you work tonight."

"Will you be at the bar?"

"Do you want me to be there?"

"You ask a lot of dumb questions."

"Won't I cramp your style?"

"Did you last night?" Chad caressed Jeremy's face tenderly.

"I don't know. You tell me."

Chad rolled his eyes dramatically. "Yes. You were awful! Patoui! Don't come back!"

"Such a drama queen." Jeremy smiled.

"Oh, honey. You have no idea." Chad sighed loudly.

"I'll walk with you if you're going in the direction of the club. It's where I left my car."

Chad sat up, closing his pants. "I don't even have your phone number." He took his mobile phone off the nightstand and turned it on. It beeped with missed messages. "Hang on." Chad put the phone to his ear to listen to voicemail.

"Mama's worried sick! You aren't answering your phone! Call me or I'll send out a search party for you!"

Chad checked the time of the call. He texted Jett an answer. *'I'm fine. Will call u in a sec.'*

"You okay?" Jeremy asked when Chad's expression changed.

Four other voicemail messages were left and he shivered at the phone number they came from. "I have to get a new phone and change my number."

"Ex stalking you?"

"No. Never mind." Chad became confused and anxious, looking around the room but not knowing what he was doing.

"Chad?"

"Huh?"

"I'm a good listener."

"I don't want you involved." Chad stood, searching for his jacket.

"Involved in what?"

"Stop being nosy." Chad snapped at him but didn't mean to. The expression of hurt on Jeremy's face upset him. "Sorry. I'm just a little freaked out still."

"I'd ask you about what, but I don't want to be 'nosy'." Jeremy finished dressing and put his jacket on, stuffing his hands into his pockets.

Chad didn't want Jeremy to become entwined with the mess he'd left behind. Or thought he'd left. "Let's go." He opened the bedroom door and waved to Nan and Le who were playing video games together in Nan's room.

Jeremy walked down the stairs first, with Chad preoccupied behind him. It was crisp and blue outdoors, and for October it felt unseasonably warm to Chad. He was used to Midwest fall and winter.

The Diamond Stud

Just as Jeremy was about to say something, smiling and parting his lips, Chad jolted at the sight of a car with Ohio license plates parked right in front of his home. "No!" He cowered back and felt the blood drain from his face.

"What?" Jeremy grabbed him, shaking him.

"Oh God!" Chad scanned the area in terror. "I have to get something. I have to get something!" Chad shook off Jeremy's grasp and ran back into the house.

~

Jeremy inspected the car. It was a silver van with Ohio plates. Nothing looked out of the ordinary to him. He spun on his heels and jogged up the narrow staircase, back inside the flat, trying to find Chad.

When he spotted him with a handgun, Jeremy choked and stopped short. "What the fuck are you doing?"

Chad tucked it into his waistband behind his back, covering it with his jacket.

"Are you really with the FBI? Or are you completely crazy?"

"You need to leave. I can't risk anything happening to you."

Jeremy couldn't believe how much Chad was shaking, how anxious he appeared. "What's with the van?"

"Go. I swear I don't want to be responsible for you getting hurt. Please."

When tears ran down Chad's cheeks, Jeremy closed the bedroom door and sat him on the bed. "What the hell is going on? Do you want me to call the police?"

"I don't know. How could they find me?" Chad began crying.

Jeremy hugged him, trying to comfort. "Who? Who found you?"

"I tried to hide. I tried."

"Shh. Calm down." Jeremy wiped at Chad's tears with his fingertip.

Chad straightened his posture and composed himself. "I'll deal with it."

"With what? With a gun? Tell me so I can help you."

Not answering, Chad stood, left the room, and walked down the stairs.

Jeremy was sick with worry.

Before Chad left the apartment house, he took the gun out of his waistband holster and opened the door a crack, looking through it. Jeremy held his breath.

Chad exited the house and inspected the van closely, both his hands were on the gun, which was pointing down. He blew out a loud breath of relief and hid the gun.

"Is it not the one you thought it was?" Jeremy was completely lost. *FBI? Criminal? Madman? Take your pick.*

"No. It's not." Chad crouched down, rubbing his eyes.

Jeremy knelt beside him. "You're okay." He ran his hand over Chad's back.

"I'm so paranoid I can't deal with it."

Pedestrians were approaching them from both sides. Jeremy helped Chad to stand and asked, "Do you have a permit for that thing?"

"Not here."

"Are you with the cops or FBI?"

"No."

"Then unload it and put it back in the house or you'll go to jail."

Chad took a closer look inside the van, walking around it as if making sure. When he seemed satisfied he was mistaken, he entered the house again.

Jeremy waited near the bottom of the stairs, staring at the vehicle, unable to fit the puzzle pieces together.

The Diamond Stud

A teenage boy and girl climbed into the van and pulled away just as Chad returned. Jeremy watched him to see if he knew the occupants. "Well?"

Chad shook his head. "I don't know them." He seemed worn out when only a moment ago he was Mr. Happy-go-Lucky.

"Come on. Let me walk you to the salon." Jeremy held his hand.

In reflex, Chad shook it off and gave the surroundings a petrified scan.

"It's okay to show affection here, Chad. But if you don't want to hold my hand, I understand."

"I'm sorry. I do want to." Chad reached for him.

They walked in silence towards the shops on Market Street. Jeremy had a feeling Chad wouldn't tell him what was haunting him until he was ready.

~

The sick feeling in his gut was making him weak. Chad knew his fears were unfounded. Or were they? Didn't it stand to reason he would live here in the Castro District? Was that really a big mystery to the homicidal lunatics he'd left in Ohio? No. Where else would he go? Where would an abused gay man go for solace? Though the country had a few isolated gay communities speckled across its states, Chad was aware the most obvious destination for him was San Francisco. He couldn't afford LA and the gay West Hollywood area.

Lost inside his head, Chad felt Jeremy stop walking. He looked up and realized he was standing at the salon entrance.

"I can stay with you."

"No. It'll bore the snot out of you. Bleaching takes an hour or more."

"Up to you."

"Where do you live?"

"North Berkeley."

"In an apartment?"
"No. A condo. I own it."
Chad stared at him. "Are you rich?"
"No." Jeremy smiled. "But I do okay." He drew Chad back from the entrance as people tried to get by them.
"I'm a schmuck. I don't even know what you do for a living."
"I'm a CPA."
"I'm sorry I never asked."
"You didn't want to talk. Remember?"
Chad felt like crap. He leaned against the window of the salon and covered his face.
"Stop beating yourself up, will you? I'm not going anywhere."
He dropped his arms to his sides. "Promise?"
"Promise."
When Jeremy went to kiss him, Chad again reacted badly, looking around.
"Uh. Okay. Well, enjoy your salon session. I'll see you later."
"No. Wait." Chad had to face his fears. Had to. "Come here." He grabbed Jeremy's jacket lapel and pulled him close. They kissed, no tongues, but a series of loving pecks. "I'll call you."
"Can I have your number?" Jeremy removed a fancy iPhone from his lining pocket.
"Hang on. I'll call you on my wonderful generic cell phone." Chad took it out and said, "Tell me your number. I forgot to type it in earlier. I guess I got distracted."
"I understand." Jeremy gave it to him.
Chad dialed it, hearing Jeremy's ringtone.
"Got it." Jeremy looked at his phone. "See ya later."
"Later." Chad watched him go. Jeremy spun back to wave again, giving him a sweet smile.
I like-like you, Jeremy. A lot.

Chapter 10

A smock and towel around his neck, Chad put the phone up to his ear while his hair bleached in foil wrappers. "Hello, my brown sugar Mama."

"Finally! Okay, where on the map are you?"

"I rented a great room right in the middle of the Castro District. When are you coming to visit?"

"I told you, no cash, no vacation time...poor me!"

"I miss you, Jett." Chad flipped through the cheesy celebrity magazine on his lap.

"I miss you too, so much. My BFF left."

"Hey...*Rufus* is doing a concert here...oh, hang on. This issue is five months old."

"Where are you?"

"Getting my tips done, then my eyebrows waxed."

"Thought you said getting your *tits* done."

"Nope. Not going transsexual on you. Still like playing with my balls."

"Hey, in California anything goes. You can have tits and balls."

"So true." Chad tossed the magazine onto a pile. "I met a guy."

"You meet hundreds of guys, you diamond stud."

"Yeah, but this one I *like*-like."

"So soon? He swept you off your size eleven feet?"

"I got a job at this fab bar. The owner is a total fuzzy bear who let me dress up and do a number. I did *I Will Survive*."

"Tell me about, what's his name?"

"Jeremy. So we're Chad and Jeremy. Does that ring a bell?"

"No, Tinkerbell. What's it supposed to ring?"

"Never mind." Chad sighed. "A van with Ohio plates was parked in front of my house this morning."

"No!"

"It wasn't them, but what were the friggin odds? Seriously, Jett. I nearly had a conniption fit."

"There is no way. No way they will schelp out there and find you. You do realize that, don't you?"

"No. I don't realize that. You know how serious this is. They will snuff me out. They want me dead for so many reasons."

"How are they going to find you? Did you get a listing in the phone book? You're not that careless."

Chad's stylist, Fabio, walked over, opening the foil flaps to check on his color. Chad asked him, "Am I cooked?"

"You're cooked. Come. Rinse time."

"I have to go, Jett. I'm done turning blond."

"Are you keeping this number?"

"No. I have dozens of voicemails coming in. I'm terrified to listen to them."

"Play them for the local police."

Chad thought about it. "I could." He walked to the sink where Fabio was waiting. "It is a hate crime. They have to take that stuff seriously here."

"They do." Fabio assured him, nodding as he overheard.

"Oh, honey..." Jett whined, "Mama is so worried for you."

"Then come out and be my bodyguard."

"I wish I could. Let me go. Boss-ette is about to see me on the phone and give me a tongue lashing, and not in a good way."

The Diamond Stud

"I keep forgetting you work weekends too. Bye, my sweet chocolate bunny."

"Bye, my white Elizabeth Taylor diamond."

Chad hung up and stuffed the phone into his pocket.

Fabio wrapped another towel around his shoulders and gently leaned him back over the sink. He tugged the foil out of Chad's hair. "Is someone harassing you here? In the Castro?"

"Not yet. Hopefully it'll stay long distance."

"I'd report it."

"I already have over and over. That thin piece of paper they call a court order won't stop a bullet or a bat to the head. They need to make them out of Kevlar."

"I don't know where you reported it, but in this state?" Fabio wet Chad's hair down. "They will arrest a bully or someone tormenting you because you're gay."

Chad thought about it. "Will they extradite from the Midwest?"

"Huh?"

He blew out a frustrated breath of air. "Never mind."

~

The gym had all the equipment Chad needed, plus classes for all kinds of new fads in exercise. What he needed was free weights and a treadmill. And he had that here and more.

Chad stood before a mirror, hefting two dumbbells over his head. A skimpy black fishnet tank top and tight-fitting mini hiker shorts exposed all of his curves and bulges. Not to mention nipples. He brought two outfits with him; one for if he thought the place was gay-friendly and the other if it wasn't. In the Castro District, it should have been obvious. But Chad made no assumptions.

The last time he wore an outfit even slightly risqué to a gym was in Dayton. He was chased out of the locker room by three good ole boys who had roughed him up. From then on he switched the hour of his workout, covered his body with baggy sweat suits, and hid his frosted hair with a knit cap. He'd been tempted to change gyms, but there wasn't another one for miles, and he had paid six months in advance.

Doing an exercise that worked his latissimus dorsi, Chad raised the dumbbells to the side, seeing the thick muscle flare out under his arms.

An attractive older man gazed at Chad's reflection. He was wearing a white t-shirt and cut off blue sweats. The gray tuft of his chest hair was showing at the scallop neck of the shirt, and his head was shaven close to give it style though his hairline had receded.

Chad set the weights down and tugged on his silver curb link necklace, loosening it up as it stuck to his sweaty neck. "Hi."

"Hi."

If I liked older men, I'd like you. Chad figured the guy was a huge gym-junkie, judging by his large biceps.

"Are you new here?"

"Yes. I'm Joe." Chad reached out his hand.

"Hi, Joe, I'm Bert."

"So? Are you the house regular?"

"Where do I know you from?"

Chad was taken aback and felt a twinge of worry. "You know me?"

Bert snapped his fingers. "Twin Pecs."

A huge sensation of relief filled Chad, but he wondered if his alias would be questioned. He was 'Chad' at the bar. "Right."

"Are you working tonight?"

"Yes." Chad smiled catching the guy giving his nuts a good leer. He glanced down, seeing clearly the outline of his own cock and balls. "Do you see something that interests you?"

"Absolutely." Bert stepped closer. "But I don't want to interfere with your workout."

The Diamond Stud

"How long have you got on yours?" Chad checked his watch.
"That depends."
"Oh?"
"How long will you be?"
"I just started, but I can take a...*bathroom* break." Chad thrust out his hips.
"Why don't we do that?"
Chad set the weights back on the rack and followed Bert to the locker room. Before he closed himself into a toilet stall, Chad said, "Can you hang on one minute?"
Bert nodded.
He walked to his locker and spun the combination lock. Checking to see if Bert was out of hearing distance, Chad dug his phone out of his clothing and turned it on. He noticed a missed call from Jeremy and listened to the message.
"I just wanted to make sure you were all right. Are you all right?"
Chad dialed his number. "Hey."
"Hey. Any more heart attacks?"
"No. Um, are we in a committed relationship?"
"Huh? I don't know. Are we?"
"Well, that's why I'm asking you. I don't know what one sexy night qualifies us for." He spotted Bert peering at him from around the wall. He mouthed, 'One minute' and held up his finger.
"I don't know either. We aren't allowed to talk."
"Ha. Ha." Chad adjusted his cock in the tight shorts. "So? What's the verdict?"
"Wait a minute. Are you asking permission to be with someone else?"
Chad blinked. "Yes. I thought I was doing the right thing. I really am clueless where we're at."
"What are you going to do?"

"You're getting defensive. Don't yell."
"Where are you? Who is he?"
"Calm down, Houston." Chad looked behind him quickly to see if anyone was listening in. "So you are a possessive bitch, right?"
"I'm going to hang up if you keep it up."
"So...I shouldn't have called to ask. I should just have had my blowjob?"
"Get lost!"
When the line disconnected, Chad stared at his phone. "Hello? Jeremy?" He redialed. "Did you hang up on me on purpose?"
"Are you going to let another guy blow you?"
"Honey! That's what I'm asking you!" Chad shook his head in confusion.
"No! Okay? No!"
"Don't get your undies in a twist." Chad caught Bert's glance again.
"Where are you?"
"Gildies. Why?"
"I'll be right there."
"You will? Why?"
"You want a blowjob?"
"Another silly question." Chad tucked his fingers down his shorts.
"Be there in five. You think you can keep your penis out of another guy's mouth for that long?"
"Sweet Jesus! That's why I'm calling you. You see? That's what I get for trying."
"Don't. Okay? You wanted me to tell you. So I'm telling you. NO!"
Chad held the phone away from his ear because Jeremy's volume was so loud. He paused and put the phone back to his

head again. "Am I getting this right? One amazing night of lust and we're a committed couple? Is that what we are?"
"I'm on my way. Will you just go lift weights and wait?"
"Sure."
"I said no. You got that?"
"I thought I was the Dom and you were the sub."
"Not funny."
"Okay. I'll be pumping iron until you can pump my rod."
"Bye."
Chad disconnected the phone and put it into his locker.
"What's going on?"
"Looks like I'm in a committed relationship. I guess it happens in one date here." He slammed the metal door with a reverberating clang and locked it.
"What? Some guy wants you all to himself after a one night stand?"
"Yeah. How about that?" Chad returned to the workout area.
"Hang on." Bert stopped him.
"Yes?" Chad batted his lashes at him teasingly.
"You don't have to listen to him. It's up to you."
Chad went into a 'Thinker' pose playfully. "Hmm. Up to me." He eyed Bert. "Twenty-nine year old boy toy who fucks and sucks like a porn star, or a...how old are you?"
"Never mind." Bert stormed away.
"Yeah, that's what I thought. 'Never mind'."

~

Jeremy was thankful he found a parking space. He didn't know why he was so angry. Chad had called him to ask. He didn't have sex first, and deny later.

Am I unreasonable to be so possessive? I know the guy one day!

"Yes. Tough shit." He grabbed his gym bag and raced to the entrance. He stopped at the front desk. "Hey. Do you do one day guest passes?"

"Sure. If you sign up I can get you a seven day pass."

"Sign up?"

"Do you know a member? They can get you one free day."

"Hang on." Jeremy looked into the weight room. He spotted Chad in a very seductive outfit and shook his head. *Well, that explains the propositions.* "Chad!"

He spun around and smiled. "Bout time!"

"Come here."

Chad climbed off the piece of equipment and approached him. "Is there another problem, Houston?"

"I take it you're going to milk that one to death."

"I know what I'd like milked to death."

"Is he with you?" the employee at the desk asked.

"Yes." Chad grabbed Jeremy's arm. "Now be nice and let him in."

"Just sign here." The man moved a clipboard over. "I can give you a tour of the facility."

"No thanks." Jeremy signed the guest sheet.

"Oh, allow me. I can show him the ...uh...ropes. Yes, that's it. The ropes." Chad hooked Jeremy's elbow and tugged him to the locker room.

Jeremy noticed an older man watching, a pinched look on his face. He could well imagine the older clientele swooping like hawks on his blond, stud-muffin dove.

Before Jeremy had even picked out a locker to put his belongings in, Chad backed him into the handicapped toilet stall. Jeremy reached out to prevent from falling over the bowl.

Chad took his gym bag and hung it on a hook. "So? You and I? Are we like-like together?"

The Diamond Stud

"I'd like-like that. Would you?" Jeremy noticed Chad's dick thickening through the clingy fabric. "Look at you." He shook his head in admonishment pinching one of Chad's exposed nipples. "Fishnet tank? How seventies."

"No! I got this from an International Male catalog last month. Girl! Update your shopping habits. Retro is back. I almost bought a lava lamp."

"You're so blond! Blondie!" Jeremy roughed up Chad's hair.

"Hey! Fabio made sure it wouldn't move. I can't even sweat out the mousse he stuck in it." Chad swiped at Jeremy's hand playfully.

He may have been annoyed at Chad on the way over, but he wasn't now. Jeremy lunged at him, slamming Chad against the stall's flimsy wall. He connected to his lips and ground his crotch into that scandalous pair of shorts.

"Mm!" Chad reacted to the advance, gripping Jeremy's ass and humping him.

With great reluctance, Jeremy parted from Chad's mouth and kissed his way to his erect nipples. He lapped at them through the mesh and chewed his way downwards.

"Jeremy-Jeremy...I like-like your style."

While crouching low, Jeremy flipped Chad's cock out of his shorts and into his mouth. He inhaled his musky scent which was mixed with a masculine aroma of soap or moisture cream. The nubs were short on Chad's body from being freshly shaven.

He ran his fingers over the tiny tattoo near the base of Chad's cock and cranked up the speed and pull of his blowjob. Chad let out a vibrating guttural moan and Jeremy tasted his pre-cum.

"I want to scream," Chad said in a breathy whisper.

"Mm mm," Jeremy indicated 'no'.

"Come on. A wild howl." He shifted his weight onto the other leg. "I'm gonna spurt! Let me tell the world!"

"Mm mm!" Jeremy tried to shake his head no.

"Bert! I'm coming!" Chad choked on his words and shivered as he came.

Jeremy swallowed the load and sucked out every drop.

"Get a room, Joe!" was hollered from outside the door.

"Why?" Chad answered. "You didn't want us to."

Jeremy stood and wiped his mouth. "What are you doing?"

"Telling Bert I got what I wanted without him."

"Bert?"

"Old guy who offered to do me. That's why I called you." Chad thumbed over his shoulder and tucked his cock in his shorts.

"Old guy?" Jeremy took his gym bag from the hook and opened the door.

"Him." Chad pointed.

Jeremy noticed the same older man who had stared at him when he arrived, giving them an irritated glare. "Be nice. You don't want to make enemies."

"True!" Chad sprinted towards Bert. "Sorry, man. I was rude. Accept my apology."

Jeremy gave his mouth another wipe, hoping he didn't have cum dripping from it.

Bert seemed to deflate and shook Chad's hand. "It's okay, Joe. No hard feelings."

Joe? Jeremy tilted his head curiously. *Who is this guy? Chad, Joe, FBI? Guns?*

Once Bert left, Chad smiled sweetly at Jeremy.

"Joe?"

"Never mind."

~

After they stopped off at a corner grocery shop, and paid the price of convenience over big named stores, Chad's pockets had emptied. All the tip money from last night was gone.

The Diamond Stud

Jeremy helped him with his paper sacks, bringing them up the stairs to Nan and his shared flat.

"Hello?" Chad called as he entered. No answer meant Nan was out. He put the bags on the counter, and took off his jacket. "I have to catch a nap sometime before I go to work."

"Okay. I can leave anytime you want me to." Jeremy began unloading the food, putting things into the refrigerator.

"You don't have to leave, unless you hafta'."

"I don't 'hafta'." Jeremy smiled.

"Good. Give me that brie. That's lunch. Where are the grapes and crackers?" Chad hunted in the bags for the items. He removed the grapes and opened cabinet doors to find a bowl.

"Why did you tell the guy at the gym your name was Joe?" Jeremy opened the box of water crackers, munching on one.

Using a colander to rinse the fruit, Chad dumped the grapes into a bowl, stuffing a few in his mouth. "Mm. Sweet." He brought the cheese and fruit to the dining area and went back for two knives and plates. "Here. Cut the cheese."

"You should do stand-up." Jeremy took the knife and opened the plastic wrapper on the brie.

"I do stand up. I piss standing. I fuck standing, and sitting, and lying down on my face, and lying on my back…"

"Okay, 'Joe'." Jeremy relaxed at the table, cutting a wedge of brie and taking a stack of crackers.

Chad snapped off a section of grapes putting them on Jeremy's plate. "I just think there are some situations where using an alias is a good idea."

"Are you ever going to tell me who threatened you back in Ohio?"

"My brother did." Chad waited to see his reaction.

Jeremy stopped eating. "How? What did he do, exactly?"

"I have a list. Would you like to see my list?" Chad started walking to his bedroom.

BargainBookStores.com   4630 Danvers Drive
Grand Rapids, MI

Order #: 464108
Name:
Seller Order:
Ship Method: International
Order Date:
Email:
PO #:

564109

QTY	LOC	Item: ISBN	Condition	Price
1	C11	1456353187 - The Diamond Stud by	New	£9.05

Subtotal
Shipping
Total

Thank you for your order!

Questions: auk@bargainbookstores.com

Returns: http://bargainbookstores.com/content/Amazon_UK_Returns.htm

0274006 RRDRF

TO REORDER YOUR UPS DIRECT THERMAL LABELS:

1. Access our supply ordering web site at UPS.COM®
   or contact UPS at 800-877-8652.

2. Please refer to label #0274006 when ordering

"Just give me the gist of it." Jeremy stopped him, pointing to the chair adjacent to him.

After cutting up several wedges of cheese and placing them on crackers, Chad said, "He assaulted me, threatened to kill me, got my dad to disown me so he would be the sole heir, not that we're rich, but..."

"Your brother did this to you?"

"Yes. He and his unemployed, white trash wife. Second wife, I may add. She was a gold digger who 'oopsy!' met a lazy slob by accident. She thought my brother was a good catch. Uh. No. He's a sexually-deviant lazy pig." Chad nibbled the cheese. "His first wife caught him cheating with his present wife. They had two kids who got totally fucked up in their divorce. It was the War of the Roses between those two." Chad ate a grape. "The first wife is still taking him to court over ten years after their divorce, making him pay enormous lawyer bills." He stared at Jeremy. "You getting all this?"

"Unfortunately."

"Well, the beast got fired for sexual harassment. He's old, obese and either unemployable or too lazy to try to get a job. Dad said he didn't put in job applications because the unemployment checks were bigger than what he could get at a 'real' job." Chad rolled his eyes dramatically. "They suck off the government's tit and whine about the democrats. Serious mental cases. Dwayne, that's my brother's name, came up with a plan so he'd never have to work again. He made my dad move in with him for his pension checks and social security money. They're squeezing what little they can get out of him." Chad ate a cracker topped with brie. "They poisoned his mind. He's getting forgetful so he's easily manipulated. Once Mom died, my brother got very cozy with my dad. He told Dad I was a pervert, that I had sex with underage boys and should be a registered sex offender."

The Diamond Stud

"Why?"

"I don't fucking know. Either to just discredit me in Dad's eyes or because he was jealous that I was gay, didn't spawn children of the devil, or have two women to support. Not to mention I was making a decent living bartending in the only gay area in Dayton. I was a source of embarrassment I suppose." Chad held up a grape and fed it to Jeremy. "Meanwhile, he's turned into a monster. He's deranged and has convinced my dad he's too feeble to care for himself. So now they all live together and Dad is supporting everyone."

"Does your dad still work?"

"No. It's all coming out of his pension, social security, retirement accounts, you know."

"That's really sad."

"No kidding. But Dad believes everything my brother Dwayne says. It's like Grima Wormtongue as the chief Counselor of King Theoden of Rohan, in *The Lord of the Rings*."

"Does his wife work?"

"Ha! Are you kidding? She's a convicted felon. She stole from every employer she had. That bitch has never worked an honest day in her life, but she flatters dad, you know, 'I love you, Grandpa…'." Chad shivered in exaggeration. "Saccharin tipped toxic waste."

"She calls him 'Grandpa'?"

"The two trolls spawned a demon together. A seriously disturbed ten year old who goes around the neighborhood saying everyone sexually molested her. Hmm. Where does she get those ideas? Not from me! I stay the hell away from all of them."

"Jesus! Thank fuck you moved!"

"Yeah, I thought that too. I have no idea why I put up with it for as long as I did. But being beaten so badly I was in the hospital, and now with Dwayne threatening to kill me? I had no choice."

"You did call the police. Right?"

"Hell yeah. They made out reports, served papers… It didn't do anything but enrage my old man. It was like all Dwayne said to Dad had come true and I was the source of all their trouble. Dwayne's first wife said he was an abuser, but no one believed her. I do now."

"Did he get arrested?"

"No. He played up how I was the sicko, that I wore dresses and touched little boys. You know homophobic cops. They didn't even bring him to the police station. They had a chat with him and served him the court order. If I could imagine it? They probably did it over a round of beer discussing handguns."

"So you think he'll hunt you down?" Jeremy broke a cracker in half and stuck a wedge of brie on it.

"We need wine." Chad stood and opened the bottle he had bought. "Anyway…Yes. He will if he can. He probably thinks I still want some claim to my dad's stuff, the nasty packrat he is. He's like an episode of *Hoarders*. The house Dad lived in was loaded with garbage and filthy. You could barely walk from room to room. I spoke to my lawyer, and he said, if my brother takes over my dad's account while he's alive, pretty much he has taken all his money. My lawyer's advice was to get away from all of it. He said with my dad's savings carrying all four of them, plus Dwayne's child support and alimony to the ex, whatever is left will be sucked dry anyway."

"That's really sick, Chad."

"Don't I know it? And they say I'm the sick one." He brought two stemmed glasses of red wine to the table.

"Thanks." Jeremy ate another grape. "What are you going to do? I assume you've kept your address and location a secret."

"Yes, so far. But I have to go to the DMV and get a new driver's license, you know, and get bills sent here. I mean how hard is it to find me once I get settled in?"

The Diamond Stud

"I don't know. I've never tried to find someone." Jeremy sipped the wine. "At least I know why you told that guy your name was Joe."

"I've done that the entire journey here. But my Pathfinder still has Ohio plates. I have to get rid of those too."

"By state law you have to do it soon. You have ten days from the day you establish residency."

"Holy shit. I'll do it Monday." They continued to eat quietly, Chad still felt exhausted from the moving and driving, and tasks that lay ahead were draining him. "I have to rest." He stood, taking his plate and empty wine glass to the sink.

Jeremy gave Chad his dishes and put away the remainder of the uneaten food. "What do you want me to do?"

"A striptease and then a solo act." Chad wiped his hands on a towel. "Oh, while singing the theme song from *Glee*."

"I don't know the theme song from *Glee*."

Chad headed to his bedroom. "Does that mean you'll still strip and jerk off for me?"

Jeremy chuckled.

Chad removed his shoes and socks, lowering the blinds to close out the sunlight. When he glanced over his shoulder, Jeremy was getting undressed, staring at him.

"That's a lousy strip act."

"I'm not good at that stuff. I feel like a geek." Jeremy folded his shirt over a chair.

"Like this." Chad pivoted his hips and raised his shirt exposing his torso. He accompanied his actions with a cliché stripper ditty, no words just syllables. "Da, da, da...dee, da, da da..." He got Jeremy's immediate attention. Chad showed off one nipple, thrusting his hips out as his 'singing' grew in volume. He dragged his shirt over his head and twirled it around, grabbing his crotch and humping his hand.

He threw the shirt at Jeremy, and it landed on his head. Jeremy sniffed it before he slid it off. Chad ran his hands down his shaven chest to his waistband. He wished he had on Velcro rip-away pants. It would be so much fun. He undid the top button and tugged the zipper tab lower and lower, in time with his song. For the finale, Chad gave Jeremy his back and yanked his jeans and briefs to his ankles, wriggling his ass. He slapped a hand on each cheek and ground his hips around, looking back at Jeremy seductively.

Jeremy was riveted, standing still.

"Huh." Chad shrugged. "Men usually attack me before I'm totally naked." He shook his jeans off his ankles and felt arms encircle him from behind. "That's better."

Jeremy dragged him backwards to the bed, climbing on top of Chad, straddling him.

"Looks like you're the Dom." Chad raised his hands over his head. "Spank me, Master." He threw his head back and moaned sensually.

"How did I get so lucky?" Jeremy placed a palm on the each side of the bed next to Chad and sat on him, pressing their balls together.

Chad stared into Jeremy's dark eyes. "There's nothing lucky about me. So your luck is bad. All bad."

Jeremy stretched out to lay on top of him, resting his elbows on either side of Chad's head. He pecked his lips and smiled. "You're about to get lucky."

"Mm." Chad cupped his head and met his mouth. They kissed gently, exploring each other's tongues and teeth. "My delicious boy toy...grrr."

Jeremy laughed but didn't argue.

Chad spread his legs. "Take me, Master. I want to be fucked and fucked, and fucked..."

The Diamond Stud

Hoisting himself back to a seated position, Jeremy reached into the nightstand. He removed a strip of condoms and the gel.

"Like this." Chad tapped Jeremy to let him reposition.

Jeremy had the wrapper off a rubber and waited.

Chad rolled to his side, bending one knee. He noticed Jeremy had softened slightly at the disruption in tempo. With both hands, Chad cupped Jeremy's balls and rolled his fingers up to the tip of his cock, over and over, as if he were stroking a cat.

A whimper-like breath escaped Jeremy and he stopped in his tracks to enjoy it.

His length stiffened once more. "Now I don't want to stop."

"Don't stop," Jeremy said, holding the rubber between the tips of his fingers.

"Now I want to suck it!" Chad laughed, increasing his speed as he reached deep between Jeremy's legs and ran his hands over his balls to the tip of his dick.

"Holy fuck that feels good."

"I give in. Uncle." Chad scooted lower and pointed Jeremy's cock towards his mouth. "I can't resist a package like yours, honey." He licked the slit and then down the underside.

Jeremy sounded like a wolf howling. "*Oooohhh...*"

Chad joined him. "Awoooo!"

"Shut up." Jeremy laughed. "Where was I? That's right. About to make you my bitch. Again."

"That's it, girl. You're bad, you're bad..." Chad did a little dance move on the bed, using only his arms. When Jeremy shoved him back with a straight arm to the chest, Chad blinked and felt his cock wag. "That'a boy!"

"You like it rough?" Jeremy squeezed the bottle of lube onto his fingers.

"Pretend you're cowboy Charlie, and ride me like a mad bull."

"Cowboy Charlie?" Jeremy tossed the bottle into the drawer and ran his slick fingers against Chad's rim, slipping in.

A rush of shivers raced through Chad and his dick came alive instantly. "Yeehaw...cow-poke me with that brandin' iron, Houston, Texas."

Jeremy made a stifled chuckling sound and scooted closer.

Chad returned to the position on his side, reaching out to help Jeremy fit between his knees like a missing jigsaw piece.

Jeremy straddled Chad's open legs, and crept up Chad's body until he was inside him.

With the penetration Chad closed his eyes and relaxed, hearing Jeremy's respirations accelerate.

"Christ, this is good. I can get really deep." Jeremy pumped his hips a few times.

"That's why I like it." Chad squeezed, Jeremy's arm. "Do your thang, love-machine."

Jeremy pumped his hips faster, holding Chad for balance.

The internal massage was setting Chad's teeth on edge. He grabbed his cock and started fisting. He caught Jeremy's gaze switching back and forth from their connection to his jerking off.

"I am *so* not going to last." Jeremy's cock throbbed strongly inside Chad.

Chad didn't even bother responding. He cupped the end of his dick and came, closing his eyes and filling his palm with his spunk.

"Oh, shit!" Jeremy hammered his last few thrusts and ground in as he hit orgasm.

Holding his semen in his hand, Chad admired Jeremy's sexual snarl and taut muscles. A last pump inside, and Jeremy pulled out, holding the base of the condom. "Wow. That was intense."

The Diamond Stud

"No kidding. Maybe having sex with the same guy more than once is fun." Chad got to his feet, trying to keep the creamy puddle in his hand.

"Ha. Ha." Jeremy snapped the rubber off. "Ow."

"I've never seen a rubber injury. What the hell did you do?"

"Nothing." Jeremy massaged his cock and looked uncomfortable.

"If you have the clap you may as well tell me now." Chad used his clean hand to open the door, headed to the bathroom.

"I don't have the clap. Shut up." Jeremy followed him, holding the spent condom away from his body.

"Herpes?" Chad turned the water on in the sink, rinsing the sperm away.

"No."

"Crabs?"

"No! What the hell's wrong with you? I just snapped the rubber on the end of my prick."

"Have you ever had the crabs?" Chad used a washcloth to wipe the lube from his bottom.

"No!"

"I have. Eww. Got 'em from a nasty boy in Cincinnati back in the nineties. Hang on a minute. He was an accountant for the IRS. You sure you don't have crabs?"

Jeremy hung his dick over the sink and washed up. "One dirtbag had crabs and now all accountants do? Did you just tell me that?"

"His head was completely shaved and his eyes bugged out when he fucked. I didn't want to look. I swear I thought they would pop out and go rolling on the floor."

Jeremy took the towel from Chad to dry his crotch. "You really don't have to tell me all this."

"His dick went west. I mean, like this." Chad curled his index finger. Never saw one that shape. It was like his wiener was trying to look back at him."

"God!" Jeremy cringed. "Are you trying to wig me out?"

"It was like screwing Mr. Clean, but he wasn't. Know what I mean?"

Jeremy exaggerated a shiver, shaking off his arms and walking back to the bedroom.

"And he hummed." Chad followed him. "A hummer. A hummer with a bent dick." As Chad entered the room, Jeremy was getting under the blankets, ignoring the conversation. Chad shut the door and light, joining him. "He stalked me for a year. I'd get emails and text messages from him for more sex. I deleted them but he never got the hint."

"Nap time."

Chad put his hands behind his head. "He was deep in the closet. He loved porn and kept inviting me over for gay videos and curved penis sex."

Jeremy rolled over to give him a look of exasperation.

"What?" Chad asked.

"Do you want to hear about all my ex's?"

Shrugging, Chad said, "Sure. It could be fun."

Jeremy moaned and rolled to his side, facing the wall.

Chad snuggled up, spooning him. He parted Jeremy's ass cheeks and stuck his soft dick between them. "Nighty-night."

"Goodnight, Joe."

Chad smiled and held Jeremy close. "Joe and Jeremy. Nope, just doesn't have the same ring to it." Chad began to feel sleepy. "Did you set the alarm?"

"For what time?"

"Nine?"

"Nine? It's only three in the afternoon. Believe me, I won't sleep 'til nine."

The Diamond Stud

"You sure? I can't miss my shift."

Jeremy moaned and groped at the digital clock, feeling for the buttons. Chad watched the numbers blink.

"There."

"I like-like you, Jeremy."

"I like-like you too."

Chad sighed and fell asleep.

Chapter 11

Jeremy felt disoriented. The room was dim and the bed was shifting behind him. He looked over his shoulder and saw Chad twisting around under the sheets.

"Chad?" Jeremy could see he was having a bad dream. "Chad, wake up." When Jeremy touched him, Chad jolted and nearly fell off the bed. Jeremy grabbed after him to stop his tumble. He felt Chad's boiling heat and sweat from his nightmare. "You're okay. I'm here."

Watching the terror slowly vanish from Chad's dilated eyes, Jeremy kept stroking his hair and neck gently. "Do you remember it?"

Chad adjusted his position so he was leaning against the headboard and pillows. "Same one, again and again."

"You don't have to tell me." Jeremy sat upright next to him, leaning on his shoulder, holding his hand.

"I was closing at the bar in the Oregon District."

Jeremy expressed his confusion.

"The only gay area—one block long—in Dayton."

"Oh." Jeremy knew he wasn't going to like this story.

"Two guys came at me with a baseball bat."

"In the dream?"

"No. In reality. In the dream, I keep fighting back. I think my subconscious isn't content to let me play the wimp."

"You were beat up by two guys with bats?"

The Diamond Stud

"One guy with a bat. The other just used his fists and feet."

"When did this happen?"

"Last year on Halloween. So almost one year ago."

"Baby. I'm so sorry."

"I was in the hospital for weeks. I had really lousy health insurance so it nearly broke me financially as well."

Jeremy clasped Chad's hand in both of his, massaging the back of it.

"I think my brother had something to do with it. He seemed to know the details and told my father, even before I did."

"Did it hit the news?"

Chad laughed sadly. "No. There were no reports of gay-bashing in Dayton. No way."

"Did they catch the bastards?"

"No. I couldn't remember them well enough to describe them. White trash rednecks with baseball caps and denim jackets. That was about all I remembered." Chad rubbed his chest stubble. "What time is it?"

Jeremy twisted to look over his shoulder. "Only five."

"I can't sleep anymore."

"We napped for two hours. That's not bad." Jeremy shut off the alarm. "Come here." He snaked his arm around Chad's back and snuggled him close, kissing his hair. "I'm glad you're here in San Francisco."

"Are there any gay bashings here?"

"I suppose there are some, but not like the Midwest. I'd be terrified to be 'out' there."

"Have you ever lived anywhere else?"

"No. I grew up in northern California. My parents live close by."

Chad hunted under the blanket for Jeremy's cock and toyed with it. "Are you out to your parents?"

"Yes. I came out at my twenty-fifth birthday."

"How long have you known you were gay?"

"Since I was eleven. How about you?"

"When I was four, I tried on my mom's high heels and dresses."

"I was a late bloomer." Jeremy smiled, hugging Chad tight.

"Have you ever been targeted because you're gay?"

Jeremy thought about it. "I keep a very low profile at work, so nothing there. But once in a while I hear a comment or two."

"Hear a comment or two?" Chad sat up straighter and stared at him.

Jeremy felt embarrassed he'd not had to endure what Chad did. "I come from a very open-minded family, Chad. Nothing like yours."

"Wow."

"You survived it. You should be very proud of yourself."

"I haven't survived shit. I still don't think I'm safe."

"Why would they follow you here? Doesn't that seem like a lot of time and effort?"

"What else has my brother and his dimwit-caboose-butt-dildo-wife have to do? They both don't work. It's either spend all day in a recliner watching Jerry Springer with a plate of cold pizza on your stomach, or hunting me. I think Dwayne could justify anything to get dad to finance him. He's desperate to not have the will contested."

"You sure it's not a lot more money than you think?"

"Sweetheart, to an unemployed waster, even a hundred thousand is a fortune."

Jeremy tried not to get distracted by the way Chad was fondling his genitals. "But don't you think he already knows he has your father's money?"

"They obsess about me. You have no idea the phone calls I get. I've become those ass-wipes' full time job." Chad stopped playing with Jeremy's nuts. "Let me show you." He climbed out of bed, dug through his clothing and returned to his spot with his mobile phone.

Jeremy sat up higher, dreading hearing anything from 'Dahwayne'.

After pushing a few buttons on his tiny phone, Chad handed it to him. "Listen to this."

Jeremy winced, but took the phone. *"You faggot! Leave! If you're not already out of this state, fuck off! No one wants you here, do you hear me? So pack your shit, and get out! If I find you around here, you're dead! So leave! You've done enough to make everyone think there's something wrong with this family. And there is! You! So move! Pack your shit and move!"*

Jeremy heard enough. He felt sick and stopped the message from playing. He scrolled the screen and noticed the date. "That was four days ago. Does that mean he doesn't know you've moved?"

Chad took it back and stared at the tiny LCD screen. "This one is from today. I haven't listened to it and I don't want to." He gave Jeremy the phone again.

"I really don't want to hear it."

"Okay." Chad shrugged.

"But I will." Jeremy put the phone to his ear. *"Don't think since you left without telling anyone that this is over. I will find you. I will hunt you the fuck down. And I will make sure I never have to hear your name or have anyone ask about you ever again. I want you dead! You can't hide, you cock-sucker! I want to write your obituary!"*

The sense of violation and disgust in Jeremy was strong. He ended the message and said, "You have to play that for the police."

"Was it bad?" Chad appeared pale, putting the phone on the nightstand.

"Yes." Jeremy felt his eyes burn from his worry.

"Did he say he'd kill me still?"

"He doesn't know where you are." Jeremy embraced Chad, holding him tight.

"If you were a gay man living in the Midwest, where would you go? Isn't it obvious?"

"You can be anywhere. There are gay communities in New York, Florida, Seattle…"

"Nope. They'll know I came here."

"Why?" Jeremy released his hug and sat back so he could see Chad's face.

"I sort of threatened to move here once before."

"You think that let the cat out of the bag?"

"Sometimes I talk too much for my own good." Chad leaned his cheek on Jeremy's chest, digging his hand under the blanket to his cock again. "I pretend I'm brave and full of myself when I'm verbally attacked."

"That's understandable."

"Dwayne said 'California gives tofu eaters a bad name'."

"What the fuck does that mean?"

"It means he's sick in the head." Chad wrapped his legs around Jeremy's, sealing them on one side.

"Can we stop talking about him?"

"My pleasure."

"Speaking of pleasure." Jeremy ran his hand down Chad's naked back. "Your fingers are giving me an erection."

"Duh!" Chad licked Jeremy's nipple and resumed pressing his head against it.

"I don't remember getting this much sex in a relationship before."

"Please tell me that was a joke."

"No. I wish I was joking. My last boyfriend refused to touch me."

"Because…"

The Diamond Stud

"No clue. He was into it in the beginning, then...nothing."

"Gawd. I'd be lost without sex. Maybe I'm a sex-aholic. You know. Like the guy from X-files."

"I'd do him." Jeremy unfocused his gaze.

"In a heartbeat. Mm!" Chad moved the blankets back and enveloped Jeremy's cock.

"Oh...I hope you continue to like-like me, because you're spoiling me rotten." Jeremy nearly dissolved into the pillows as he swooned. There was nothing like a hot wet mouth to turn him into putty.

Chad held the base of Jeremy's cock with two hands and sucked until his cock popped out of his mouth with a loud noise.

Jeremy blinked. "What are you doing?"

"Does it feel good?"

After a moment to consider, Jeremy said, "Yes."

Chad continued popping Jeremy's cock in and out of his mouth. The suck and release plus the friction on the head of his cock was unusual, but bringing chills to his skin. He swallowed loudly as the quick tempo brought a sense of risk to the pleasure.

Jeremy had an urge to tell Chad to stop, but the stimulation outweighed the strange act. "I don't think I can come like this."

"I'm not ready for you to come." Chad dove back down and sprang up with a *Pop!* of his lips.

After another five pops, Jeremy stopped him. "Err...can we move on, lollipop?"

Chad smiled at him. "Yeah. Mind if I go rim diving?"

Choking at the absurdity of the question, Jeremy made a move to spread his legs. Chad snuggled between them and Jeremy's sack was lapped at hungrily.

"Hello? Anyone home?" Nan's voice came through the door as he arrived home.

"In here eating Jeremy!" Chad called back.

"Sounds good!"

Jeremy shook his head. "I have never met a man like you before."

Chad raised his head from between Jeremy's thighs. "Is that a good thing?"

"I think so."

"I hope so."

Jeremy moaned as Chad pushed his legs farther apart and dove in.

~

Talking about his family problems had distracted Chad. Though he was devouring Jeremy, attempting to lose himself in the act, voices in his head were doing a good job making him unhappy.

He stopped, wiped his mouth and leaned on his elbows.

Jeremy raised his head off the pillow and asked, "Wanna screw me?"

Chad knew he wasn't hard, and didn't know if he could get hard with the thoughts in his head.

"Chad?"

He stared at Jeremy's cock as it deflated slowly.

"How about you just rest until your shift?" Jeremy patted the spot beside him.

"*I* can make *you* come." Chad tried to snap out of his pensive mood, holding Jeremy's cock.

"I'm okay for now."

"I'm sorry." Chad crawled higher on the bed and propped his head up in his palm.

"What are you sorry about? Do you think I'm so self-absorbed that I can't understand what's going on?"

"You don't want to be involved with a guy with this kind of crap going on in his life."

"Can I decide that?"

The Diamond Stud

Chad met his gaze. The affection was so obvious, it was as if Jeremy were telling him he like-liked him out loud. "Are you coming to the bar later? Or are you sick to death of me?"

Jeremy gave him a look of exasperation. "You really haven't ever dated a guy twice?"

"Once." Chad smiled sadly. "My best friend Jett and I tried to go steady for two weeks. We both cheated and gave up. But at least I got a best friend out of it."

"So...a couple of weeks and you'll be done with me? Is that the plan?"

"I'm terrified. You're a smart, financially secure CPA. Can't you see the neurotic five year old lurking in me?"

"Terrified of relationships? Commitment? Or what you left behind in Ohio?"

"Yes. Yes. And yes. I'm a thirty-eight year old whiny little girl."

"Thirty-eight?"

"Gawd!" Chad flopped to his back and covered his face. "Did I say that? I meant twenty-eight."

"I don't care how old you are. But now I know why you keep referring to me as your boy toy." Jeremy scooted closer and rested his hand on Chad's chest.

"May as well be in a managed care facility with a walker."

"Here comes the drama."

Chad flung his arms into the air, hamming it up. "A drama queen! A diva! That's me." Chad had a thought. "Oh! What am I going to wear tonight if Wayne wants a number?" He sat upright like a shot.

Jeremy pushed him back down again. "I don't think that bar is known for its entertainment."

"He made a lot of money last night." Chad bolted upright again.

"Okay. Want to go shopping?"

"I wish. My spending spree came to an end at brie and crackers."

"I can buy you something."

Chad spun around and stared at him. "You're my boy toy, not the other way around."

"Consider it a loan."

"No." Chad climbed out of bed.

"An early Christmas gift?"

"No!" He took a look at the black wig trying to smooth the hairs out.

"You can't wear the same outfit."

"Sigh," Chad said while breathing out loudly. "I wanted to go redhead tonight."

"At least let me buy you a wig." Jeremy swung his legs over the side of the bed.

"Hang on." Chad walked out of his room naked. He stopped at Nan's bedroom door. "Knock, knock."

"Yes?"

"Do you own any wigs, Nan?" Chad pressed his ear against the door and could hear the telltale signs of a gay porn video's bad music and play-acted grunts.

"No, sweetie!"

"Does Le?"

Le answered, "No!"

"Oh. Hi, Le. I didn't know you were there. Okay. Thanks anyway." Chad walked to the bathroom and flipped up the toilet seat to relieve himself.

Jeremy poked his head in. He was wearing his jeans. "No luck?"

"I'll do something with the black wig. I can tease it to look like a Jersey housewife." Chad flushed the toilet and reached into the shower stall, turning on the water. "Want to join me?"

"Uh. Do I stink?" Jeremy sniffed his pits.

"No." Chad laughed at him as he stepped under the spray. "I have to shave." He caught Jeremy leaning against the wall watching. Chad sprinkled him with water playfully, making Jeremy recoil and wipe his face.

Chad spread cream on his chest and removed the stubble with a razor.

"I never shaved anything but my jaw."

"You don't have to. You're not hairy. And...you're not a drag queen." Chad stopped moving to ask with a wicked lilt, "Are you?"

"Never dressed as a woman."

"Try it, you'll like it." Chad braced his foot on the corner of the wall and shaved his leg.

"Me? Nah."

"Does my ass need a shave?" Chad poked it at Jeremy. He got a spank on the rump.

"No. You don't have a hairy ass."

"I liked that." Chad wriggled. "One more."

Jeremy gave his cheek another cracking slap.

"That went right to my dick. How am I supposed to shave my balls with this thing sticking up like that?" Chad pushed his cock down, allowing it to spring upright.

Jeremy reached into the shower, turning Chad to face him, sucking him happily.

"That will only make it harder."

"Sorry." Jeremy held it by the base, popping it into and out of him mouth loudly, like Chad had done to him.

Chad blinked. "I like-like that!"

Jeremy laughed. "I can't suck you if I'm laughing."

"Sure ya can." Chad thrust his hips out and back. "Latch on like a guppy. I'll do all the work."

Jeremy stepped back and roared with hilarity.

Chad continued shaving his nuts in the interim. "You're too easy. Jett was the only other person who got my sense of humor."

"I wish I could meet Jett." Jeremy dabbed at his eyes and resumed leaning on the wall to watch.

"Me too. He's fucking awesome. I swear there were some nights I wouldn't have survived if it weren't for him."

"Survived? What do you mean? You don't mean literally, right?"

Chad rinsed the razor and used the cream on his armpits, deliberately not answering.

"Chad?"

He shaved the hair from his pits and said, "I would wax everything, but it's a fortune and ouch! It hurts. Had my bikini done once. Never again." Lastly, he took a fresh razor and shaved his face, all without looking in a mirror. Chad had done this routine so many times, he never had to look.

Jeremy's countenance had changed from jovial to preoccupied. He held a towel for Chad, who shut the water and stood dripping. "Thank you, baby-doll." He scrubbed it over his hair. "Still blond or did my bleach rinse out?"

"You can't rinse out bleach."

"I was joking. See? Most of my humor is lost on mere mortals." Chad stepped out of the shower stall. "Don't pout. It will give you wrinkles."

"I'm trying not to but..."

"No buts, unless it's one of these." Chad wriggled his ass at Jeremy.

"Let me buy you a new wig."

Chad draped the towel over the curtain rod and removed moisturizer from the cabinet. "Why? A sympathy wig? Is that like a sympathy fuck?" He spread cream from his toes to his face, massaging it all over his skin.

"No. It's an 'I like-like you' gift. Maybe I can borrow it for Halloween."

"Halloween? Is that coming already?" Chad massaged the cocoa butter balm into his shaved balls, catching Jeremy watching.

"Want me to do that?"

"Thought you'd never ask." Chad handed him the bottle.

Jeremy took a generous amount of cream and rubbed his hands together. "I feel like we've been trying to orgasm since our nap and it's not working."

"Three times the charm." Chad opened his stance for balance.

Jeremy used one hand under Chad's balls, the other on his dick. "Nubs." Jeremy smiled.

"No! How can there be nubs when I just shaved?"

"Shut up and kiss me."

"My Dom is back!" Chad coiled his arm around Jeremy's neck and connected to his mouth. The kissing morphed from casual lip-smashing to frenzied tongue dueling as Jeremy's handjob brought Chad near climax. "I'm about to blow my load." Chad tightened his hold on Jeremy, licking his lips and jaw as the sensation in him drew close to the edge. "Don't make a mess of Nan's walls."

"I got ya."

Chad peeked down to see Jeremy cupping the end of his cock. "Houston, we have blast off." He opened his lips and thrust his hips hard into Jeremy's tight grasp. Chad felt the tingles from the climax rush throughout his body and culminate in his balls, where it had started. He grunted softly while Jeremy milked him. "That was nice."

Jeremy gave him a last long pull and rinsed his hands in the sink.

"My dick has never had so much cocoa butter on it." He tapped his jaw to think. "Nope. I take that back. I've given it the same treatment recently. My turn?"

"Does this apartment have two bathrooms?"

"Yes. Why?"

"I just didn't want to hog this one while Nan and Le were here."

"You don't want to come?" Chad pouted. "I repulse you? You think I'm too high maintenance?"

"You're right. You do have a strange sense of humor." Jeremy opened his jeans and dropped them down his legs.

"Look at that bush!" Chad grabbed it and Jeremy said, "Ouch!"

"Yup. That's what waxing is like. Horrible." Chad put a generous dollop of moisture cream in his palm.

"We should have done this in bed." Jeremy spread his legs and held onto the pedestal sink.

"More fun this way. It's like doing it in the locker room at gym class."

"I never did this in gym class."

"Me neither." Chad coated Jeremy's cock and balls with the cocoa butter cream. "You'll be soft as a baby's behind."

"I'd rather be hard like a twenty-nine year old CPA while his boyfriend is giving him a hand-job."

"Boyfriend?" Chad met Jeremy's gaze. "Am I your boyfriend?"

"You're not?"

Absently toying with Jeremy's cock, Chad thought about it. "I suck at that shit. You sure?"

"I'm sure I want to come. Can we talk after?"

Chad continued to manipulate Jeremy's genitalia to get it erect, but he had to fight hard on his own distraction. "Okay,

The Diamond Stud

here we go. Nice dick, Houston, straight as an arrow and nearly seven and a half, right?"

"I have no idea. Man, that feels good." Jeremy moaned.

"No idea? Honey! Every man measures it." Chad fisted it faster, using his slippery fingers between Jeremy's legs.

"Ugh!" Jeremy grunted in pleasure. "Not me! Wow, that's good."

"Come button time." Chad pushed his finger into Jeremy's rim and gave it deep hard friction.

"Fuck!"

Chad aimed his cock at the sink basin. Jeremy's legs tensed and he ejaculated, spattering the ceramic.

"Your plumbing is in good working order, hottie. Great force behind that load of jizz."

"Fuck..." Jeremy rested both hands on the sink.

"Nothing like good ole fashioned mutual masturbation." Chad turned on the water, rinsing his hands and the sink basin. "Now I need another nap."

"No. Let me take you out for dinner and a wig." Jeremy tugged his pants up.

"Dinner and a wig? You sure know how to treat a lady. I could get spoiled...boyfriend." Chad flipped his wrist.

"Get over here." Jeremy grabbed Chad's face and planted his lips on his.

Chad blinked and made a noise of surprise. After the sumptuous kiss, Chad caught his breath. "Whoa..."

"Come on, my diamond stud. Let me woo you." Jeremy opened the bathroom door, and led Chad out by holding his limp cock.

"My wish is your command. Where did I meet you again?" Chad was definitely in *like-like*. Could it be love?

"Funny, DeSoto. Very fucking funny."

"You know my last name?" Chad gasped.

After a quizzical look, Jeremy said, "You told me. I won't tell, I promise. No one will hurt you when I'm around."

Chad entered his bedroom and hunted for clean clothing. "Is that right? Do you have a black belt? A concealed permit to carry? Israeli self-defense training?"

"Chad."

Chad glanced at Jeremy who was buttoning his shirt.

"I will do my best to protect you."

Though the sentiment was meant well, Chad shook his head as he smiled. Nothing could stop a bullet intended to kill him. No one knew that better than he did.

Chapter 12

Jeremy was fascinated with the whole concept of buying Chad his wig and outfit. It wasn't until Chad was seated before a mirror and being helped to put on a flaming red wig, that Jeremy noticed his eyebrows were extremely well groomed. Either waxed or plucked, but Chad definitely had done something to narrow them. They arched high and tapered at the end. Jeremy caught his own reflection from behind Chad and compared his.

"Thinking of a wax?" Chad smiled flirtatiously, obviously seeing Jeremy touching his eyebrows in contemplation. "Don't. Honey, I knew a uni-brow. Believe me, you don't need any touch up. And you're not a *queen!*" Chad threw out his arms dramatically, hitting the sales person in the chest. "Oops. Sorry. I get carried away. I think I'm Robert Preston in *Victor/Victoria.*" Chad helped adjust the wig. "It's so Lucille Ball! What do you think, Jeremy? Hm? Too puce?"

Jeremy lost himself on the transformation. "How can you look like a woman? You're six foot tall."

"Six two, but who's counting?" Chad said in an aside comment to the man adjusting his wig, "He never measured his own dick. You believe him?"

The clerk laughed, continuing to fluff the hair, spinning the ringlets in his fingers. "Six and three quarters on a good day. Oh well, what God didn't give me in length, he made up for in style."

"How do I love San Francisco," Chad said, holding the young man behind him in a backwards hug, "let me count the ways...six, six and a quarter, six and a half..."

Jeremy chuckled. "I guess all gay men know their size, huh?"

"Not all." The clerk stared at Chad in the reflection. "Just the paranoid ones."

"Do you know your size, Chad?" Jeremy spotted a rolling stool and pulled it close to sit beside him.

"I'm not one to brag." Chad touched the wig gently, in a feminine way.

"Do tell." The clerk brought over another wig.

"Nearly nine!" Chad gave the new wig an exaggerated gasp of adoration. "Ooo! Yes! Yes. Take this one off."

"Knew you'd love it."

"What's your name?" Jeremy asked the young man.

"Tiffany." He removed the red wig and placed it on a mannequin head.

"Where do you perform?" Chad asked, tucking his blond tresses into the netting as it slipped out.

"I was on cable TV! I won a lip-sync contest." Tiffany placed the wig on Chad's head.

Jeremy hadn't explored much of the drag world or cross dressing community. He suddenly wondered if he led a sheltered life. Tiffany was tiny and appeared to be a Pacific Islander. Jeremy imagined the transformation into a female would be simpler for him, than for big, robust Chad.

Chad squealed and batted his lashes. "I'm so happy for you! Tiff, that's to die for." Chad spun to look at Jeremy. "I love this one. Do you?"

"You look good in all of them." Jeremy felt his cheeks blush.

"He's my boyfriend." Chad touched Jeremy affectionately. "Do you have one of those?"

"A few." Tiffany smiled. "I never get tied down."

The Diamond Stud

Jeremy studied Chad's reaction to the reply.

"Honey, I get tied down whenever anyone has a rope!" He winked at Jeremy.

"I like this one." Jeremy touched the silky hair of the voluptuous light brown wig. "You need a new outfit to go with it."

"Sequins!" Tiffany said.

"Sequins are so yesterday." Chad pursed his lips. "How about red leather?"

"For your size?" Tiffany flopped his wrist. "You'd need a custom fit. When do you need it? I know an amazing seamstress."

"Tonight."

"Not that amazing!" Tiffany walked away from where they were seated.

Jeremy watched him vanish into a back room. He leaned closer to Chad. "What are you in the mood to eat for dinner?"

"I like everything but greasy Midwest all-you-can-eat buffets." Chad bloated out his cheeks. "Oink."

"You won't get that here in the Castro." Jeremy glanced back to make sure they were alone then went for a kiss.

After they parted lips, Chad asked, "Would you do me in high heels and a wig?"

"I would if you want me to, but I prefer you butch."

Chad's eyes went wide and he burst out laughing. "Did you just use the word 'butch' to describe me?"

"Yeah." Jeremy caressed Chad's cheek.

After a long exhale, Chad said, "I sure do like-like you, *Jer.*"

"I'm very glad you do."

"Ta da!" Tiffany appeared with a gown draped over her arm.

Chad leapt to his feet and touched the gold lame. "Where did you get this?"

"We have a few stashed in back. It's on consignment, but barely worn."

Jeremy rolled the stool back to observe the process of buying a dress. He remembered going to the department stores with his mother, but he must have been nine or ten at the time, maybe younger.

Chad held it up to his chest.

"It stretches. That's the beauty of the fabric." Tiffany helped hold it up. "What size bra do you wear?"

"I can't believe I'm having this conversation!" Chad's expression was awe-struck. *I can tell I'm not in Kansas anymore, Dorothy!*

As Chad and Tiffany walked to a dressing room, chatting in excitement, Jeremy smiled and said to himself, "Well? You found a Midwest drag queen, *Jer*...how about that?"

~

After dinner at a Greek restaurant Jeremy had suggested, Chad returned to the apartment alone with his new outfit and wig. "Hello?" He called out as he entered the apartment, listened for a reply and didn't hear one.

He hung up the dress and placed the wig box gently on his dresser. Removing the wig to admire it, he turned the Styrofoam head to face him, found a marker pen, and made a smiling face on it with almond eyes surrounded by long lashes. "There. Much better." Chad looked through his wardrobe to decide what to wear for his bartending shift. Regrets of not packing all his clothing when he left Dayton soon surfaced. But when you're being hunted, you either fight or flee. Suddenly Chad felt like a coward.

He located his empty suitcase and dug through the zipper pouch on the side. He had stuffed a wad of paperwork into it, mostly old receipts for bills so he could call them and stop service. Since he hadn't done any of that yet, he sighed and sat

The Diamond Stud

on the bed, sorting through which calls to make first thing Monday morning.

With a pile forming on the bedspread, Chad needed moral support so he called Jett. Before he even dialed the number, the phone indicated more text messages and voicemails. It made Chad shiver in anxiety. He ignored them.

When Jett answered Chad could hear background noise. "Honey! You out doing the town?"

"Hello, girl! I always have time for you."

"Jett, can you hear me in all that chaos?" Chad felt as if he were shouting.

"Hang on."

Chad checked his battery level quickly on his phone and put it back to his ear.

"I'm at your old haunt, stud. The drinks will never be the same. Do they water them down?"

"Nope. You just drink like a great white."

"Never!"

"You sober enough to listen to something?"

"Yes, precious honey child."

"If I call my apartment manager Monday, and find out if he still has my clothing..."

"Oh dear." Jett sighed loudly.

"Yeah. Never mind."

"No! No, baby. I'll ship your things. How much are we talking?"

Chad glanced at the few items he'd traveled with. "Loads."

"What did you do? Leave with the clothing on your back?"

"Close. I was terrified. I swear, Jett, I had to get out."

"I know. I know...poor thing."

"The manager's name is Mike Simmons. He's not too nasty. He may still be holding some of my stuff, you know, for legal reasons or something. I mean, he has no idea I bugged out."

"Hang on, sugar. If he has no idea you 'bugged out' why should he have your clothes?"

Chad felt disoriented. "How long have I been gone from my apartment?"

"A week tomorrow."

Cold sweat broke out on Chad's skin.

"Sugar?"

"I paid my rent until the end of October."

"Then no one should have removed any of your things."

"Then how did my brother find out I left?"

"That lazy white trash stalker? You asking me that for real?"

"Can you help me hire someone to pack the rest of my clothing and ship it? I'll pay of course, Jett."

"Just your clothing? What about all your worldly possessions?"

"You take them. Or give them to charity."

"Don't make any more rash decisions, Chad. Have you thought about it?"

"The place I live in now is furnished. I have one bedroom."

"I can't believe those bastards chased you out of Ohio like that."

Chad began to feel sick to his stomach. He checked the clock and had to get ready for his shift at the bar. "Please help me, Jett."

"You know I will. But you asked me on a Saturday night. I have no idea who I can be in touch with tomorrow."

"Monday is okay. And you'll need Mike to get you in. Unless I send you my keys in Fed Ex." Chad removed his keychain from his pocket and looked at it.

"Send me the key. I'm not involving anyone else in this."

"I'm terrified to have you go to my place alone."

"I won't be alone. I'll take my cousin Deshawn with me. He looks like a gangsta."

The Diamond Stud

"I love you, Jett. And I owe you."

"You don't owe me anything but a night on the town in San Fran if I ever get my ass out there."

"I'll buy you tickets with my tip money."

"Don't buy anything yet. I have to see what time off I can scrounge. The suckers I work for are so *not* into family-time days off."

"I'll text you my address. And I'll send you a money order once you figure out how much it's going to cost."

"Okay. Let me go back inside the bar. I'm freezing my tits off."

Chad smiled. "What are you wearing, girl?"

"My Lady Gaga outfit. And I'm cold!"

"All right, my delicious chocolate bunny. Get inside."

"Back at ya, white diamond stud!"

Chad made kissing noises and disconnected the line. Worry set in at the favor he asked. It was a big one. Before he slid off the bed to get ready for work, he checked the text messages. "Oh, no." The threats were increasing in violence. Chad didn't even dare listen to the voicemail. "I've moved, you morons!" Chad shivered and put the phone on the nightstand. "Leave me alone! I don't want a dime from you filthy bastards! Just forget I exist!"

~

Jeremy checked his watch as he strolled down Market Street. He had managed to find street parking nearby, which was a miracle. He stopped to inspect a storefront Halloween window display. The novelty shop had a mannequin with a nurse's uniform wearing a mask of 'Jason' from the horror movies, holding a bloody cleaver. She seemed to be aiming for a child's mannequin that was dressed in a princess costume but with a demonic head and holding bloody scissors. Around the made up dolls were rubber masks, plastic weapons and enough accessories to make any trick-or-treater the stuff of nightmares.

The theater was showing *The Rocky Horror Picture Show* at midnight. As Jeremy continued on his way he said to himself, "It'll be Christmas before I know it." He exaggerated a shiver. "Then tax season." He cringed.

He arrived at the pub and waited as two men entered. One held the door open for him. "Thanks." Jeremy smiled and hoped there was an open seat at the bar. He unraveled his scarf and looked for his man.

He spotted him, looking like every gay man's fantasy with his diamond earring and frosty blond, shaggy head of hair. Chad was wearing a sleeveless denim shirt, worn and torn to a soft frayed sky blue, and matching shredded jeans which appeared spray painted on they were so tight. Jeremy felt his entire body react. If he hadn't already slept with Chad, he would have assumed Chad was way out of his league.

As he approached the bar, in an attempt to get his lover's attention, he noticed between his smiles, Chad's face fell into a preoccupied pout. He and Trent were pouring, shaking and stirring their magic potions, trying to keep up with demand.

It was only just after ten, and the crowd was still not at its peak. Jeremy opened his jacket and stuffed his scarf into his pocket. When a stool at the bar opened, Jeremy walked closer to it, asking the man beside it, "Are you just taking a pee?"

"No. Go ahead." The man put on his coat and left a tip on the counter.

"Thanks." Jeremy removed his jacket and hung it on the back of the seat. He relaxed with his elbow on the bar and was surprised to see Chad was still so busy, he hadn't noticed him. Trent was up to his tricks, grabbing Chad's bottom as he scooted by, making Chad jump and scold him.

The Diamond Stud

"What can I get you?" Trent asked, wiping the counter and setting down a coaster.

"Chocolate-tini?"

"I got it, T'." Chad nudged Trent over with a push of his hip and leaned over the counter to Jeremy. "Hi, boyfriend."

Jeremy's body heated up instantly. "Hi."

"What did you ask Trent-the-Groper for?"

"Chocolate-tini."

"Mm." Chad pecked Jeremy's lips and went to work making it.

Jeremy shouldn't have been surprised he got the kiss. After all, he got a two here last night as well. He glanced around and noticed quite a few men had spied it.

Before he set it down, Chad tasted it, licking his lips seductively. "Good!"

Jeremy stopped Chad before he rushed to fill the next drink order. "You okay?"

"Talk later." Chad hurried to a man waiting near them.

The fact that Chad hadn't said he was okay, upset Jeremy. While he sipped his drink Jeremy stared at Chad, trying to believe he was safe here and there was no way anyone would find him.

Chapter 13

Nearing the end of his shift during his break, Chad approached Wayne. "No number?" Chad said. "You sure, Wayne? I have a great outfit and a new wig."

"It's just not our style here. We're more laid back."

Chad reacted emotionally. "But I have all my stuff."

"Maybe we can do it for Halloween." Wayne held the nape of Chad's neck. "This is a quite bar for older guys. Maybe you can ask around for another place that caters to more drag-oriented customers."

"But they loved me last night." Chad dabbed at a tear.

"I know, Chad. They did. Not tonight. Okay?" Wayne stepped back from him. "You want me to get you anything?"

"No." Chad sniffled and spun around so Wayne wouldn't see him fall apart. He had five minutes left on his break.

Juan was busy loading the glass washer behind him. "You okay, blondie?"

"Wayne doesn't want me to lip-sync tonight. I bought a new outfit."

"Aww…poor thing. Go have a shot of tequila. On me." Juan reached for his wallet and handed him a five.

Chad hugged him, kissing his cheek. "Can I get you one?"

"Later."

"I'll bring back your change." Chad headed to the bar.

"No, you put it in the tip jar."

The Diamond Stud

Chad threw him a kiss. He tried to ignore the crowd waving at him for their order.

Trent leaned to his ear. "Let me get it for you. You're still on break. What do you want?"

"Cuervo." Chad handed Trent the five and glanced at Jeremy who was staring at him.

"Get back there or you'll never get your five minutes." Trent cupped Chad's bottom and marched him out of the public area.

Before he hid from view, Chad glanced back at Jeremy. Jeremy obviously grew concerned, his mouth turning down at the corners.

Trent handed Chad his shot of tequila and a wedge of lime. "Extra large, like you." Trent glanced at Chad's crotch.

"You're making my boyfriend jealous." Chad bit into the lime before he shot the booze down.

"Boyfriend? In this job?" Trent peeked back at the men all trying to order drinks in both their absence. "You can get your cocked sucked by a different man every night."

"Been there. Done that." Chad threw the alcohol down his throat and shivered. "Here." He handed Trent his empty glass with the lime rind sticking out of it and walked out from behind the counter to where Jeremy was sitting.

Jeremy swiveled in his chair, facing Chad in anticipation.

Chad stood between Jeremy's knees and held his waist, kissing him. He could hear Jeremy's purr over the music and conversation, feeling it vibrate his lips. He felt Jeremy squeeze his knees, holding him tight. Chad pecked him a few times and said, "Break's over."

"When's your drag number?"

Chad made a sad face. "Wayne said no."

"No!"

"Yes. No." Chad backed up and walked behind the bar. He was instantly hit with orders as Trent tried to escape for his break.

Knowing his emotions were all screwed up because of the turmoil he was dealing with, Chad kept fighting back a ridiculous sensation of welling up with tears. He spotted Jeremy's compassionate gaze.

Jeremy mouthed, 'I'm sorry.'

Chad shrugged, getting busy with his customers.

By three am, Chad, Trent, Juan and Wayne were cleaning up for the night while Jeremy waited by the door patiently.

Trent said, "You know, Chad, there're loads of bars that do drag contests."

"Oh?" Chad turned the chairs on top of the tables as Juan mopped the floor.

"Loads of them. Honest. And you can do a better act with a stage and really loud music."

"True." Chad glanced at Jeremy whom he assumed could hear from where he stood. "But...will there be a bunch of good ole boys with bats waiting outside for us girls?"

Everyone around him stopped what they were doing to stare at him.

"Was it something I said?" Chad caught Jeremy's worried look.

Trent laughed uncomfortably. "Did you just ask if guys would be waiting to beat you up after your performance?"

"Yes." Chad didn't think it was an unreasonable question.

"Where the fuck did you live before you moved here?" Trent continued draining the beer taps as Wayne shook his head sadly.

"Hell." Chad dabbed at his eyes again.

"No shit." Wayne bagged the money from the register for deposit. "No one will be waiting to hit you with a bat, Chad."

The Diamond Stud

"You sure?" Chad began falling apart.

Jeremy hurried to comfort him. "You're all right." He rubbed Chad's back.

Trent asked, "Did someone beat you up?"

"Yes." Chad's teeth chattered. He hugged Jeremy closer.

"Go." Wayne nudged Chad. "Go get some rest."

Chad stood away from Jeremy and used his shirt collar to dab his eyes. "I'm fine. Let me finish helping." Struggling not to sob like an infant, Chad continued what he was doing, catching the other three men exchanging worried glances.

With Jeremy beside him, Chad walked to Jeremy's car, his outfit draped over his shoulder on a hanger covered in plastic, and his wig in its small case in his hand.

Jeremy stopped at a silver BMW and used a fob to unlock it. He took the items from Chad and hung the dress up on a hook over the back driver's side door and placed the wig case on the seat.

Chad dropped into the front passenger's seat tiredly, rubbing his face. Once Jeremy joined him, he asked, "You want to come to my place?"

"Sure." Chad fastened his seatbelt.

When the engine started, opera music was playing. Jeremy lowered it.

"What was that?"

"Don Giovanni."

"Mozart."

"Very good!" Jeremy pulled out of the parallel parking space and drove down the empty street.

"Don't be impressed. I know it because of the movie, not because I go to the opera."

"It's still good." Jeremy held Chad's hand as he drove.

"Sorry. Where did you say you lived again?"

"North Berkeley."

"North Berkeley." Chad yawned. "I'm not in good shape tonight. I'm sorry."

"Stop apologizing. You were on your feet all night and you've been through a lot of shit."

"Still going through." Chad slouched low in the seat.

"What's the latest?"

Chad felt his temples throb with a headache. He used both hands to massage them. "Um. I called Jett to see if he could go to my apartment and pack my remaining clothing. I didn't bring much."

Jeremy was quiet as if thinking about the information.

Chad stopped rubbing his head and resumed holding Jeremy's hand, bringing it to his lap to toy with.

"What can I do to help?"

"Nothing. You think I'm sending you back there?" Chad choked at the absurdity.

"Can I hire movers to do it for you?"

Chad spun around on the seat to face him. "Stop paying for everything. It's making me feel like a charity case."

"I'm not doing that. I just care for you."

"Stop." Chad released Jeremy's hand with a shake.

They were silent for the rest of the drive to Berkeley.

Chad tried to wake up as Jeremy slowed the car, obviously having arrived home. He read 'Bonita Avenue' on a street sign and sat higher in the seat to get a look. "Which one is yours?"

"That one." Jeremy parked directly in front of it.

Chad spotted a sweet home with a gazebo and sitting porch lit by an outdoor light. Getting out and walking around the car to help with his drag clothing, Chad kept looking at the neighborhood, and could tell it was upscale.

He followed Jeremy to the front door. Jeremy pointed a key fob at it. A beep was heard from inside. Chad kept silent as

The Diamond Stud

Jeremy unlocked the door and used a code for the security system. Lights were already lit from an automatic timer, but as he walked through the house, Jeremy turned on more. "Can I get you anything?" He stood at a coat closet and hung up his jacket, reaching for Chad's.

Chad folded the plastic bag containing his dress over a dining room chair and gave Jeremy his jacket, his mouth hung open as he admired the interior. "Oh. My. God. Jeremy Houston!" Chad spotted stone counter tops in the kitchen which had brand new stainless steel appliances. A fireplace was inset in the living room, complimented by hardwood floors and an oriental area rug. Similar to Nan's apartment, but bigger and higher quality.

"Check this out." Jeremy waved him over and turned on a light in a bathroom. "The tub has jets."

"Gaaak!" Chad leaned in and ogled the tile work and recessed lighting. "Did a designer do this?"

"Yes, and me. I completely remodeled it."

"Is it a rental?"

"No. I own it."

He remembered Jeremy telling him that previously. Chad did indeed feel like a charity case. He was nearly ten years older than Jeremy and living like a college student, hand to mouth. "What are you doing with a fuck-up like me?"

"Cut it out." Jeremy maneuvered out of the bathroom around Chad. "Can I get you coffee? Water? Booze?"

"A sink, a toothbrush, and a bed."

"Okay, sweetie," Jeremy said, "Get comfy. Everything you need is there." He nodded to the bathroom and turned down the bed, tossing the throw pillows in a pile. "Let me lock up for the night."

After Jeremy left the bedroom, Chad gave the contents another look. The bed had a high dark wood headboard with matching foot, a lush gold and brown overstuffed quilt and pillows gave it a rich texture. The window treatments were a mixture of blinds, a sheer curtain as well as scalloped dark gold drapes. Tasteful abstract artwork adorned the walls. Chad stood in the bathroom again, investigating the extra large bathtub/Jacuzzi.

Chad hadn't dated anyone steadily previous to Jeremy. He didn't count the two weeks with Jett as a real relationship. And he and Jett had similar lifestyles and incomes, so Jett's apartment was like Chad's, one bedroom, cluttered, and crammed with too much stuff.

What a mess I made of my life.

Chad began to wonder where he had gone wrong. He had been preoccupied growing up gay. That aspect of his life had always seemed to overshadow everything else, including his education and ambition. He dropped out of high school when he was bullied relentlessly. If it wasn't for his mother's pressure, he would never have gotten his GED. Even as a teen, Chad had clung to her for support. She knew he was gay before he did. And he was so terrified of his brother and father, he never came out to them or publicly, until he was in his mid-twenties and living on his own.

Chad had bartended since he was twenty-one. It was all he knew. That, and dressing in drag.

"Chad?"

He spun around to see Jeremy looking worried. "Please talk to me."

"I'm fine." Chad looked around the sink area. "Which toothbrush should I use?"

Jeremy opened a cabinet and gave him a new one.

As Chad tore the cardboard backing, Jeremy stood behind him, smoothing his hands over his naked shoulders. "I love this outfit on you."

"This?" Chad looked in the mirror over the sink.

The Diamond Stud

"Uh huh." Jeremy kissed and licked Chad's deltoid muscle. "My 'denim' stud."

"It's falling apart." He tossed the packaging into the trash.

"I know." Jeremy wrapped his arms around Chad, slipping his hand down his open shirt collar to his nipple. "That's why it's so sexy."

"Toothpaste?" Chad asked, holding up the brush.

Jeremy tugged at the mirrored cabinet, removing the paste and offering to squeeze some out for Chad.

Chad held the brush steady as a swirl of white, green and red topped the bristles. He ran it under the water and stuck it into his mouth.

Jeremy put the tube down on the vanity and tugged the tail of Chad's shirt out of his jeans. Chad leaned a hand on the sink, staring at Jeremy's actions in the mirror. His shirt was raised and Jeremy covered Chad's back in kisses, sending a chill up Chad's spine. He spat out the toothpaste and rinsed his mouth. When he put his toothbrush next to Jeremy's in the holder, it felt as if they truly were connected. Never before had Chad shared a toothbrush holder, with his own toothbrush, with another man.

Propping both palms on the sink, Chad felt Jeremy smoothing his hands down his bottom to where a rip in the material had left a gap on his left cheek. Chills rushed over Chad again as Jeremy knelt down, running his tongue between the white threads to his skin. Jeremy went on a journey down Chad's worn pants to every gap and tear in them. Chad didn't even realize he had a hole in the crotch until Jeremy's fingertips touched his naked balls.

As Jeremy poked and prodded, Chad grew hard, getting a second wind. Jeremy chewed and sucked at the tear on his bottom, while twirling his index finger against his balls. It was getting more difficult to not be an active participant, but it felt so good, Chad waited.

When two fingers began probing between his legs, Chad heard the weak material give slightly. "I had no idea when I went commando that there was a hole there."

"Your ass and balls were sticking out all night."

"My balls were sticking out?" Chad spread his legs and looked down.

Jeremy removed his hand for Chad, so he could see.

Chad thrust out his hips to get a view. "Son of a bitch."

"I've wanted to stick my tongue in there since I first noticed."

"I need to patch it. I had no idea."

"Sure you didn't." Jeremy spun Chad around so he was backed up against the sink, licking at the soft wrinkled skin as it pushed through the hole.

"Honest. I don't usually expose those to strangers."

"And I have swampland in Jersey to sell you."

Chad chuckled. "Not including hook-ups."

"Now I believe you." Jeremy held Chad's sac in two fingers and tugged it out even more.

"Want me to just take them off?"

"The urge I have to rip them open is overwhelming."

"Do you know how to sew? They're all I have to wear home."

"I'll learn." Jeremy gave the two edges a yank and opened the gap.

Chad held his breath, hoping Jeremy did indeed own a needle and thread. It was bad enough looking gay. Chad didn't need to be arrested for indecent exposure or clobbered because he was an exhibitionist. He gave his crotch another inspection. "Jesus!"

Jeremy sucked his balls outside of the worn jeans, mouthing them as he dug his fingers into the hole in the rear. Chad had no doubt that the rip on his behind was growing larger as well. When Jeremy's whole hand cupped his bare cheek, Chad knew the jeans were a lost cause.

The Diamond Stud

Jeremy leaned back to look. "Wow."

"You're killing me. My cock is bent."

"How do you wear jeans so tight?" Jeremy smoothed his fingers over where Chad had become erect.

"I won't anymore. You killed this pair. And they were my faves." Chad touched his testicles. "Looks weird to see them sticking out like that."

"Looks fucking sexy." Jeremy lapped at them.

Chad made an attempt to reach into his pants and upright his dick. "I'm sticky."

"Good." Jeremy took the skin of Chad's balls in between his lip-covered teeth and pulled gently.

"Why don't you just get me in bed?" Chad tilted his head in the direction behind Jeremy. "It's right there."

"Are you tired? I'm sorry." Jeremy backed up.

"Oh no you don't! You got me into this state, you get me out of it." Chad grabbed the back of Jeremy's head and connected him to his crotch.

"Yes!" Jeremy dug his hand into the tear on Chad's behind again, getting to Chad's ass crack.

More fibers giving way made Chad cringe. He finally opened his pants and yanked them wide. His cock sprang out. "I'm free!"

Jeremy enveloped it instantly.

"Good boy. Now…let's just back this way. Come on." Chad inched towards the bed. "That's it…let the old man lay down."

"Shut up," Jeremy laughed as he replied. "Go get naked."

Chad took off his shoes and socks, peeling the tattered jeans down gingerly. He held them up to have a look, able to see right through the back tear to the one in the groin. "Oh dear, oh dear. Call Sally the Seamstress."

"I'll fix them." Jeremy undressed quickly. "Don't worry."

"I can sew. I just don't have my kit with me."

"Chad?"

"Hm?"

Jeremy was lying in bed naked, patting the spot beside him.

"Oh. Lookie loo. Aren't you handsome?" Chad took off his shirt and crawled in. "Hey fella, do you know the horizontal bop?"

Jeremy scooped Chad up around his waist and intertwining his legs, connecting their bodies.

Chad stared into his dark eyes and felt his stomach flip at the passion he was reading. He dropped the silly banter and kissed him. Jeremy climbed over him, straddling Chad's hips, using his cock to rub hot friction on Chad's.

I love you. I love you.

Chad didn't know why he felt such a strong bond with Jeremy. They just connected on every level. Chad wondered if his fear of someone getting hurt because of their association with him was subsiding. Maybe the one night hook-ups and failed relationships were a symptom of his worst nightmare; the person he loved getting harmed. Like his mother.

~

Jeremy felt Chad's kissing change. He stared down at him in concern. "Are you too tired for this?"

"No." Chad bit his lip and his eyes appeared watery.

Jeremy made a move to slide off him.

"No. Fuck me, lover."

"You sure?"

"Yes." Chad rolled over to his stomach and wriggled his ass in the air.

"Chad." Jeremy had lost momentum and knew Chad was exhausted.

"I want you in."

Chad gave him a silly smile, but Jeremy had a bad feeling. "Come here."

The Diamond Stud

"Where did I go?"

"I mean here." Jeremy directed Chad to lay on his side and once again, connected their legs and bodies close. "Goodnight, stud."

"What?" Chad blinked. "I'm not fuckable?"

"Are you kidding me? You're hotter than hell."

"Then put your cock where your mouth is. So to speak. If you could put your cock in your mouth you wouldn't need me."

"Even at four in the morning, you're hilarious."

"I warned you about my sense of humor."

"You did."

"Hang on. You're cuddling me?"

Jeremy gaped at him. "No good?"

"Maybe for post-coital."

"You're up for making love?"

"Oh for Christ's sake." Chad crept down Jeremy's torso and took his whole limp cock into his mouth.

"*Ooo*-kay." Jeremy couldn't figure Chad out, and knew he needed to stop trying. Chad drew hard suction and fisted Jeremy's cock at the base. It didn't take long for Jeremy to get hard again. "You want me to come in your mouth?" He began to edge the climax.

"Mm!" Chad wedged himself between Jeremy's thighs and groped his balls excitedly.

Jeremy stared at Chad's high cheek bones as his lips were wrapped around his cock. When Chad's lashes parted and his bright blue eyes connected to Jeremy's stare, Jeremy felt his groin swirl with a climax. He jerked his hips involuntarily and Chad cranked up the action while Jeremy came. "Fuck!" Jeremy grabbed Chad's head and thrust his cock deeper as he continued to ride the wave.

Once Chad had milked him for the last drop, he leaned up on his elbows and gaped playfully at Jeremy. "I'll be full for a week."

"Here we go." Jeremy smiled. "The comic is back."

"Forget breakfast tomorrow. What a load, Houston!"

"Get up here."

"Where am I?"

"You need to come here." Jeremy fluffed Chad's pillow. "Let me do you."

"You kidding? I'm out of steam, and spunk. I need to close my eyes." Chad crawled higher on the bed.

"Okay, babe." Jeremy made sure he was tucked in before shutting the lights. "Sweet dreams."

"I'll try. But no promises."

Jeremy kissed Chad's nose and closed his eyes.

Chapter 14

Since they had gone to bed late, Chad had woken at eight, but quickly sunk back to slumber. Rousing again two hours later, Chad noticed Jeremy propped up on the pillows, staring at him.

"How long have you been awake?"

"Not long." Jeremy brushed a lock of hair back from Chad's forehead.

"Bed head?" Chad touched his hair.

"Yes, but it's sexy on you."

Chad rolled his eyes playfully. "Sure, just like morning breath."

"Do you want to continue sleeping?"

"I'm good. I'm not the type to sleep a day away."

"Anal?"

"Absolutely!" Chad expressed his enthusiasm and wriggled under the sheets. "When you smile you have dimples." With the tip of his finger, Chad touched Jeremy's face. "I wish I had dimples. All I have is this slight cleft on my chin."

"Very Captain America."

Chad smiled. "Comic books? No. For real?"

"I dabble."

"Screw that. Dabble. You're a collector who goes into a buying frenzy on eBay."

"You spying on me?" Jeremy grinned like a guilty little boy.

"I didn't get the grand tour last night. How many bedrooms does this place have?" Chad spider-crawled his fingers under the covers to check if Jeremy was sporting morning wood.

"Two bedrooms, and a small den I use for my computer...and comic collection."

"Knew it." Chad wrapped his palm around Jeremy's dick. "Knew you had a woodie too."

"I always do, looking at you."

"Don't you say all the right things!" Chad batted his lashes. "A regular Don Juan."

"Hardly. I'm usually really shy."

Chad ran his fingers over Jeremy's length, making it bob. "You weren't shy with me."

"I was a little. I was shocked you picked me out of the crowd."

"Why? You're adorable."

"Adorable? Not handsome?"

"Same thing, isn't it?"

"No."

"Jeremy! You're gorgeous. Are you trying for an ego stroke while I'm stroking your big unit?"

"Not intentionally. But it's nice to hear you say it."

"What on earth could make you feel self-conscious?"

"My height."

Chad blinked and stilled his hand. "You think you're short?"

"Five-nine?"

"Honey!" Chad made a noise of disapproval. "That's not short. I went with a little person once. Now, that was a hook-up I will never forget." Chad expressed sensual pleasure for affect, closing his eyes and moaning.

"You're a crack up. I never know if you're telling me the truth."

The Diamond Stud

"Honest!" Chad held up his hand in a vow, but quickly dug under the blankets again to fondle Jeremy. "I don't lie. Oh, unless it's about my name. Or my fucked up family...or..."

"I get it." Jeremy laughed, relaxing as the massaging from Chad grew more focused.

Thinking about all the phone calls he had to make, the possibility of renting a storage unit if he had too many boxes coming from Dayton, and deciding when to go to the police to see if they could help him, made Chad lose track of his actions.

"You're doing it again."

"Huh?" Chad snapped back into reality.

"Let's shower and I'll make breakfast."

Chad gripped Jeremy's cock tighter. "I'm not done playing."

"You sure? You sort of went off in your head."

"I do that. I'm in need of therapy. I keep a tiny analyst there."

"A shrink."

"That was too redundant. I couldn't say a tiny shrink."

"You should write comedy."

"Write comedy what?" Chad threw off the blanket so he could see what he was doing to Jeremy's body.

"I don't know. Stand up? Sit-coms?"

Chad choked at the irony. "Yeah. My life's a laugh a minute." He began lowering on the bed to suck Jeremy.

"My turn to give you a BJ."

"Six-nine?"

"We can do that again."

Jeremy scooted lower on the mattress and Chad straddled his face with his knees. "It shows off your multi-tasking skills, Mr. CPA."

"One of my many talents."

"I've only just begun to explore your tip." Chad licked his slit. "I mean, tip of your iceberg."

"You always make me laugh when I'm trying to blow you."

"Accept my apologies. Blow me away." Chad shifted to his elbows and sank Jeremy's cock into his mouth, holding the base and balls in both hands. He felt Jeremy do the same with his soft length, and began a gentle rhythm of orally fucking him.

Chad closed his eyes as Jeremy caressed his balls and ass, while deepening his suction. He went into autopilot, drawing on Jeremy's cock while humping. At the taste of Jeremy's pre-cum, Chad began jerking off Jeremy's cock as he sucked. The stimulation of Jeremy coming close to climax was pushing Chad over the edge. He deliberately concentrated on what he was doing and Jeremy's response to it, blocking any intruding thoughts out of his mind.

Jeremy's hips bucked and Chad felt his cock pulsate as he came. He thrust his hips through the tight friction of Jeremy's hand and wetness of his mouth. Moaning, arching his back, Chad kept Jeremy's dick inside his mouth as he came, holding it still. Jeremy's full-mouth whimper made Chad's skin tingle. He milked Jeremy's cock for another drop and opened his eyes, sitting up.

"Wow. Nice one." Jeremy used the back of his hand to wipe his mouth. "Never get tired of it."

"You passed the test twice now for giving and receiving simultaneously. Some men fail miserably and need to come before they can make you spurt." Chad climbed off the bed and straightened his stiff back.

"I haven't done that often enough with other men to have a comparison test for you."

Chad reached out to haul Jeremy to his feet. "Then there's only one whore in here, because Elvis has left the building."

"Don't call yourself that." Jeremy spanked Chad playfully.

"Okay. How about a slut?" Chad made his way to the bathroom.

"Mr. DeSoto. Cut it out."

The Diamond Stud

"Gawd, that makes me think of my father. Ew!" Chad entered the bathroom and loaded up his new toothbrush with paste.

"Sorry. I assume he's as bad as your brother." Jeremy took a stack of clean towels out of a linen cupboard in the bathroom.

"More mental abuse than physical." Chad spat out the toothpaste and rinsed his mouth. "He used to ask me if I took my stupid pills when I was a kid. He made my mother's life so miserable she was on Prozac."

Jeremy gave Chad a frustrated expression. "I'm sorry, Chad."

"Why? You weren't the abuser me and mom lived with. He was." Chad stared at the jets coming out of the side of the tub. "I swear that makes me want to soak."

"We can. Are you in a rush?"

"A rush to…?" Chad flipped open the toilet seat to pee. "I don't even know what I'm doing any longer. I need another job if all I have is a Friday and Saturday shift at Twin Pecs."

"Let me fill the tub then."

Chad gave his dick a shake to get off the drops and put the lid back down to sit on. "It needs bubbles."

Jeremy appeared to think. He knelt down and dug through the cabinet under the sink. "I knew I had this." He handed Chad a children's bubble bath bottle with a plastic superman head as a top.

"Oh my God, Jeremy!" Chad admired it, wiping a layer of dust off of it. "You are adorable. Yes. Adorable. Sorry. This nailed it."

"Is there enough in there?"

Chad dumped the contents under the running water. "A little dab'll-do-ya." He sniffed the air. "Bubblegum? No!"

Jeremy went for a smell. "Sorry."

"Don't be. It's so funny." Chad capped the bottle. "Save this for the room with the comic book collection."

"I think that's why I bought it originally." Jeremy put the bottle on the vanity. "Let me make us espresso so we can sit and drink while we soak."

"I feel like I'm at the Ritz!"

"Be right back."

Chad smiled but it soon faded. The noise of the water filling the big bathtub lulled him into a stupor. He stared at the white foam as the peaks became high and swayed with the churning water. Absently he touched the back of the diamond stud in his ear to make sure the fitting was tight. It was a habit he'd had ever since he spent the money for the pricey little stone.

He stood at the threshold, staring into the bedroom. While Jeremy was busy with the coffee, Chad made the bed, replacing the many throw pillows. Once it was done, he picked up his clothing and inspected the jeans. "Shit." He walked out of the room to find Jeremy, seeing him standing naked, using an espresso maker.

"Don't steam your prick," Chad said.

"I won't." Jeremy noticed him holding the pants. "How do they look?"

"Unwearable. Do you have a sewing kit?"

"I do. In the study." He made a move to go get it.

"Just tell me where it is."

"Down that hall, first door on the right. There's a closet on the left side of the computer desk. On the top shelf is a box with needles and thread. It has spools and bobbins patterns on it, so you can't miss it."

"Okay." Chad walked down the short hall and into the den Jeremy used as a home office. It was immaculate with rows of books, perfectly matched for binding and size, and when Chad approached he realized they were in alphabetical order. A shelf of action figure dolls, still in their packaging caught Chad's eye. As he opened the closet, expecting a mess like his back in

The Diamond Stud

Dayton, he was stunned to see the entire contents organized and lined up. "Are you a madman or a genius?" Chad instantly found the sewing box. It was metal a cookie-like tin, yellow with sewing paraphernalia drawings all over it. He removed it and opened the lid. No mass of threads and needles, patches, and buttons. Even the contents were neat and tidy.

Chad returned to the kitchen where Jeremy was topping off the espresso with foamy milk. "Do you have OCD?"

Jeremy blinked. "I don't think so."

"My God. Look at this sewing kit." Chad opened it and showed Jeremy.

"What am I looking at it for?" He rinsed the steamed milk container and wiped down the espresso machine.

"It's perfect. Mine is a shambles."

"Do you have what you need?"

"I don't know. I was so impressed by how organized it was I didn't look."

Jeremy carried the two cups back to the bathroom.

Chad placed the sewing box and his jeans down on the bed, following him. "Is the tub full enough?"

"We need to get in. I can't tell until we displace the water how high it will need to go to cover the jets."

Chad climbed in slowly. "Nice and hot."

Jeremy handed him a mug, climbing in opposite him. "Looks good." He shut the water and pushed a button.

Chad heard whirring noises then a jet at his back began blasting and bubbling. "You are spoiled rotten."

"I never use it." Jeremy sipped his coffee.

"I'd be in it until I was pink and wrinkly." He peeked down. "I mean even more than normal."

Jeremy smiled at him.

Chad sighed loudly and scooted down, bending his knees so he was straddling Jeremy's legs. He sipped the strong coffee and asked, "Did you put something in it?"

"Pumpkin spice. No good?"

"Do you do eggnog lattes for Christmas?"

"Yes."

"I love you!" Chad blew the hot espresso and sipped more. When Jeremy didn't laugh Chad tilted his head. "I'm sorry. Did I insult your barista talent?"

"Huh? No."

Chad tried to think. *What did I say?* Then it dawned on him. "Oops. I said the 'L' word. Did I freak you out?"

"Nope."

"Anyhoo..." Chad wanted to bypass his faux pas in a hurry. Not only was he not sure how he really felt about Jeremy, he'd known him all of two days. "What's on the agenda for today? Do you have anything you have to do?"

"I could do some errands later. You know. Food shop, stuff like that."

"I can help."

"Sure. If you want to."

"I don't mind. And I'm stuck until tomorrow to look for a job or take care of shutting off my utilities and stuff from O-hell-o."

"Are you going to make out a police report here?"

Chad frowned. "Probably."

"We'll do that first."

"If I go see Officer Friendly, I have to stop home for clothing that won't show off my round and nubblies."

"We can do that." Jeremy smiled. "But I can patch your jeans."

"Okay, boss." Chad finished his coffee and placed the cup on the floor beside the tub. He sunk lower, putting his heels on the ledge on either side of Jeremy. Jeremy downed the contents of

The Diamond Stud

his mug and did the same, massaging Chad's calves in the foamy bubbles.

"I've died and gone to heaven." Chad closed his eyes and moaned.

"You need a little nurturing."

"Are you the guy to do it?" Chad peeked at him.

"I could be."

"Yes. You certainly could be." Chad reached under the water and returned the favor, rubbing Jeremy's foot.

Chapter 15

Jeremy used his teeth to cut the thread. He held up the jeans and inspected the work. Chad was lying on the bed, tickling his back and shoulders while he played seamstress. They had debated who should do the repair. Jeremy insisted he do it since he ripped them. "I think they look very trendy."

"Let me see."

Jeremy handed them to Chad, packing away the needle into the box.

"Jeremy Houston! It looks like a sewing machine did it."

"That's me. The sewing 'machine'." Jeremy stood and left the room to return the box to the closet. When he came back to the bedroom, Chad had the jeans on, touching the areas Jeremy had patched with denim fabric.

Chad spun to look at his ass in the mirror on the dresser. "I couldn't do better myself."

"Thank you. I like the illusion that they're ripped, but the fact that there's still faded blue denim under the white threads."

Chad reached between his legs to feel the crotch hole.

"Is it rough inside? Chaffing your balls?" Jeremy asked.

"No. Soft as butter. Like my package."

Jeremy closed the gap between them and massaged Chad's groin. "You're right. It feels really soft."

"If you keep that up." Chad blew out a breath playfully, saying, "Phew! Not for long."

The Diamond Stud

"Want to come?"

"This is what I get for dating a younger man." Chad swayed with him.

"Are you really that hung up on our age gap?" Jeremy didn't think of Chad in terms of numbers.

"It's ten years, boy toy. When I was in high school you were playing with your dollies."

"I still play with dolls."

"You don't play with them. You keep them in their original boxes and stare at them."

"True." Jeremy reached to drape his arms over Chad's shoulders. "You hungry?"

"I am."

"I can make pancakes here or I know a fabulous breakfast café but there will be a line on Sunday." Jeremy couldn't gauge the thoughts in Chad's head when he didn't reply. "Hello? Anyone home?"

"Huh?"

"Where did I lose you?"

"What's this area like? You know."

"I know? No, I don't know."

"I mean, if two guys were just eating together, but one looked slightly queer..."

"Chad."

"Huh?"

"You're safe here. No one will hurt you."

"So this area is gay friendly?"

"Yes. It's nicknamed the gourmet ghetto. It's very gay friendly and there are a lot of gay owned restaurants and retail stores."

"So...no need for a guy to wish he had taken his gun with him?"

"I'll make pancakes." Jeremy took a step to the bedroom door.

"No. No, I can go out."

"You sure?" Jeremy was miserable Chad had been hurt because he was a gay man. "I don't want to make you uncomfortable."

"I trust you. If you say it's okay, it's okay." Chad tucked his denim shirt into his pants, again checking the rear view. "And I'm not showing skin, right?"

"No. Do you want to borrow a pair of briefs?"

"I'm fine, as long as nothing is hanging out." Chad fussed with his hair. "I look so gay."

"Chad, sit down." Jeremy tugged him to relax on the bed, standing in front of him. "Have you ever thought of going to therapy? Don't take offense, but being beaten up and threatened because of your sexual choice isn't easy for anyone."

"I did. I am. I mean, I did." Chad pointed like he was showing Jeremy a direction. "I had a therapist and he gave me anti-depressant meds."

"Are you on them?"

"Not since I moved. I can't remember where I put them."

"I can recommend you a doctor to get a new prescription."

"Are you taking any?"

"Not at the moment."

"Did you?"

"I did Zoloft in high school."

Chad looped a finger through a belt loop on either side of Jeremy's black slacks, rocking him. "I'm glad. Then you won't think I'm some kind of wacko-case."

"Everyone in California is on happy pills." Jeremy kissed Chad's forehead. "Come on. They have incredible omelets."

Chad nodded, but Jeremy knew he wouldn't feel comfortable in his own skin, or in San Francisco, for a long time.

The Diamond Stud

~

Chad entered the BMW beside Jeremy. He took his mobile phone out of his pocket and turned it on even though it terrified him.

"You have to get a new number."

"It's on the list." Chad hoped only Jett called him, but he knew that was wishful thinking. "Fuck. They won't let up." Chad cringed to see new voicemail messages. "I'm gone, Jer. Why won't they leave me alone?"

"Do you want me to listen to it?" Jeremy drove down the street.

"I suppose if I'm going to make out a police report, someone has to."

"After we eat we'll head to the police station in your area."

Chad moaned and went limp in the seat. "Why, why, why…"

"Greed? I mean, you said your brother wants all your dad's property and money, right?"

"Pretty much. But he already took over my father's bank accounts and snatched his possession. Everything the old fucker owned."

"He may still think you have some claim to it legally."

"He wants me dead. I am not kidding you, Jeremy. Dwayne won't stop until I'm dead."

"He doesn't know where you are."

"He'll use Dad's money and hire someone to find me. You'll see." Chad rubbed his forehead, his stomach knotting up.

"Is he that desperate for what your dad has?"

"Yes! I told you. He's a lazy unemployed piece of white trash, married to a convicted felon who spawned a sexual deviant *Damian-ette*, and two freaks of nature from a previous marriage." Chad stared at Jeremy's profile as he drove. "Did I mention his two demon seeds from the first breeder? One cuts herself just to get attention. She keeps a very special piece of glass to do the deeds. She hoards everything like my father does. A packrat of the worst degree. I mean, she keeps everything; dirty feathers from birds, pieces of old rags...psycho stuff. She wants to be a tattoo artist, is into branding, dying her hair fire engine red, and accuses my brother of sexually assaulting her as a baby. She spreads this stuff all over Facebook. She's only fourteen years old."

"Jesus!"

"It gets worse! My 'nephew'..." Chad cringed. "God, I am so nauseated to claim any connection to these misfits...but, he's the next Columbine-shooting-spree mastermind. He talks about guns, going out to kill everyone, and is bigger than my brother in girth. He's all of twelve. Seriously, Jeremy, it's Jerry Springer on a stick."

"And your brother is supporting the entire group of mental cases?"

"No. Dad is! That's why Dwayne is so desperate. I take that back, he's *more* than desperate. He's homicidal. His ex-wife still, I said *still,* brings him to court weekly over money. That's after nearly fifteen years of them being divorced. My father's been paying his lawyer bills the entire time. Then Dwayne had the nerve to buy an enormous house because his felon-hellion of a wife—she's what Jett and I call a 'want-want', by the way. She thinks she needs to pretend she's wealthy. Thus the stealing of everything not nailed down from every employer who was unlucky enough to hire her." Chad tried to calm down, but couldn't.

"So Dad is paying their mortgage so they don't get repossessed. You think Dwayne wants me in the picture?" Chad always hyperventilated when he spoke of the mess he had of a family. "They have nothing to do all day but watch daytime TV, eat carbohydrates and sugar, and sponge off my dimwitted dad while they plan my assassination."

The Diamond Stud

"Calm down. We'll notify the police about it."

"And do what?" Chad couldn't stop panicking. "Throw yet another piece of paper at him this time with the seal of California on it and hope he doesn't come here for fag-hunting season?"

"They take hate crimes very seriously here, Chad." Jeremy pulled into an overflowing parking lot.

"Hate crimes. Domestic violence. I've already heard how serious all this is and still I'm about to get whacked." Chad spotted a person backing out of a parking space. "There."

"I thought I was going to have to hunt one down on the street."

Chad unfastened his seatbelt and took a look at the café. It was mostly glass and easy to see inside. Jeremy parked and before Chad climbed out, Jeremy held him back. "I'll do what I can."

"I know. Thanks." Chad handed him the phone. "See if they know where I am."

Jeremy exhaled loudly and took the phone.

"Push that button to hear the new voicemail." Chad shivered visibly and tried to stop, staring at the expression on Jeremy's face as he pressed the small phone to his ear. They met eyes.

Chad didn't like the look on Jeremy's face when the message played. He could hear the garbled tones from where he sat. It made him cringe.

Jeremy said, "Your brother guessed you came here."

"Fuck!"

"Chad, San Francisco is a big place. You're a needle in a haystack." He handed Chad the phone.

"What did he say?"

After a sigh, Jeremy said, "The same shit as the last message." He opened the car door. "Come on. Let's eat something."

Chad turned off the phone and slipped it into his jacket pocket. He gave the area a thorough inspection, expecting gunfire from a sniper.

Jeremy put his arm around Chad's back and directed him to the main entrance. "Look." Jeremy pointed to a poster in the window. It was a pink triangle overlapping a red stop sign with a message that read, 'Stop Hate Crimes'.

"I think I'll like living here."

"I think you will too."

Since they were between the breakfast and lunch crowd, there wasn't a long line.

Chad stuffed his hands into his blue jean pockets and gave the occupants a paranoid glance. It was a mixed group of young couples with small children, and men. When Chad received a flirtatious smile from a handsome man, he instantly let his guard down and relaxed.

"You've got an admirer." Jeremy brushed his arm against Chad's.

Before they were seated, Chad touched Jeremy's hand. "Is it okay?"

"More than okay." Jeremy clasped Chad's fingers tightly. When the hostess approached, Jeremy said, "I'd like a special table for me and my boyfriend."

"Awesome!" She giggled and waved in the direction of an open table. "Right this way."

Chad felt more and more at ease. "Thank you." He took off his jacket and slung it on the back of the chair.

"Love those jeans. They look like my favorite pair at home." She handed them menus.

"They are mine too."

"Coffee for you two lovebirds?"

"Yes, thanks. With cream." Jeremy winked at Chad.

The Diamond Stud

"I'll get them for you. And your waiter will be right over to take your order."

Chad waited until she walked away. "So, 'boyfriend'. What looks good?" He opened the menu.

"You do, Chad."

Chad threw him a kiss.

~

After their brunch, Jeremy used his iPhone to find the police station nearest to Chad's apartment. He parked on the street and shut off the car. "I assume it's open. I can't imagine police stations close."

"I hate this. I swear, the cops in Dayton looked at me like I deserved what I got."

"They won't here. At least I hope not." Jeremy climbed out of the car and waited for Chad at the entrance. Chad was looking at his mobile phone, Jeremy assumed he was finding the correct voicemail for the police to listen to.

Jeremy pushed the door and it swung open. "Good. They are open." He glanced at the posters on the walls in the small lobby area. "Go up to that window."

Chad gave Jeremy a nervous glance and walked to the uniformed officer behind heavy glass. "Hi. My family wants to kill me."

While Chad tried to explain his circumstance, Jeremy stood beside him for moral support. The officer said, "Someone will be out to take a report for you."

"Okay." Chad noticed a men's room. "Can I use that?"

The officer said, "I'll buzz you in."

Chad gave Jeremy another forlorn look before he entered the men's room.

Jeremy strolled around, reading the pleas for information regarding murder victims and wanted suspects. A door opened and a woman officer stepped out with a clipboard. "Are you the man who wants to make a report?"

"No. He just went into the men's room. He'll be right back."

She nodded.

Another minute later, Chad exited the bathroom looking frazzled. The woman officer said, "I'm Officer Smith and I'm going to take the report for you. Right this way." She opened another door with a key and Jeremy spotted a round table with a few chairs.

"Do you want me to come with you?" he asked Chad.

Chad's eyes went wide as he grabbed Jeremy's arm and dragged him inside. "You're not going anywhere."

Jeremy sat down, opening his jacket and waiting quietly.

Chad held out his phone. "There are a dozen threatening messages on this. All you have to do is listen."

"Let me get some information first." She began writing on her form, lowering the volume on her shoulder microphone to her police radio.

Jeremy fought back his own nerves as Chad explained more details to the police officer than he had previous to him. It was ugly. The hatred, intolerance, and greed from a blood sibling was like nothing Jeremy could conceive of. He came from a loving home where his sexuality was accepted, even if it wasn't exactly what his parents had wanted from him. They understood it. They even joined PFLAG.

Jeremy watched the expression of the officer as she listened to the voicemail. Chad fidgeted anxiously, shifting in his chair and tugging at his earring.

She placed the phone down and wrote notes on the paper. "Threatening to kill is a felony offense."

"Why didn't he get arrested by the local police then?" Chad appeared cold, wrapping his jacket closer around him.

The Diamond Stud

"I don't know. Ohio law may differ. When he was served papers, what did the court state was the reason?"

"I don't remember. I blocked it out. I swear, I can't deal with it."

"Okay." She reached out as if to calm him. "I want you to write a statement for me."

"A statement? Another one? A lot of good the last one did me."

"It's not mandatory. But it will help if he comes across California's state line."

Chad exchanged a look of pain with Jeremy. Jeremy said, "Do it."

Chad took the pen he was handed, gave a split second to compose his thoughts, and began scribbling. Jeremy gave the officer a sad look. She returned it and continued to listen to the other voicemails Chad had collected on his phone.

~

Chad began getting light-headed as he described the events that had occurred leading up to his brusque departure from Dayton and including the current phone threats. He figured the beating with the baseball bat by thugs—even though he could never prove his brother had put them up to it—and the abuse he had suffered at the hands of Dwayne and his batty wife had already been documented. He had kept the original police incident number in his wallet to prove to authorities that he had, indeed, tried. Nothing seemed to work.

He tapped the pen on his lip, suddenly noticing Officer Smith and Jeremy sitting very patiently, but staring at the ink on the paper, nearing three pages in length. "It's a novel."

"Don't worry about it. You write what you need to write," Officer Smith said.

"I hope it has a happy ending." Chad huffed out an exhale of anxiety and then in big letters at the end of his statement he wrote, '*The reason for my brother's abuse and threats is homophobia and GREED.*' He then signed the bottom and slid the pile of pages towards the officer.

She took a moment to read it as Jeremy reached out to hold Chad's hand under the table. Chad took it, assuming the cop wouldn't be allowed to make a derogatory remark. Not in this age of political correctness. Even if she wanted to shoot her stun gun at him, she had to be polite and smile.

Once she read it she asked, "You believe this has to do with your dad's money?"

"Oh my God yes!" Chad took back his hand from Jeremy's grasp so he could gesture with it. "You have no idea. I could write ten more pages just on his laziness and the need for control Dwayne has over everything my dad does." Chad removed his wallet and took out a business card. "Write this information down. This is the police report number for what I did in Dayton."

She took the card and jotted the report number on the paperwork. "Do you have a copy of the court order?"

"It's at home. I did take it to California with me, but I don't have it with me now."

"Photocopy it and mail it to this precinct, in care of me. I'll see to it it gets filed with this report."

Chad took the card from her with her name on it. When he met her eyes he felt real concern and it surprised him. The police he dealt with in Ohio treated him as if he had leprosy. "Thank you."

Officer Smith glanced at Jeremy first before she said, "I'm gay and I can relate."

That shocked Chad even more. "For some reason, I feel so much better now." Chad held the card to his heart before he put it into his wallet with the one from Dayton.

The officer rose to her feet and held the paperwork in her hand. "If anything else happens that concerns you, call 911 if it's

The Diamond Stud

urgent, and use this case number as a reference if it's just more threats via voicemail." She pointed to a number written on the paperwork. "I wrote it on the card with my name."

Chad felt slightly afraid to ask but he did, "Can I defend myself?"

"If your wellbeing is in imminent danger, and I can't stress the *imminent* fact enough, then yes."

Jeremy said, "You'll be okay. He won't find you here."

Chad asked the officer, "Can I use a P.O. box address for my driver's license?"

"Yes."

Jeremy opened the door and waited for Chad. He shook the officer's hand. "Thanks. Really. I appreciate you not sneering while you listened to me."

She smiled wryly. "No sneering from me, promise."

Chad hugged her, feeling her heavy bulletproof vest. He stood back and gave her a teary smile. She waved and was buzzed back inside another door near where the reception window was.

Reaching out his hand, Jeremy led Chad back out to the street where the sun was shining and the afternoon had warmed up to a delightful seventy degrees.

"I need a drink. A joint. A hit of heroin. Something." Chad walked to where Jeremy had parked the car.

"I can't help you with anything but the booze."

"Sold."

Once they were seated in the car, Jeremy cupped Chad's face tenderly. "You'll be okay."

Though Chad nodded, he wasn't so sure.

Jeremy located a parking spot close to Chad's flat. They had stopped on the way for a bottle of wine at a market and Chad had it on his lap, twisting the brown paper around the neck neurotically. He felt completely spent and didn't know if the day was a total waste of time or could actually improve his situation.

"Do you want me to come in?"

Chad held back on opening the car door and climbing out, and gave Jeremy his attention. "Up to you."

"I feel like I'm stifling you."

"How?"

"Taking up all your free time?"

"I don't work first thing tomorrow. Do you?"

"Yes, but I don't have to head to the DMV, call a mover, find another job, get a new phone number…"

"Augh!" Chad moaned dramatically and mimed chugging the wine down.

Jeremy laughed softly. "I assume Nan has a cork screw."

"If he doesn't I'll shoot it out." Chad opened the car door and met Jeremy at the apartment. Before he opened the lock, Chad gave the area a good scan. He had done the same precautionary measure for nearly fifteen years, he wasn't about to stop now.

Getting the message, Jeremy spun around as well, searching. "What does the asshole look like?"

"Five ten, three hundred plus pounds, dark hair that he dyes to cover the gray, but keeps the temples white, and a goatee."

"And the felonious twit he married?"

"Seriously hideous wedge hair cut, short at the nape of the neck and long at the chin, dyed a bad home-job reddish black, and she's shaped like a pear. Like hugely big on her bottom half with pencil thin arms and a flat chest." Chad spread his hands out to indicate a big ass. "Bad skin coated with pasty glue-like makeup…Gawd, you can't miss her in this area. They both would stick out like a couple of douche-bag hicks at a gay pride rally." Chad waited as two men passed, holding hands. "But they hire people to do their dirty work. Dwayne wasn't the one who

The Diamond Stud

beat me unconscious with a baseball bat. He paid someone to do it."

"Let's get inside." Jeremy took the bottle so Chad could use his key in the lock.

As Chad entered the flat he called, "Nanny? Oh, Nanny?"

"Hey, Chad." Nan and Le were cuddled on Nan's bed playing video games.

Chad stopped at the door. "Hi, Asian doll."

"Hi, Chad and Jeremy." Le smiled.

Jeremy leaned in and waved.

"We bought wine. Do you want to share?"

"Sure." Nan asked Le, "Okay if we stop?"

"Sure. You losing!"

"I'll be in the kitchen pouring." Chad smiled as he headed to get glasses and a corkscrew. He noticed Jeremy reaching out to take his coat. Chad didn't even remember he was wearing it and handed it to him. "My mind is gone. I'm taking after my nasty old man."

"Never." Jeremy left his view. Chad figured he was going to toss the coats on his bed.

Nan appeared in the doorway. "How was your time together? I tried not to worry about you last night." Nan opened the refrigerator and removed the last of the brie and some sharp cheddar he had obviously purchased on his own. Le sat down at the dining room to watch the preparation.

"I think calling you Nanny is appropriate. It's just that you look nothing like Fran Fine."

Nan chuckled.

"My God. He gets me." Chad filled four glasses.

"Love that show." Nan emptied a box of crackers into a bowl and brought it with the cheese to where Le and Jeremy were sitting.

"We just ate brunch." Jeremy slid the plate closer to Le.

Chad carried two glasses of wine to the table, going back for the other two. "Jeremy has a great house in North Berkeley."

"That's such a nice area." Nan sat down, topping a cracker with a slice of cheese.

"Cheers." Jeremy raised the glass.

Though Chad didn't think he had a reason to be 'cheery', he tapped everyone's glass.

"You okay?" Nan asked, loading up another cracker.

Chad caught Le's concerned gaze as well. "What could be wrong? I just came from the police station to report my own family wants to write my obituary."

Jeremy reached out to touch Chad in comfort while Le and Nan exchanged worried looks.

"I can't talk about it anymore." Chad gulped the wine and refilled it to the brim.

"Why you not join us for video game?" Le asked. "Will take mind off trouble."

"I don't play video games." Chad drank the second glass faster than the first. "I'm old, baby-doll. Over the hill."

"Shut up." Jeremy shook his head.

"How about new Blu-ray?" Le asked. "Just released action thriller?"

"Do people get assassinated because of their sexual choices?" Chad tilted the wine glass up to drink the last drop. He noticed the other three staring at him, appearing very unhappy. "See? I'm the life of the party, aren't I?" He stood, set his glass in the sink and walked down the hall to his room. Not a peep was heard from the other men, but Chad could imagine their exchanging of bewildered looks.

~

Jeremy rubbed his face and noticed both Nan and Le waiting for some kind of explanation. He peeked behind him, seeing Chad had gone into his bedroom. "He's just having a bad day."

The Diamond Stud

"He knows he can talk to us, right?" Nan asked.

"I'm sure he does. Thanks, guys." Jeremy washed both his and Chad's glasses and went to join Chad to see if he should go home or not. He knocked on the partially opened door and pushed it back. Chad was seated on the bed with the revolver in his hands, staring at it.

Jeremy did not have a comfort zone with guns. He stopped short. "What are you doing?"

"I have to get a concealed weapons permit. I just don't know how long it will take."

"Can you put it away?"

Chad met Jeremy's eyes. A chill of terror washed over Jeremy, as if he were seeing a side of Chad he had not previously. A vigilante who would not be beaten again. He made a wide path, avoiding being in the invisible line of fire and sat beside Chad. "Let the police handle it."

"They can't. I tried that route."

"If you were going to shoot your family, you left them a long way behind."

"I feel them. They're coming."

Jeremy couldn't argue the point. Though he doubted it, he knew the messages certainly indicated they may. And Chad had good reason to worry. "They're not at the door at the moment. Please. Put the gun away."

"Get up."

As if he'd been scolded, Jeremy stood slowly. Then he realized Chad tucked the handgun between the mattress and the box-spring. "Crap. Is that where you keep it? Loaded?"

Instead of answering, Chad kicked off his shoes and curled on the bed in the fetal position.

Jeremy did the same, spooning Chad. Though he wanted to say, 'Don't worry', Jeremy did worry. And the sentiment would be hollow and worthless. "I'm here." He ran his hand down Chad's arm to his hip.

Chad turned to look at him, holding him close and hiding his face in Jeremy's neck. "Why, Jer? Why?"

"We know, don't we?" Jeremy dug his arm under Chad's body to hold him closer. "Do you think if you had an attorney write up a certified letter that you are relinquishing all your ties to the family, that Dwayne would be convinced you don't want any of your dad's money?"

Jeremy felt Chad shift in his arms. Chad leaned back so they could see each other's eyes. "I never thought of doing that."

"Would that be enough to get him to lay off?"

"I could disown myself. Right? Like say I've never been born to that idiot and that my brother is no longer my brother? I mean, can a person do that?"

"Maybe you can divorce your dad and in the process that gets you off the hook with your brother."

The look of astonishment on Chad was evident. Jeremy shrugged. "I can call around. It's at least an idea."

"I need a job. The 'A' word always means billable hours." Chad held his hand on Jeremy's mouth. "If you offer to pay I'll spank you."

Jeremy lowered Chad's hand from his face. "If you don't let me do this for you, *I'll* spank *you*."

Chad shook his head no, but tears filled his eyes.

"What's your peace of mind worth, Chad?"

"I can't. I know you such a short time. You already bought me a wig and dress." Chad dabbed at his eyes.

"It's a loan." Jeremy shrugged. "I want you to be able to function without a loaded gun constantly in your thoughts."

Chad gripped Jeremy in a vise-like hold, kissing him.

Jeremy perked up and responded, feeling boiling heat coming from Chad as he rolled on top of him. The amount of attachment

The Diamond Stud

Jeremy felt for this adorable, vulnerable man was growing each hour they spent together—Friday night, all day Saturday, and now Sunday too. Jeremy never hung out with one man an entire weekend. He never wanted to before, and no one ever expressed an interest in doing so with him.

He wasn't bored, needing to get his space or part ways. On the contrary, Jeremy could not get enough of Chad DeSoto. He was like no one else Jeremy had ever encountered. A man so complex, Jeremy knew it would take decades to unravel him.

~

Yes, Jett Warren was his best friend and ally, but Chad had never before met a man with the savvy to think outside the box. Though Jett stood by him in his darkest hours, nursed him when he was released from the hospital, and more than once became a safe haven for Chad when he was terrorized, Chad had never been able to find an answer to the miserable question of *How*? How to get out of this terrible mess?

Perhaps he did now.

Partly in gratitude, and mostly for the delight of having sex with a man as wonderful as Jeremy, Chad sat up straddling Jeremy's hips, grinding his ass on top of his crotch. "Hello, Houston. Need a deep hard fucking?"

Jeremy's eyes sprang open and he laughed.

"Ground control to Major Houston. Commencing countdown, engines on." Chad took off his shirt and tossed it aside. He held his pectoral muscles like breasts. "Am I sexy?"

"Fuck yeah."

"I'd let you take off my pants, but these jeans have been through enough shredding." Chad hopped off the bed and shimmied out of them. "They are a reflection of me. Tattered. Schmatta, schmatta, schmatta."

Jeremy kept laughing as he undressed, shaking his head. "I swear sometimes I feel as if you're speaking a different language."

"Too young to know the Rolling Stones?" Chad rolled his eyes. "Oy!"

"That is not the Rolling Stones." Jeremy used his feet to kick his clothing to the bottom of the bed.

"Is too. *Shattered.* Go look it up on your iPhone, smart man." Chad dug in the nightstand for a condom and the lube. He lay back on top of Jeremy, using his knees to part Jeremy's thighs.

"Is this my reward for giving you a good suggestion?"

"This is both our rewards for the like-like thing going on, boyfriend." Chad made sure both their cocks were upright and snuggling together, then kissed and licked Jeremy's lips.

"God, you are so hot." Jeremy bent his knees around Chad's hips.

"That's me. The Diamond Stud."

"Who gave you that name?" Jeremy chewed on Chad's earring.

"I did. What? No good?"

Using a deep purring voice, Jeremy asked, "Who gave you the stud?"

"Me again. A gift for surviving the beating."

"I'll stop talking now."

"Good idea. I think I deflated."

"I can fix that."

Chad raised his hips and Jeremy grabbed his dick and jerked it. "That'll work." Chad deliberately let go of his thoughts and concentrated on the physical touch. He was good at it. If he hadn't learned to separate the two, he'd never orgasm again in his life.

Leaning on one hand, Chad witnessed the fisting of his cock, which made him even harder. Jeremy's cock was trying to take

The Diamond Stud

part in the action, raising off his body and hitting Jeremy's knuckles. "That feels so yummy." Chad glanced at the condom and back at Jeremy's ready cock. "I wish I was Samantha and could twitch my nose and that condom would magically be on you."

"Why?"

"Because I don't want you to stop playing with my dallywagger."

Hearing Jeremy's laughter was by far the best medicine for his aching heart. Chad held off on sheathing Jeremy's cock for the moment, and used both hands to hold himself up high enough for Jeremy to do his thing. Though the urge to close his eyes was strong, Chad kept his gaze glued to the wonderful hand-job he was receiving. Jeremy had a terrific way of squeezing right at the head and moving his skin down the shaft, quick and sharp. It was making Chad need to come, and he knew if he let go from holding onto the edge he was riding, he would.

"Keep that up and I'll spurt my jizz all over you, boy toy."

"Spurt." Jeremy pinched one of Chad's nipples.

The 'zing' to his groin from the tweak started a climax Chad could not control. He locked his elbows, arched his back and jammed his cock as hard as he could into Jeremy's tight friction. His cum spattered in a wide angle over Jeremy's abdomen.

"Agh!" Chad gave an exaggerated expression of sensual pleasure. "Might as well face it, I'm addicted to...your palm!"

"And so well versed in so many songs."

As Chad replied, he thrust his hips with each word to emphasize his sentence, "It's. The. Drag. Queen. In. Me!" On the last word he opened his mouth and threw his head back dramatically. "*Ahh!*"

"Damn. You are seriously gorgeous, blondie."

"On that note." Chad scooted back, made Jeremy straighten his legs under him, and rolled a condom on Jeremy's cock.

"Now the *pièce de résistance*." Chad took the gel and drew a thick line of lubrication up Jeremy's cock. He tossed the tube aside and gave Jeremy's dick a good fisting as he coated it with lube.

"Oh, man..." Jeremy grabbed the bedding in his fingers and Chad felt all his muscles tighten under his legs.

"Oiled like a sixty-nine Chevy." Chad used the residual to wipe on his own ass, and aimed Jeremy's stiff dick upwards, then he sat on it.

"Chad...holy shit."

Working his way downwards, Chad wriggled and humped until Jeremy was in deep enough to get off on the penetration. Chad enjoyed the sensation, always had liked being a bottom, and made a concerted effort to relax and savor the internal contact. He again propped himself up with both arms, a hand on either side of Jeremy's waist, and began a rhythm, riding him up and down.

"How's that, boy toy?" Chad liked the expression on his lover's face.

"*Ohhhh*," Jeremy crooned, closing his eyes. "I seriously am in like-like with you."

Chad smiled. He knew what Jeremy really meant. "You just love my ass."

"That too."

Keeping silent, Chad used Jeremy's stiff dick like a pogo stick, moving up and down, deeper each time, until his ass was able to hit Jeremy's body under him.

More low whimpers echoed in the small bedroom as Jeremy climbed the ladder to climax.

Chad reached behind him, continuing the motion of his loving, and located Jeremy's balls. He gave them a good fondling, tugging on them and trying very hard to get at Jeremy's ass, which took a contortionist. He wasn't quite that flexible.

The Diamond Stud

He spotted Jeremy staring at him and asked, "Ready for lift off, Houston?"

"Anytime you are, stud."

Chad placed both hands on the bed again and stared at Jeremy's sheathed cock as it entered and exited his own body. He upped the tempo, hearing Jeremy's accelerated breaths and feeling his cock throbbing inside him.

"Chad! Wow! Shit!"

Chad knew that was as obvious a sign as he could hope for. He gave Jeremy's cock more deep quick thrusts, heard Jeremy choke and felt his body go into an orgasm.

"Mm! Feel that bad-boy throb!" Chad wriggled on top of Jeremy, hoping to extend the waves of pleasure.

As Jeremy recovered he reached out his arms for Chad to come closer. Chad detached from Jeremy's cock and dropped to his side to take the weight off of Jeremy's thighs.

"My God." Jeremy still gasped, holding his chest.

"Gonna live?" Chad began working the spent condom from Jeremy's softening cock.

"Oh, fuck yeah. You are a god."

"A god? Well, I'm the god of gay men everywhere. Their token sacrificial lamb." He managed to get the rubber off and stood. "Time to get un-sticky."

"I can't move."

"If you don't mind a lube and spunk covered hand, here." Chad reached out.

Jeremy took it and was hauled off the bed. Before they left the bedroom to clean up, Jeremy scooped Chad up in an embrace. "You are the best thing that has ever happened to me."

The irony made Chad roar with hilarity. "Oh, honey! I'm everyone's worst nightmare!"

"No. Never."

Chad received Jeremy's kiss and stared into his dark brown eyes. Even though he felt the tasks that lie ahead were monumental, Chad knew in reality, Jeremy was the best thing that had ever happened to him as well.

Chapter 16

Jeremy had gone home.

Chad was lying wide awake in his bed, dreading Monday morning and the amount on his 'to-do' list. Jeremy had offered to take time off, but Chad didn't want to become a burden. He already felt as if he were using and abusing Jeremy's good nature.

Le had left late as well, and Chad knew Nan had work in the morning. Like most normal humans, they all appeared to do the nine-to-five job. Chad, being a bartender most of his life, slept late, lived in the dark, and felt as if he could easily be a vampire.

I wish I were. I know who to dispatch quickly. Then the thought of actually touching Dwayne, even to kill him with his teeth, was too revolting to imagine.

Chad tossed...and turned.

He punched the pillows, threw off the blankets, curled up in them, counted sheep, and finally gave up. He left his bedroom, being very quiet, and searched the cabinets in the kitchen and dining room for a shot of alcohol, something stronger than wine.

A tiny bottle of Chivas Regal had enough to fill a small shot glass. He stood in the kitchen in the dimness and poured the remainder into a juice tumbler.

When the light came on, Chad felt as if he were caught with his hand in the cookie jar. He squinted his eyes against the brightness, held up the bottle and said, "I'll buy you a new one."

Nan reacted as if he never expected him to be standing there. He gawked at his naked body before straightening out his expression. "Finish it. It's been in there since last Christmas. I'm here for the anti-acid meds."

"Here's to your heartburn and my insomnia." Chad threw the shot down his throat and cringed. "Yech!"

"Yeah. I figured it was crap by now." He shook a bottle of pink liquid and opened a drawer for a spoon. "I wish I could strut around nude. I'm just too self-conscious. And I don't have your fucking body."

Chad dumped the empty bottle into the recycle bin and rinsed the juice glass, drying his hands. "I guess I don't care if friends see me. I mean, I perform on stage in drag with my ass cheeks hanging out constantly." Chad leaned his elbows on the counter near Nan as he took reluctant teaspoonfuls of the medicine. "That looks worse than what I just drank."

As if he were sickened by the flavor, Nan shook his head making a sour face. "Gross." He capped the bottle and put the spoon in the sink. "Le and his love of hot food. There's a big difference to me between Asian hot, and Hispanic hot."

"I think you're both hot." Chad laughed and crossed his arms over his chest, leaning back on the edge of the doorframe.

Nan stared directly at his groin.

"I don't want to tempt you." Chad lowered his hands, thinking being naked was not a good idea. He never expected to bump into Nan, and since he had been seen naked before by him, he hadn't thought it would make things awkward.

"You tempt Le. He wants a three-way really badly."

"That's very sweet. He's a cutie." Chad began heading to his bedroom.

"You can't sleep, Chad?"

He stopped and looked back. "No. I'm freaking out about a lot of things right now."

The Diamond Stud

"Do you want me to massage your back?"

Chad chuckled, saying sarcastically, "Yeah, that's a good idea."

"Plutonic." Nan held up his hands. "To try and help you sleep."

"I appreciate the offer. But being touched by another gay male has never been 'plutonic'." Chad closed the gap and pecked Nan on the cheek. "But you're a doll for offering."

"I'm here for you. Anytime."

"Kisses." Chad threw him a kiss and closed the door to his bedroom. He curled under the covers, glanced at his mobile phone and wondered if Jeremy was asleep. *Yes. He must be. He's got nothing to worry about.*

~

Jeremy stared at the ceiling. It was rare for him to have insomnia. But tonight, worrying about Chad, he could not sleep. After a few hours of spinning like a top and no success shutting his eyes, he put on his robe and booted up his laptop. Using the dim light from the nightstand lamp, Jeremy looked up local attorneys and the right of a child to 'divorce' his parent. Most applied to emancipation or under-aged children. Was it rare for an adult child to request to be set free from the ties that bound father to son? "Yes." Jeremy had no idea how he would feel if he and his dad were on such bad terms that he never wanted to see, hear, or speak to him ever again. Top that to be saddled with a brother from hell. The empathy he felt for Chad was weighing heavily on him.

He tapped away on the keyboard, sending out queries with the thought of following up while at work. He had to do something to get Chad safe. Maybe he couldn't perform a miracle, but Jeremy had always believed in the court system. He had to. If he lost faith in any more government related systems, he'd lose his mind.

After an hour on line, Jeremy rubbed his face in exhaustion. It was nearly four. He shut off the computer, and the lamp, trying to get a few hours sleep.

~

By eight a.m., Chad sat at the dining room table with a map, telephone directory, and pad and paper, while Nan poured them both a cup of coffee. "Use my Satellite Navigation system, Chad. I won't need it today."

"What if it gets stolen?"

"Lock it in the glove compartment."

Chad chewed the back of the pen, staring at all the maps he printed from Nan's computer. "You don't mind?"

"No. Not at all." He topped both cups with milk and sat down beside Chad. "I remember when Le moved here." Nan read over Chad's long errand list. "At least yours doesn't include immigrations and a green card."

"True." Chad picked up his cup. "Thanks for the coffee."

"You bought it. I never buy French Vanilla. But it's good."

"Oh. Right." Chad wondered when he would be able to think straight again. It was as if all his brain cells were on strike.

"Let me get it for you. I have to head to work."

Chad nodded, staring at his hands warming on the mug, trying not to worry. His mobile phone vibrated and the sound brought terror. He picked it up from where it lay on the table next to him and realized it was Jeremy. "Hi, babe."

"Just called to wish you good luck on your day."

"Thanks. Nan is loaning me his navigation system."

"Good. You sure I can't—"

"No. Do not take time off. I'll be fine."

"If I needed help getting settle here, you would help me, right?"

"Right. But don't take off work. Let me do this by myself. I'm sick of feeling helpless."

The Diamond Stud

"I get it. I do."

For a moment Chad listened to Jeremy not speaking on the other end, just finding comfort he was there.

"Chad?"

"Yes, love of my life?"

"Leave the gun at home."

Chad jolted and peeked down at his waistband. He had the gun in its holster already clipped to his jeans and hidden by a denim shirt.

Nan placed the navigation system on the table next to him. "Gotta go. Good luck." Nan kissed his cheek and left.

"Chad?"

"I'm here, Jeremy."

"Is Nan there?"

"No. He just left." Chad heard the door close and Nan's footsteps on the stairs going down.

"Put the gun back. You can't take it into the DMV or any government offices, and you don't have a permit to carry it."

Chad unhooked it from his belt and placed it on the table. "I'm crazy to think they know where I am, right?"

"You're not crazy. But it is highly unlikely. Last night when I was tossing and turning, I sat with my laptop and looked up attorneys who specialize in child/parent divorce."

"You couldn't sleep either?"

"No. Anyway, a few looked promising and are local. Do you have a pen?"

Chad picked up the one near the pad he was using. "Go ahead." He jotted down a few names and phone numbers.

"Listen to me," Jeremy said, "Take all your police paperwork with you if you go to the attorney. Oh, and you need either a passport or birth certificate for the DMV forms. Do you have either?"

"Both."

"I'm a phone call away. I can drop everything. You got that?"

Chad's lip began to quiver. "Yes."

"You sure you don't want me to help you out?"

It was as if Jeremy heard his weakness over the phone. Chad sat up straight and imagined he was a soldier ready for battle. "I got it."

"Call me later. Oh, and get a new phone number. That will end most of the current misery."

"That's top on my list."

"Good luck."

"Thanks." Chad hung up and finished his coffee, gathering the paperwork for his long day.

He filled a small rucksack with the navigation unit, his paperwork, and various directories with phone numbers and maps. Reluctantly he stuck the gun back under the mattress. Before he left the room, he looked at himself in the mirror on the dresser. He had an impulse to remove the diamond stud from his right lobe. Look less gay.

He took it out, stood tall and gave himself a 'mean' man expression. "You have to be kidding." He pushed the earring back into the hole. "Girl! You are so gay!"

As a last minute thought, he found his wool cap and wore it to cover his frosty blond locks. His leather jacket on his back, his rucksack over his shoulder, Chad locked the door and headed to where he'd parked his car.

His paranoia was strong. After all, his Pathfinder still had Ohio license plates. "Not after today you won't." He gave the area a determined scan before getting into the car. As he plugged the navigation system into his power outlet, someone rapped a knuckle on his window. He jumped out of his skin and reached for a gun that wasn't there.

"You pulling out?"

The Diamond Stud

Chad huffed in terror, trying to recuperate. The man seemed to be interested in his parking spot. "Yes."

"Sorry to scare ya, man." He walked away.

"Scare me?" Chad choked. "You nearly made me pee my pants!"

It took him a while to figure out how to get the addresses into the electronic mapping system. The first destination was the post office to get a PO Box address.

He pulled out and noticed the man must have found another spot because there was no one waiting to pull in. Trying not to believe that was cause for any anxiety, Chad figured he had just taken too long, and another spot must have opened up.

The voice from the navigation system began guiding him. He drove to the nearest post office, trying not to stress over the long list he had to complete.

~

The last thing Jeremy could do was concentrate. The desire to continue to text Chad, call him, and make sure he was okay, was giving him a classic case of ADD. He couldn't focus on his work, and may as well have taken the day off.

By noon his mobile phone finally rang. He didn't recognize the number but it was local. "Hello?"

"It's me. I got a new phone."

Jeremy instantly felt relief. "Good. We'll have a party and take a hammer to your old one."

"Uh. No. It didn't work that way. They just put some new magic card in the old cheapie. You know what I mean?"

"Oh, right. Well, so the morons can't even contact you any longer."

"Nope. Four people have my number. You, Jett, Wayne, and my aunt."

"Your aunt." Jeremy didn't know about an aunt.

"Yes. She's cool. She knows what's going on."

"Okay. I hope you made it clear to her not to give anyone your number."

"Yes, sir! God, how I love when you dominate me."

"You sound in better spirits."

"I am. I got a PO Box and new phone number, now I'm sitting at the DMV waiting. Waiting, oh, did I mention, *waiting* for my number to be called?"

"Welcome to California. You pay more and wait longer, but we're *so* worth it!" Jeremy's stress level dropped with Chad's good mood.

"I know! My God, the amount everything costs here. Mama mia. I need more work. Speaking of that. When I called just now to give Wayne my new number, he said I can have a few shifts mid-week if the alchy-traffic picks up."

"Good. Very good."

"Oop! That's me! Time to trade in the *Birthplace of Aviation* for *Find Yourself Here!*"

"Yes, find yourself, hopefully that means no one else can find you."

"Your mouth to God's ear. Kisses, hot thang."

"Keep me up to date."

"Will do."

Jeremy punched a few buttons on his phone to identify Chad's new phone number on his call list. "Hang in there, baby. You're almost there." Jeremy knew a letter to Chad's brother from a lawyer, releasing all claim to the family, would most definitely end the torment. After all, it was about money. Yes, Dwayne hated the fact he had a gay brother, but thinking Chad may have claim to a penny of his father's estate was the real heart of the matter.

"Greedy bastard. Greedy, greedy, bastard." Jeremy shook his head.

~

The Diamond Stud

Chad was in the parking lot with an employee from the DMV who verified his car's identification number while he unscrewed the plates. "Good riddance to you horrible things." He sat on his butt on the tarmac and removed the two bolts, then the license plate. "Here's one of the Wright brothers on a plate for you, honey."

She laughed. "You say that as if you're happy to get rid of them."

Chad stood and brushed the dirt off his jeans. "You ever been to O-hell-o?" He walked to the front of the car and did the same to the second license plate.

"No." She smiled sweetly at him. "Bad?"

He made a face in exaggeration. "All I can say is welcome to California!" He waved his arms around and then got busy removing the bolts.

"I guess it's hard being a minority, isn't it, sweetie?"

Chad smiled wryly at her. "We both know that, don't we, my brown-sugar-bunny."

The woman giggled and became shy to his gaze. "Why are all the good looking ones gay?"

"A good woman like you can turn me." Chad winked at her. He removed the second plate and stood. "Take Wilbur and Orville for me, please," he said, handing it to her.

"Come on. Let's get you some sparkly new license plates. It'll go perfect with that nice diamond stud ya got there."

He followed her back inside the packed motor vehicle station. "You talking about my earring? Or...?" He fluttered his eyelashes at her.

"You're trouble." She pointed her finger at him.

"Yes, you got me. High maintenance." Chad smiled. "Don't need this anymore." He took off his cap. "You're on to me."

"Like I said. If you're pretty, odds are..." She typed on her computer, placing the old plates under a shelf and handing him new ones in a brown folder.

Chad removed them. "Hmm. Can't see an easy way to memorize this. What's with all the numbers?"

"Don't ask me. I only work here." She filled out more forms. "Okay. That's your car taken care of. Now we have to take care of you."

"You have! You are!"

"Come on, handsome. Time for your picture."

Chad fussed with his hair, trying to catch up to her as she headed behind the counter to the end. "Picture? I feel like a mess. Do I have hat-head? Is there a hairdresser? A makeup artist?"

"You don't need one. Believe me."

Chad glanced around the area and caught more smiles than scowls. *Wow. That's a first.* He stood in two, outlined foot imprints in front of a blank wall, gave the nice lady a big grin and she snapped the picture. "Let me see!" He raced towards her. She showed him the image.

"Oh, honey." Chad shook his head. "I'll be embarrassed to show anyone."

"Stop talking junk. It looks great." She handed him an elongated form and said, "Now go over there and take this test."

"Test? No one said there'd be a test. I didn't study. I had no idea." Chad took the paper and realized it was a quiz on traffic laws.

"It's easy. Don't worry. When you're done, you come back to me."

Chad did worry. *Test? I have a test?* He walked to a wall with standing booths and pens. Near it was what looked like an officer or a security guard. Chad imagined he was there to prevent cheating. He tucked his hat into his pocket and read the

instructions, worn out and ready for a nap. The last thing he needed was the effort to focus. The week of hotel and driving hell on Interstate 80, terrified of his own shadow, and now working through his relocation was making his head hurt.
A test. Now I have to take a fucking test! Just shoot me.

~

Jeremy filled his coffee mug in the employee lounge. It was nearing five and he felt like a mother hen with a newborn chick. He returned to his desk and checked his mobile phone again. His behavior was getting neurotic. One thing he knew about himself and relationships, he took them seriously. Perhaps that was one reason he shied away from them. Or men shied away from him. *Am I clingy? Or just concerned?*

Though he had the urge to keep track of Chad, he didn't text him every five minutes. That would scare to death even a man without homicide threats. Just as he was about to put his phone away and finish up a few items before he went home, it rang. He snatched it and looked at the ID. With a sigh he said, "Hi, Mom."

~

Chad now had California license plates on his Pathfinder, a temporary California driver's license in his wallet, and his Ohio license was punched with a hole, which was fine, since Chad planned on burning it, like a draft card in the seventies. A new invisible address, a new phone number, and an appointment with an attorney pending, Chad felt a little of the fear lighten.

He had never been so exhausted in his life. Though he could think of a few more details to take care of, such as going to the bank, or walking around more local bars and restaurants for another job, Chad couldn't do it. Burn out had hit.

He found a parking spot near the apartment and shut off the engine. Before he got out, he sent Jett a text making sure he got his phone number. Jett immediately called him.

"Hello, girlfriend."

"Hi, Jett-love-of-my-life."

"Well, I asked around for what it would cost to move your stuff. You sitting down?"

"Oh no." Chad slouched behind the wheel.

"It's not the amount you have, sugar, it's how far. These Ohio movers are afraid to drive out of a three hundred mile radius."

Chad imagined Jett's expressions and gestures of dismay.

"I had to call a real mover. You know. A *real* one." Jett huffed loudly.

"Phooey." Chad rubbed his face. "I don't want to hear this."

"Two to three big ones! And I'm not talking Ben Franklins, honey."

"I can't. I could buy a whole new wardrobe at the second hand shop for a few hundred."

"I know. I thought he was out of his mind. You want me to mail you a box at a time?"

"Oh, God, Jett. That is too much labor for you to do."

"A labor of love…"

Chad choked up and dabbed his eye. "I'm about to blubber like I did when I watched *Fried Green Tomatoes*."

"I cried for a week over that one. You just tell me what to do."

Chad couldn't fight the tears and they came flooding out.

Jett tried to calm him over the phone. "Don't cry. There is nothing to cry about. You are in sunny C-A."

"I know, Jett. But I can't think anymore. I even had to take a test to get a driver's license. I almost didn't pass it." Chad sniffled and coughed, rubbing at his running eyes. "I can't get my brain to work. You tell me what to do."

"Lovey-dovey…do you own anything you can't part with? That is a must have?"

"Beside you? No."

"Do you say all the right things, girl!"

"Seriously, Jett. You know my shit. What? A few worn out pairs of skin-tight pants…my drag outfits…International Male undies…"

"You just named your must-haves. You let me sort through your things."

"Even mailing boxes here… Jett, it's too much money for you to lay out."

"I have some mad money saved for a rainy day. You pay me back when you can."

Chad rubbed his face and couldn't get under control.

"Baby. I wish Mama could be there. I would hold you. You poor thing."

"It's hitting me all at once." Chad looked for something to wipe his face and ended up with an old tissue from his jacket pocket.

"You been through hell. I know. You think I don't know?"

"I miss you."

"You got no one there? No one?"

"There's that guy, Jeremy, I told you about. And Nan, my landlord slash roommate." Chad wiped his eyes. "But you were with me when I was beaten black and blue. You held my hand when I had tubes sticking out of me."

"And I am holding your hand again. Close your eyes. I'm with you, Chad."

"Baby. Why didn't you and me make it?"

"We did!" Jett laughed.

"I mean…you know."

"I can't go into a relationship. I love my freedom. You do too. You and I, we can't fool ourselves. We're cock-mad. We can't say no to a pretty girl with a nine inch lure."

"I know." Chad nodded, still wiping his eyes and nose with the remnant of a tissue. "I have to try this time. This Jeremy-guy, he's too good to screw around on."

"So the diamond stud is retiring?"

Chad smiled, and it felt good after the cry. "I don't know. Maybe a hiatus."

"If he lasts longer than a few weeks, I want to know about it."

"You will. Believe me." Chad looked around the neighborhood. "I feel like a sitting duck. I should get inside."

"Where are you?"

"In my ride. I just got back from all my need-to-do's. Got C-A plates now, girl. Spell it. Cee-Ay!"

"I am so jealous!"

"Use that rainy-day money to come see me."

"It ain't that much!" Jett laughed. "I can mail you a few boxes by pony express."

"I'll mail you plane tickets the first minute I catch up on bills."

"Why don't you just go get a massage instead? You take care of you. I will get my big buttocks out there. You don't worry about it."

"Big? Your perfect bubble butt? Just thinking about it makes me squirm in my thong."

"Don't you get me going. Okay, my white Liz diamonds…you just don't worry. You let your big sister deal with your stuff. I remember what you couldn't live without."

"I know you do. No one knows me like you, my brown-sugar-muffin. Just tell me every penny you spend. Deal?"

"Deal. Kisses…"

"Kiss-kiss." Chad disconnected the call and read how much the pay-as-you-go cost him. He sighed and grabbed his rucksack, heading to the apartment to collapse on the bed.

The Diamond Stud

As he used his key in the door he heard conversation. He closed it behind him and noticed both Le and Nan stop talking, staring at him. "Hello, girls."

Nan stood and approached him. "What happened?"

Chad set his rucksack down near his room and tried to smile. "I'm a big baby."

"Honey." Nan embraced him. "You know you can talk to us."

Chad rocked him, catching Le's concerned expression over Nan's back.

"I get you wine." Le stood from the dining table and vanished into the kitchen.

"Come sit." Nan held Chad's hand and led him to the living room. He stood behind him and massaged his neck.

Le gave Chad a glass of red wine, crouching down to remove Chad's boots. "My word...I'm not in Kansas anymore, Toto. Where's the hate I used to loathe and abhor?" Chad realized how lucky he was. "I love both of you." Chad raised his glass in a toast and sipped it.

"Why you cry?" Le sat beside him, rubbing his leg.

"I was talking to a friend back..." Chad stopped. "I almost said 'home'. That horrible place is not my home."

"You home now." Le scooted closer.

"Kisses." Chad smiled at his sweet face.

Le met his lips. Chad blinked and nearly spilled his wine. He backed up and said, "Easy Asian doll. I meant figuratively."

Nan made a disapproving sound and sat on the opposite side of Chad that Le was. "Stop showing Chad how hot you are for him."

"Sorry." Le suddenly appeared like a bad little boy.

"You were saying?" Nan caressed Chad's cheek lovingly.

"My best girlfriend, Jett...she's just been such a dream through this move. I just turned on the waterworks when I spoke to her." He sipped more wine.

"You have girlfriend?" Le asked.

Nan gave Le a playful whack on the arm. "Anyhoo..." Nan continued talking to Chad. "We were just deciding on dinner. You must be starved."

"I am." Chad finished the wine in a gulp. "I think I skipped lunch." He thought about it. "I did. I don't think I had anything all day since coffee with you this morning."

"That's how you keep your girlish figure." Nan stood. "I know a wonderful place that delivers."

Chad gazed at Le while Nan made a phone call. "Hello, my hot Vietnamese boy toy."

"You think I hot?"

"Hell yeah. You don't think you'd get someone as wonderful as Nanny if you weren't." Chad spotted Le getting a good eyeful of his crotch. "Three-ways are cheating."

"No!"

"Uh huh." Chad touched Le's nose with the tip of his index finger. "Take it from a whore like me. They are."

Nan leaned on the threshold between rooms, staring at them as he spoke to the restaurant.

"Speaking of men. I should call mine." Chad fished out his mobile phone. "Look." He showed Le the LCD screen. "No new voicemails."

Le laughed but Chad knew he didn't get it. He put the phone to his ear after he selected Jeremy's number on his list.

"Hey. Are you surviving?" Jeremy asked.

"I came home to a welcome that made the horrible day worth it." Chad caressed Le's hair gently, seeing him savor the contact.

"I'd ask to see you, but I know it sounds possessive and clingy." Jeremy sounded shy.

"Come over, boyfriend. I need some good man on man, hard core fucking." Chad got a kick out of Le's reaction.

"On my way! Want me to bring dinner?"

The Diamond Stud

Chad asked Nan, "Enough for four?"
"More than." Nan nodded, finishing up his order.
"Nope. We're all taken care of, care of the nanny."
"Be there ASAP."
"Bring your PJs."
"A sleepover on a school night?" Jeremy laughed.
"It's fine with me, handsome."
"I'll pack a bag!"
"You come with baggage?" Chad held Le's hand on his lap, loving his infatuation.
"A light load."
"Yeah. Not like mine."
"Your five hundred pound tumor is about to be removed."
"Good guess at Dwayne's weight."
"You told me he was tipping the scale at three and I was adding his felon-wife."
"Oh. Then more like a thousand."
"Stay horny 'til I get there."
"Promise." Chad made kissing noises and disconnected.

Nan returned with the wine bottle and two more glasses, filling them all. "So? What did you accomplish today, Chad?"

Chad thanked him for the wine by raising the glass to him. "Well. I think I'm beginning to wash the stink of Dayton and the DeSoto clan, and I mean that as in 'klan' with a K—" Chad rolled his eyes as if he were nauseated. "Off my skin." Chad sniffed his pits. "Ew. I need a shower."

Le went for a sniff. "I like smell."

"If it's a 'smell' I need a shower." Chad gulped the second glass and stood. "Be back."

"We'll be here." Nan waved.

Chad knew things were finally looking up. Knew it.

~

Jeremy had an urge to stop for a bouquet of flowers. Instead he bought a bottle of wine to share. It took him a pass around the block to find an open spot. When he did he noticed two men loitering. He didn't like the look of them. They were near Chad's Pathfinder.

He wondered if he was allowing his imagination to take over simply because he was aware of Chad's situation. Jeremy turned off his headlights and ignition and waited. Butterflies filled his stomach. Though Jeremy wasn't naïve enough to believe the gay, bi and transgender population was safe anywhere, he had not felt vulnerable living in North Berkeley and never unsafe near the Castro District. Could these men have tracked Chad down and were waiting for him?

While Jeremy began to imagine scenarios in his head of what he would do, he blinked. The two men kissed, embracing each other in the shadows. "Uh, okay. Yes, I'm paranoid." He climbed out of his car, with the bottle of wine, and the two men parted, as if afraid of what Jeremy will do. He waved shyly. "Nice night for a kiss."

"Isn't it?"

Jeremy walked to Chad's apartment door and rang his doorbell. He glanced at the two men and noticed they were kissing again. That made him feel very good.

A clomping of feet on the other side of the door preceded the door opening. Chad's beautiful smile greeted him. "Hello, boyfriend."

Jeremy slung his arms around Chad's neck and hugged him.

"Miss me?" Chad chuckled.

Slightly embarrassed by his over-the-top reaction to Chad being safe, Jeremy backed up and showed him the wine. "For everyone."

"You are sweet. I can't argue that." Chad nudged Jeremy in front of him to the stairs. "You go first so I can admire your ass."

The Diamond Stud

Jeremy was about to reply when he noticed Chad look out the door, possibly spotting the couple nearby.

"They were kissing. Are they still?" Jeremy hoped the men weren't faking it to fend off suspicion.

"Who were kissing?" Chad closed and locked the door.

"They must have left. Never mind." Jeremy ascended the stairs, knowing his anxiety was unfounded. The touch of Chad's hands on his ass shook him out of his preoccupied mood. He glanced back and got a sexy wink from his stud.

~

Chad took advantage of Jeremy's bottom the entire walk up the narrow flight of stairs. By the time he was at the top, he was ready to hump. The emotions and exhaustion had left, replaced by the kindness of his friends, and a renewed sense of safety as his Ohio persona and recognizable tags were shed. Chad was thrilled he was able to become his campy self.

"Hi, Jeremy." Nan waved from the living room.

"Hi, Nan, Le." Jeremy waved back. "I brought wine."

Just before Jeremy made his way to the other two men, Chad scooped him up in his arms, putting him on his bed. He poked his head out of the room. "See ya in a minute." Shutting them in for privacy, Chad gave Jeremy a devious smirk. "Ready for some hard-core fucking?"

"Yeah. Are you?" Jeremy tried to place the brown bag containing the bottle of wine on the nightstand. "I thought you might not be up for it."

"As if!" Chad took the bottle and put it on the floor by the door, then dove on Jeremy. "A stud always wants his boy toy."

The look of pleasure on Jeremy's face was pure gold to Chad. He began devouring him with kisses, removing Jeremy's jacket as he did. He knelt over Jeremy, rolling their tongues together, revving up from the foreplay. Jeremy cupped Chad's jaw and deepened the already scorching kiss. Chad felt his crotch go damp and his cock throb. He dropped down on top of Jeremy, grinding his cock against him.

Between kisses Jeremy said, "Naked."

Chad leaned on an elbow, yanking his shirt off, returning to Jeremy's mouth for more kissing. Under him Jeremy toed off his shoes. Chad heard them drop to the floor. Next Jeremy opened his own pants and tugged his shirt up.

Chad parted long enough for them both to strip off their remaining attire, lunging for Jeremy's lips immediately after.

The roughness of Jeremy's new beard growth was rubbing him raw, but Chad couldn't get enough. They rolled around crosswise on the bed, whimpering at the hot kissing and even hotter friction.

Jeremy parted for a breath and moaned. "I am so horny."

"Grrr!" Chad humped him roughly. "Me or you?"

"I can't think. My blood is in my dick."

"Your turn, Dom." Chad flipped them over so he was on his back, spreading his legs wide.

Jeremy scrambled to get a rubber from the drawer beside them. He sat up, rolling it on while Chad dug blindly for the lube in the same drawer. Once he removed the tube he handed it to Jeremy.

"I'm about to come." Jeremy panted loudly, kneeling between Chad's legs and getting the gel around his rim.

"Come away, boyfriend." Chad held his own knees and exposed his body.

Jeremy gave Chad an expression of agony. "If I didn't just lube you up I'd dive in."

"Next time. Dive in cock first this time."

Without hesitation Jeremy connected their bodies together. Chad shivered from the penetration and the pure pleasure Jeremy was showing in the act. While Jeremy inched inside, he held Chad's cock, drawing it upwards to keep it hard.

The Diamond Stud

The growing love he was feeling for Jeremy was strengthened by the excitement of their physical chemistry and compatibility. They had made love several times, and Chad still wanted to play with him. With Chad's promiscuous history, he knew—with most men—by the second bout of sex if he grew bored.

He took the top off the lubricating gel and dabbed some on the head of his cock as it poked out of Jeremy's fist. Jeremy used it to make his hand-job more enjoyable for Chad.

"Yeah." Chad shivered as the heat inside and out was bringing him closer to a climax. "Just like that."

"Motherfucker." Jeremy hammered as quickly into Chad as he jerked on his cock. "Fuck!"

Chad felt Jeremy's cock pulsating rapidly in his ass. He swallowed a gulp of air as he was propelled into his own climax. The two of them working hard to deepen the final thrusts for maximum pleasure, Chad opened his eyes to watch the cream spray out of his slit and across his shaved abdomen and chest.

Jeremy grunted and nearly bent Chad in half as he drove in deep, squeezing his cock tightly. "That was incredible."

Chad breathed out loudly, then laughed. "I think I passed out a second from it."

"Look at that load." Jeremy milked another drop out of Chad's dick.

"Felt so good. Wow." Chad gazed at their connection. His attention was drawn to Jeremy's cut abdominal muscles, the prefect amount of hair on his treasure trail and chest, and finally to Jeremy's dark bedroom eyes. It was when they met gazes that Chad actually imagined he could fall in love. Not like-like. Love.

Before Chad got the courage to say his thoughts, which terrified him after knowing Jeremy for such a short time—not to mention, his own track record of one-night hook-ups—Jeremy pulled out. Jeremy's priority seemed to become the spent condom and cleaning up.

Nan said through the door. "Food's here, lovebirds."

"'Kay." Chad watched Jeremy work the condom off. "Jer?"

"Yeah?" Jeremy tugged a tissue out of a box on the nightstand and wrapped the mess into it.

It was there on the tip of his tongue. Chad wanted to tell him. But he didn't trust his emotions at the moment. He was vulnerable, cried at the drop of a hat. "Food's here."

Jeremy smiled. "I got that."

"A naked dash to the bathroom?" Chad gathered their clothing into his arms.

"Not much choice."

"Ready? Set?" Chad opened the door and took off running, Jeremy at his back.

"I'm glad you moved in, Chad!" Nan yelled.

Chad chuckled as he dumped the clothing on the bathroom floor and washed up.

"I'm glad you moved here too, Chad," Jeremy said.

Stopping in his tracks, Chad said, "Oh what the hell. I don't just like-like you, Houston."

"Yeah. I'm feeling more than like-like too." Jeremy dried his hands.

"Are we nuts?"

"Maybe. But life's too short to worry about love."

"Get over here." Chad looped his arm around Jeremy's waist and kissed him.

The Diamond Stud

Chapter 17

Halloween night, Chad pushed through the stage curtain to a packed house of hooting fans, colorfully decked out in their ghoulish best. He held a cordless microphone and sauntered on his high platform heels, dressed as Tim Curry in *The Rocky Horror Picture Show*. His black laced bodice showed his nipples, his long dark curling wig tickled his naked shoulders. Once he'd reached the edge of the stage, he thrust his crotch out, showing off his full g-string and belted out, "I'm just a sweet transvestite," singing with the recorded music.

The roar of the crowd blocked out both his voice and Tim Curry's. Right up front was his Jeremy, looking adorably dorky as Brad. Nan and Le were waving feather dusters at him, wearing Magenta maid's uniforms.

As Chad hammed it up, his Frank-N-Furter outfit covering much less than the screen version, he thought about his journey.

Growing up as a kid in Montgomery County, feeling freakish and alien. Bullied at school for his effeminate qualities. Beaten by his brother's thugs when he came out, dressed in drag, and admitted to the world he was gay.

Then his thoughts raced to his drive across country, the threats and greed that made him leave Dayton, and the men he had met along the way—Bill, Tim and Sal, Cowboy Charlie, Military guy-Dennis—and his new friends, Nan and Le. As the song grew more erotic and Chad began unlacing his bodice, more like a striptease act than a musical performance, he met Jeremy's gaze. Could he be the one? The soul mate for which every heart yearns?

Chad didn't know. His fears and self-doubt had made trust a difficult trait to possess.

There was no way for him to know what the future would bring. No crystal ball to tell him he had nothing left to fear. Letters from lawyers divorcing himself from his family, changes of addresses, new life, new town...would it work? He had no clue.

But from the strength of the gay aura in the city of San Francisco, and in particular the Castro District, with its abundant gay life, Chad felt hope for the first time in ages.

As his song came to its finish, Chad opened his bodice so it hung wide on his chest, and the only thing covering him was a black thong, fishnet stockings, oversized pearls, and high platform heels.

He threw his head back and raised his arms to the roar of the crowd, loving it, needing to be adored, wanted—not treated like an outcast.

With a spin of his heels he wagged his naked ass down the stage to the curtain where the next act was waiting, applauding him enthusiastically.

"How do I follow that?" Tiffany in her Columbia outfit seemed near tears as she hugged him.

"Like a drag star, honey." Chad kissed him. He watched Tiffany wow the audience, and headed to his friends in the crowd. As his towering height on the five inch platform shoes came parading past the throng, they parted wide to allow him through. Chad had his gaze on Jeremy as he made a beeline directly to him. Someone else caught his eye. Chad stopped short and his jaw dropped. It was too loud in the room to shout out or

The Diamond Stud

communicate verbally, so Chad scampered over on his heels to someone he never expected to see so soon.

He threw his arms around 'Janet Weiss' and hugged him so tightly he picked him off his feet. "Jett!"

"Hello, my precious."

Chad's eyes overflowed with tears. "How? How did you get here? When?"

Jett tilted his head to Jeremy. "Your lover thought you needed some brown sugar."

Chad held Jett to his chest, crying over his shoulder, when he caught Jeremy's smile. Chad mouthed to him, 'I love you.'

Jeremy's eyes widened in joy.

Chad leaned back to see Jett's dark gaze. "How long are you staying?"

"Just two days. You know work. I can't take extra time off, but I had to see you." Jett playfully toyed with the black curly hair wig. "Any sign of the Beast?"

"No. And I have no idea if the letter was the end to it or not. Time will tell." Chad looked at the stage as Tiffany was performing. "I should introduce you. She's delicious."

"You do that, girlfriend!" Jett held Chad by his waist.

As they watched Tiffany's number, Chad felt someone brush against him. He looked down at Jeremy and smiled.

Jeremy had to get on his tiptoes to communicate. "I need a ladder now with you in those heels."

Chad crouched down so they could talk easier. "I can't believe you flew Jett in."

"Don't be mad. I just know how much he's done for you. I thought it would be fun for you both."

"Where is he staying?" Chad noticed Jett infatuated with Tiffany, and Tiffany finally spotted Jett in the audience.

"My place. But…" Jeremy glanced at the obvious attraction between Tiffany and Jett. "That's subject to change, of course."

Chad glanced from Jett to Tiffany to see for himself. "Get your ass up there, girl!" He shoved Jett to the stage.

Tiffany reached out to help Jett up the side of the platform and they sang in a duet, looking very hot to fuck each other.

Chad held Jeremy in his arms, rocking him, adoring him.

"Did you mean what you said to me? Or was that just a thank you for bringing Jett here?"

Chad thought about it. He held Jeremy's face and gave him a passionate kiss, rolling his tongue, sucking his lips and grinding his cock into his. When they parted Chad said, "I meant it."

Jeremy leapt onto Chad, locking his ankles around Chad's hips and holding him around his shoulders.

Chad squeezed him tightly, heating up quickly at the love they shared in their kissing. Chad felt hands on his naked ass. He peeked over his shoulder to see Nan and Le trying to lead him out of the crowded area where the audience was standing, singing, and cheering to Jett and Tiffany belting out another number.

Chad let the men direct him to a backstage area, private, without prying eyes.

Nan drew a curtain as he and Le left, leaving Chad and Jeremy alone in a small dim dressing room.

Jeremy slowly slid to stand on his own two feet. He craned his neck up and said, "I need a stool."

Chad took off the high shoes and was immediately within reach for whatever Jeremy had in mind.

"Look at you." Jeremy shook his head at the outfit, or the lack of one. "You are the sexiest Frank-N-Furter I have ever seen."

"I could make a hot dog joke right now that will be utterly tasteless." Chad laughed.

"You want me to eat your sausage, diamond stud?"

The Diamond Stud

"What did I do to deserve a man like you?" Chad cupped Jeremy's cheek.

"You deserve wonderful things, Chad. I think from now on you're going to enjoy dessert. You've already been through enough crap. Sit back and eat the chocolate covered strawberries in life."

A shuffling sound came from outside the curtain. Chad took a peek. Jett and Tiffany were lip-locked, backing into their own private space. "Go get em, girls."

Jett waved at Chad dismissively and continued to find a private spot.

Chad laughed then said, "Jett, the king of the hook-up."

"Was that you too?" Jeremy toyed with the oversized beads on Chad's neck.

"Yup. You know it was."

"And? Now?"

"One day at a time, my love. No promises, no broken hearts."

Jeremy's expression soured.

"But I will try." Chad took the plastic glasses off Jeremy's face and drew him to his lips. "I will try, and try, and try." He felt Jeremy's hand dip into the front of his thong, righting his cock and stroking it. A moan came from Jett from another location in the room.

"It's all I can ask." Jeremy kissed his way down Chad's neck.

"No. You can ask anything of me. But I won't lie to you and say yes just to appease you." Chad held Jeremy's shoulders as Jeremy took his cock into his mouth. At the intense heat of Jeremy's sucking, Chad thought, *I will not cheat on you. I will not cheat on you.*

Jeremy didn't answer. Chad didn't know if he was absorbed in the blowjob, or too nervous to pursue commitment with a man as screwed up as he was.

He began fucking Jeremy's mouth gently as Jeremy held the base of his cock and drew hard on the tip. "But I do love you. That's no lie."

Jeremy moaned and sucked faster, harder.

Chad felt his knees weaken. He held onto Jeremy to keep from falling and closed his eyes as the climax grew closer.

Jeremy made a sound of pleasure and yanked Chad's thong down his thighs so he could get to his balls and ass.

Chad peered at him, seeing Jeremy's pleasure and determination. The sight of his wide cock filling Jeremy's mouth gave him the last push he needed to come. Chad widened his stance and arched his back.

Responding to cum filling his mouth, Jeremy whimpered and fisted Chad's cock into his lips vigorously.

Chad choked on his grunt of euphoria and blinked. He spotted Jett and Tiffany poking their heads into the curtained room, grinning.

Jeremy sat on his heels and wiped his mouth with the back of his hand. He gave Chad a loving smile.

Jett said, "Diamond Stud jizz. Nothing better."

Jeremy whipped his head towards the two mischievous men. "Were you watching?"

"Duh!" Tiffany flipped her wrist at him as if the question were absurd.

The noise from the front stage area erupted in applause as another number was completed.

Jeremy tucked Chad's cock back into the pouch and stood, straightening in his shirt.

"Are you happy, girlfriend?" Jett batted his lashes at Chad.

"As close to that mysterious nirvana as I've been yet."

"Good girl. Tiff and I are going back to the party. See you there." Jett held Tiffany's hand and walked away.

The Diamond Stud

The smile still on his lips, Chad held Jeremy close, pushing their crotches together. "My turn to please you?"

"It's okay."

"Uh uh." Chad spun around, yanked his thong down and wiggled his ass at Jeremy.

"Holy fuck."

"Got a rubber, handsome?"

Jeremy fumbled to get his wallet out of his pocket. He unfastened his trousers and exposed his cock.

"Hang on." Chad wrapped his lips around the head and gave it a good sucking first. When Jeremy was shifting his weight side to side and Chad tasted pre-cum, he said, "There. Better."

He offered his ass again, bracing on the wall in front of him. Jeremy managed to get the condom on and well lubricated in record time. Chad was impressed. He watched over his shoulder. "Take it, Master Houston. Show me I don't need another man in my life."

The look of resignation mixed with determination on Jeremy's face convinced Chad he had his man.

Jeremy pinned Chad to the wall and spread his ass cheeks wide, penetrating him.

Chad shivered from the thrill as the noise of dancing feet and blasting music made the foundation shake.

~

Jeremy didn't know if he should take the challenge as a dare or a threat, but he rode Chad harder than he normally would have. The booze flowing freely, the mischief and masquerade in the air, all gave Jeremy a sense of freedom. He wasn't Mr. Houston, CPA. He was the boy toy to the hottest new drag act in the Castro. Life just didn't get any better than that.

Holding Chad's narrow waist, staring at his slick cock pushing in and out of Chad's hole, had Jeremy right on the edge. He jammed in, jumping off the edge, and came. As his body swirled with orgasmic chills and his cock pulsated like his beating heart, Jeremy crushed Chad from behind, trying to convey how much he meant to him.

He pulled out, panting, staring at the filled condom tip.

Chad spun around. "Nice load! Houston, we do not, I repeat, *do not*, have a problem."

Though Jeremy felt insecure in this budding relationship, and the urge to keep giving things to Chad—helping him financially, bringing his best friend Jett out to visit, buying him gifts—was compensating for his need for love, Jeremy knew Chad would do his best to make it work too.

It's what Chad always did. Try very hard.

"Let me help you." Chad worked off the spent rubber, finding a garbage pail to put the wrapper in. "The bathroom is that way. Shall we?"

Jeremy yanked up his pants and they hurried to the restroom, washing up. He glanced at Chad as he dried his hands. "You do love me, don't you?"

Chad spun around and met his eyes. "I do."

Jeremy finished washing, and straightened his clothing. When he was through he stood in front of Chad. "I believe you."

Chad pushed the wild hair of the wig off his sweaty cheek and smiled. "I just don't know what tomorrow will bring."

"Neither do I." Jeremy knew he meant the letter and whether or not it would end the threat.

"I can't see too far into the future. I never have been able to."

"I understand."

"But I do know when a man is worth changing for. Worth a try."

Jeremy felt a lump in his throat. "No one ever said that to me before."

The Diamond Stud

"They didn't know you like I know you." Chad placed his arm around Jeremy's shoulder, opening the door and shutting the light. "Maybe we just need to go slow, and trust in fate."

Agreeing completely, Jeremy allowed Chad to escort him back to the party, which appeared completely chaotic. In a spot by the bar, Jeremy knew Chad had a good group of allies to help him make it through the rough times. Jett, Tiffany, Nan, and Le were smiling at them knowingly.

Jeremy said, "This isn't Dayton, Chad. We can be who we are here."

"Hallelujah, praise the Lord!" Chad waved his arms into the air like a preacher.

Jeremy stood slightly back as Chad reconnected with the men he had grown to trust.

Yeah, maybe no one can predict the future. But we can pray we learn from the past.

Chad glanced back at Jeremy and threw him a kiss.

Jeremy caught it, smiling.

The End

G.A. Hauser

About the Author

Award-winning author G.A. Hauser was born in Fair Lawn, New Jersey, USA and attended university in New York City. She moved to Seattle, Washington where she worked as a patrol officer with the Seattle Police Department. In early 2000 G.A. moved to Hertfordshire, England where she began her writing in earnest and published her first book, In the Shadow of Alexander. Now a full-time writer, G.A. has written over fifty novels, including several bestsellers of gay fiction and is an Honorary Board Member of Gay American Heroes for her support of the foundation. For more information on other books by G.A., visit the author at her official website. www.authorgahauser.com

G.A. has won awards from All Romance eBooks for Best Author 2009, Best Novel 2008, *Mile High*, and Best Author 2008, Best Novel 2007, *Secrets and Misdemeanors*, Best Author 2007.

The G.A. Hauser Collection
Single Titles

Unnecessary Roughness

Hot Rod

Games Men Play

Born to Please

The Diamond Stud

The Hard Way

Got Men?

Heart of Steele

All Man

Julian

Black Leather Phoenix

London, Bloody, London

In The Dark and What Should Never Be, Erotic Short Stories

Mark and Sharon (formally titled A Question of Sex)

A Man's Best Friend

It Takes a Man

The Physician and the Actor

For Love and Money

The Kiss

G.A. Hauser

Naked Dragon
Secrets and Misdemeanors
Capital Games
Giving Up the Ghost
To Have and To Hostage
Love you, Loveday
The Boy Next Door
When Adam Met Jack
Exposure
The Vampire and the Man-eater
Murphy's Hero
Mark Antonious deMontford
Prince of Servitude
Calling Dr Love
The Rape of St. Peter
The Wedding Planner
Going Deep
Double Trouble
Pirates
Miller's Tale
Vampire Nights
Teacher's Pet

The Diamond Stud

In the Shadow of Alexander
The Rise and Fall of the Sacred Band of Thebes

The Action Series

Acting Naughty
Playing Dirty
Getting it in the End
Behaving Badly
Dripping Hot
Packing Heat
Being Screwed
Something Sexy

Men in Motion Series

Mile High
Cruising
Driving Hard
Leather Boys

Heroes Series

Man to Man
Two In Two Out

G.A. Hauser

Top Men

G.A. Hauser
Writing as Amanda Winters

Sister Moonshine
Nothing Like Romance
Silent Reign
Butterfly Suicide
Mutley's Crew